W9-BIZ-749

PALM BEACH POISON

A CHARLIE CRAWFORD MYSTERY (BOOK 2)

TOM TURNER

TRIBECA PRESS

Copyright © 2016 Tom Turner. All rights reserved.

Published by Tribeca Press.

This book is a work of fiction. Similarities to actual events, places, persons or other entities are coincidental.

Front cover design by James T. Egan of Bookfly Design

www.tomturnerbooks.com

Palm Beach Poison/Tom Turner – 1st ed.

JOIN TOM'S AUTHOR NEWSLETTER

Get the latest news on Tom's upcoming novels when you sign up for his free author newsletter at **tomturnerbooks.com/news**.

ONE

Vasily and Aleksandr Zinoviev were having lunch with Churchill Ames at Delbasso's in Palm Beach. Since the Russians were picking up the tab, Ames ordered the twenty-dollar ahi tuna appetizer to start.

Rush Limbaugh, a Palm Beach resident who Ames had met at a golf outing, had called him out of the blue and asked if it would be okay if a Russian named Vasily contacted him. Before Ames could ask him what he'd be calling about, Limbaugh started blathering on about how he had shot a seventy-four the day before. Ames had seen the guy's swing and knew that had to be with ten-foot gimmes and a mulligan on every hole.

Ames and the Russians had arrived at the restaurant fifteen minutes ago. Vasily—short, stocky, shaved head—wasted no time ordering a bottle of their national beverage, which was now chilling in a silver wine cooler between the brothers. Ames didn't recognize the vodka's name when the waiter brought it over, but saw a lot of backward E's and upside-down K's on the label and figured it had to be the real deal. Delbasso's was the kind of place that stocked a customer's favorite caviar and even had—so the story went, anyway—

its own pig in France with a finely tuned snout that rooted out spec-
imen truffles.

That sounded like a bullshit story to Ames, but stories like that
were a dime a dozen in Palm Beach.

Ames said "no thanks" to the vodka when Vasily offered it, and
ordered iced tea with a slice of lime. The waiter brought iced tea with
a lemon wedge instead. Ames shook his head imperiously and
pointed a long, skinny finger at the offending lemon. The waiter scurried off and fetched a lime.

Churchill Ames was a fastidious man who had thin, bloodless
lips, perfectly parted short, straight hair, erect military posture, and
no discernible laugh lines. A canary-yellow pocket square bloomed
forth from the breast pocket of his blue blazer, and was neatly
complemented by pleated, tan gabardine pants and a blue-striped
shirt—everything extra-crisp. He was kicking himself, though, for
wasting fresh linen on the Russian mutts.

Vasily looked up from his menu and smiled at Ames. "So what do
they call you?" he asked.

Ames looked puzzled.

"He means, your nickname," Aleksandr said. It came out "knicht-
nem."

"Churchill," Ames said, not looking up from his menu.

"Not...Church or something?" Aleksandr smiled, displaying a set
of straight white teeth.

Ames looked up and shot him a patronizing glance. "No, just
Churchill," he said. Then, looking back down at his menu, "or sir."

The Russians ordered something heavy on carbs and cholesterol.
Ames chose the salade Niçoise.

"So, Churchill," Vasily said after a long pull on his vodka, "we
would like to talk to you about what Mr. Limbaugh mentioned."

The name came out *limbo*, like the dance under the pole.

"Mr. 'Limbo' didn't mention anything," Ames said, putting the
menu down. "He just said you'd be calling."

The brothers were a study in contrast. Muttsky 'n Jeffov, Ames thought, amusing himself. Vasily's huge, shaved head highlighted his cauliflower ears and fleshy lobes. He was wearing dark pants and a long-sleeved, black mesh shirt, possibly a fashion statement some-where in lower Novosibirsk. He looked as if he'd been in his share of fights. Ames guessed he'd probably won them all because he could just tell the man fought dirty. Used his sharp, pit-bull teeth, no doubt, for more than just eating dead animals.

Clearly, Aleksandr had gotten the looks. He was around six-feet-two and had a thick head of blonde, wavy hair. He was handsome and soft-looking, compared to his brother. But they both had the same eyes, emerald green and striking. Ames hadn't seen Vasily blink once since they'd sat down.

"Mr. Ames, our proposition is a real estate venture," Vasily said. "Specifically, we would like to buy the Poinciana Club."

Ames was impressed: the man skipped the foreplay and got right to it. His proposition, on the other hand, was totally absurd. It was like offering to buy the Washington Monument.

"You can't be serious," Ames said.

"Sure I am," said Vasily. It came out as "chewer." "I would think as CEO of the Poinciana Club—"

"The Poinciana is not a corporation," Ames snapped. "I am its president."

"Okay, I would think as president of the Poinciana Club," Vasily said, "you could convince the other members to sell if we make you an offer you—"

"—can't refuse?"

Vasily nodded and raised his glass of vodka. "Exactly."

"Let me explain something," Ames said, making no effort now to disguise his condescension. "Any offer you make, I assure you, I will refuse. The Poinciana Club is owned by three hundred and eight members. It is a highly exclusive club distinguished by some of the most magnificent, historically significant buildings in the country. It will never be the object of some tacky real-estate play."

Vasily ignored Ames's fusillade of withering disdain.

"We know," Vasily said simply. "We have been there. It is magnisifent—"

Aleksandr winced at his brother's butchery of the word, while Ames was horrified that the scruffy little mongrel had actually stepped foot into the hallowed halls of the Poinciana. Ames made a mental note to talk to the club manager about how this egregious trespass had been allowed to take place. How these miscreants had been able to cross the threshold into the WASP bastion reserved for men of distinction and social status, not to mention rock-solid, unimpeachable character. Men like Atkinson Bailey, Webster Mills, Townsend Applegate and, in keeping with the two-last-name tradition, Churchill Ames himself.

Vasily drained his vodka, then looked up at Ames. "My friend, the fact is buildings are buildings. What is important is that it is two hundred and eleven acres in the middle of Palm Beach."

Again, Ames was impressed with the crude vulgarian's ability to cut straight to the heart of the matter.

"Correct," Ames said. "Two hundred eleven acres in the middle of Palm Beach, which you, my friend"—he started to say "comrade"—"will never own. There aren't enough rubles in the Motherland."

"How can you say that," Vasily said, "if you don't even know what our offer is?"

"Because it's not for sale, under any circum—"

"Three-hundred-twelve million dollars' worth of circumstances," Vasily said.

Ames was stunned. "How in God's name did you come up with a figure like that?"

"Very simple: There are three hundred and eight members of the Poinciana. We will make three hundred and seven of them millionaires and you...a millionaire five times over. The extra four million to you would be in a separate, private agreement. A finder's fee, let's call it," said Vasily.

Suddenly the vodka bottle with the upside-down K's and backward E's looked very inviting to Ames.

"Mr. Zinoviev," Ames said wearily, "my fellow members and I are already millionaires. Every single one of us. Not to mention our five billionaires."

Ames had, in fact, once been a millionaire, but not anymore. His three divorces had taken their toll. The second one had almost cleaned him out. The last one, with Celia, well, to her infinite disappointment, there hadn't been that much left to clean out. Nevertheless, Ames had gone to a great deal of effort to make sure that word of his dire financial circumstances hadn't gotten out. That he was, literally, down to his last seven hundred thousand dollars. If people knew, he would be banished from Palm Beach society. He'd have all the allure of a homeless guy bunking in a refrigerator box in some desolate back alley.

To conceal the truth, Ames had come up with an ingenious story. He'd put the word out at the men's bar that when things starting going south with Celia, he started going offshore with his cash. Squirreling away a million here, a million there. Switzerland. The Caymans. All his friends shook their heads and said, "that Church, what a prick," but made a note to do the exact same thing if they were ever in that position. They all assumed he had ten, fifteen mill stashed away.

But the reality was, all he had was a lousy seven hundred thousand dollars in Fidelity mutual funds. Actually, come to think of it, no, it was only five hundred and fifty thousand. He had forgotten about losing a hundred and fifty thousand dollars during a disastrous binge of day trading.

Still, as tempting as the Russians' offer might be to him, it stood no chance of flying with the other members. The rest of the membership, except for him and Buzz Cox, really were all millionaires. And yes, there were five billionaires.

"Just out of curiosity," Ames said, "this 'real-estate venture' of yours, what exactly did you plan to do with the property?"

"Make it into the most spectacular luxury-housing development in the world," Vasily said with pride.

That's when Ames noticed Vasily's long pinkie fingernails for the first time. He wondered whether they were used to gouge people's eyes out. Then he remembered when long nails used to be a fashionable cocaine-snorting accessory way back when.

Ames sighed loudly, to convey that he was now officially bored to death with the whole harebrained conversation. It was time to wrap it up. He had a tee time in forty-five minutes and wanted to hit some balls on the range before playing. And, as much as five million dollars could help solve his personal financial problem, there was just no way it was in the cards.

"So, gentlemen"—the word almost made him gag—"the Poinciana is not for sale. Not now, not ever."

"But why?" Vasily asked.

Jesus Christ, what was the guy not getting?

Ames dialed up his haughty look again and bore down on Vasily.

"I've told you why," he said, pausing. "But if you need another reason, I'll give you one: Because it's where I play golf."

Vasily glared back at Ames. "Let me point out a few things to you, Church. One, everything's for sale; and two, there are seven hundred and fourteen other golf courses in Florida where you can play your silly little game."

"But only one Poinciana," Ames said.

"Which is why we just offered you almost half a billion dollars for it," said Vasily.

Thinking that was a pretty generous roundup, Ames got to his feet.

"For once and for all, forget it," Ames said, wiping his mouth with the cloth napkin. "Just forget it."

But Vasily Zinoviev was still not done. "So, Mr. Ames, you have no intention of speaking to the other members?"

Ames shook his head. "Absolutely none."

"Five million dollars," Aleksandr dangled it again.

"I heard you the first, second, and third times," Ames said, getting to his feet and flinging his napkin on the table.

"Sit down, please, Mr. Ames," Aleksandr said, politely.

"I have to go," Ames said. He barely had time to hit even a small bucket of balls now.

Vasily stood and leaned to within six inches of Ames's face. "Mr. Ames, you really should reconsider your decision." Then, with astonishing quickness, he shot out his hand.

Reluctantly, Ames shook it. It felt like a moray eel had clamped onto his hand.

Ames tried to yank it away, but Vasily dug in with his nails. "You have twenty-four hours to reconsider," he said.

Vasily finally released Ames's hand as his brother tossed a wad of cash down on the table. Then, the pair turned and walked out.

As Ames watched them go through the door, he looked down at his wrist. Blood was streaming onto his starched, white cloth napkin.

TWO

AMES WAS BUCK NAKED, UNLESS YOU COUNTED THE WHITE butterfly bandage on his wrist. The twenty-five-year-old woman in the chaise longue next to him was naked too. It was 10:00 on a warm Saturday night in May, and they had been skinny-dipping in his pool.

She was stretched out, looking up at the stars, and Ames was admiring her full, sag-free breasts, no visible tan line above or below them.

"You sunbathe naked?" he asked, imagining her spending her days at a nude beach, lying out on a fluffy white towel.

She nodded and flashed her coquettish smile.

"Would you like another cocktail?" Ames asked.

She reached down, picked up her glass, and finished off the last of the Myers's rum and orange juice.

"Thank you," she said, handing him the glass.

He got up, sucked in his gut, and tried to stretch out his five-foot-nine-inch frame. For fifty-five he wasn't in bad shape, but who was he kidding? She wasn't there for his body. Jessie, which might or might not have been her real name, came discreetly recommended by a friend, David Balfour. Balfour didn't usually have to pay, but for top-quality "strange," as he liked to call it, he'd make an exception.

Churchill Ames went around to his pool-house bar and reached for the bottle of Myers's. He flashed back to his bizarre lunch the day before with the Russian buffoons and thought about the five million they had offered him. He had no regrets about his decision. Not because he wouldn't have grabbed the money and run—because he would have—but because there was no way in hell that the rest of the membership would go along with it. In fact, they'd laugh it off: A million bucks per member wasn't going to catch anyone's attention. With the exception of him and Buzz Cox, who'd had a few reversals of his own lately, a million dollars was chump change to Poinciana members.

Nevertheless, he had called up David Balfour, who was on the Poinciana Executive Committee with him. "You gotta hear this," Ames said, "I had lunch with these two Russian guys who Rush Limbaugh told to call me. Clowns wanted to buy the Poinciana."

"You're shitting me," Balfour said. "Did they actually make an offer?"

"Sure did. Three-hundred-twelve million, to be exact. Works out to a million a member, but they were going to slide me an extra four mill under the table," Ames said, taking the opportunity to show how incorruptible he was.

"Christ, that's incredible," Balfour said, not impressed with the money, but with the sheer ballsiness of the offer.

Ames poured the orange juice over the rum and ice cubes. As he set the bottle on the bar, he heard a scraping sound nearby, like something hard making contact with another solid object. He looked around, but saw nothing except Jessie and her exquisite breasts as she walked toward the pool. He did a mental shrug and began mixing another drink.

ON THE OTHER SIDE OF THE WALL THAT SURROUNDED THE backyard pool, two men struggled to lift a giant Igloo cooler that had holes punched in the top by an ice pick. It wasn't so much the weight of the cooler that made the load awkward, but the way its contents shifted around unpredictably. Not to mention how careful the men had to be. What would happen if the top suddenly popped open? There were twenty-five highly venomous snakes inside and the two men could feel their shifting movements as they writhed around. The men had almost gotten used to the constant low, electric hiss. Clearly, the snakes weren't happy campers getting bounced around on top of each other.

The men had scoped out the place earlier in the day, dressed as landscapers. Their instructions were that if anyone asked what they were doing there, they were to play dumb—no-speak-a-da-English— or, sorry, wrong address. When they arrived, however, no one was around and they spent ten minutes looking over the backyard and studying the pool house. The setup was perfect because of the six-foot-high stucco wall around the property. The only escape would be into the main house. And the door to the pool house swung open and had a six-inch space below it, like an old-fashioned changing room, so it was definitely no safe haven.

The tricky part was how to release the snakes from the cooler. The men had decided just to lift it up to the top of the wall, yank open the top, then quickly tilt the cooler down and let them fall to the ground below. If they weren't riled up enough already, falling six feet would get them good and cranky.

As AMES MIXED THE DRINKS, HE THOUGHT ABOUT THE RUSSIAN in the tacky black mesh shirt. Who was he kidding? You got twenty-four hours. "Come on, pal, you're messing with the wrong guy," Ames thought to himself. Who the hell did he think he was threatening? Churchill Ames was a hard-ass litigator, a guy who'd dealt with every lowlife scumbag threat in the book.

Vasily whatever-the-hell-his-last-name-was had called earlier that afternoon, exactly twenty-four hours after the lunch at Delbasso's, and left a message saying it was important that Ames get back to him.

Important...important to who? Unless maybe the guy was going to raise his offer to a billion dollars. Now that was a nice round number he might consider taking to the executive committee.

Another thing, Ames wondered: Where were these Commie bozos laying their hands on money like that in the first place? They must have done a hell of a lot of gas-tax scams or global arms deals to have that kind of scratch lying around.

HAVING GOTTEN THE LAY OF THE LAND, THE TWO MEN DECIDED to release the snakes at the south wall near the house. That way they'd block access to the back terrace, cutting off any escape to the house. The men carefully raised the big white cooler to the top of the wall so it wouldn't scrape again. Then the smaller of the two men scrambled up the wall and perched there precariously. He saw the naked woman get out of her chaise longue, walk towards the pool, and get in.

Atop the wall, he braced himself with his legs and reached for the Igloo cooler beside him. In one swift motion, he pulled it open and tilted it down. The snakes made a thumping sound as they hit the ground, their hissing growing louder immediately.

CHURCHILL AMES, ABOUT TO JOIN JESSIE IN THE POOL, HEARD A noise. Like someone had fallen from the top of the wall, then a buzzing noise like the kind a transformer makes.

The girl in the pool screamed suddenly. Ames looked over and saw how the half-moon caught the terror in her eyes. She was running in the pool—if you could call it that—from the middle to the shallow end, trying to get out. Her hands were slapping at the water, desperately trying to make her go faster. Then Ames spotted two snakes. One slipped into the pool, barely causing a ripple near the light at the deep end. Another slithered along the eighteen-inch-wide coquina coping. Then he saw more of them. They were everywhere.

In a panic, he looked toward the house. A snake wriggled up onto the covered terrace near the back door to the inside. It looked like it was about four feet long and had a thick brown-black body. Ames was frozen momentarily, horrified by the reptilian forms writhing around him in every direction.

"Jesus! Help me!" Jessie shrieked from the bottom step of the pool.

Ames glanced over in time to see a snake's triangular head rise menacingly six inches in the air on the pool's coping. Its mouth opened, exposing the fluffy white inside. With its fangs bared, it snapped at the girl and struck her on her right shoulder. Ames realized that in her haste to get away from the one in the pool, she hadn't seen this one, which now seemed to dangle from her shoulder. It hadn't just bit her, but was squirming and twisting like some bizarre, dangling clothing accessory.

Ames thought only of his own survival now. The snakes were everywhere. He thought about climbing to the roof of the pool house, but had read that snakes could climb. For Christ's sakes, could they really chase him onto the roof like a bloodhound treeing a fox? But it didn't matter, because there was no way to get up on the roof anyhow. And now he couldn't get to the house, either, because at least three of them were prowling like sentries between him and the back porch.

All of a sudden, the girl let out a long, blood-curdling wail. She had been struck again, he suspected.

"Help me," she shrieked, her hands over her head, shaking.

He heard a shout from somewhere nearby.

"Church, what the hell's going on there?" came the distant voice.

It was John Randall, his neighbor. A guy who had called up once and complained about a party of his.

"Call the cops!" Ames shouted back.

He heard a door slam.

It was now or never. Ames dashed around the pool house toward the back of the property. He didn't see any snakes back there. It was roughly fifty feet to the wall. He ran as fast as he could. But then a snake's head suddenly rose up, its cottony mouth opened wide below its cat-like, elliptical eyes. He cut to his left to avoid it and felt a sharp jolt of pain right below his left knee. He kept running and jumped up onto the wall, his arms hoisting him to the top. He put one leg over the side, then the other, and fell to the ground on the other side.

The two men watched his escape, got down off the wall, ran over to their car, and drove away.

Their orders had been to make it clear to Churchill Ames that he should never, ever say no to their boss again.

THREE

The last fifteen years had not been kind to Cat Deville. That was when Charlie Crawford last saw him. Cat had played a concert at Dartmouth back when Crawford was a senior there. It was a lifetime ago for both of them. Cat had had Kurt Cobain aspirations and Crawford had been lacrosse captain. Now Cat had a frizzy ponytail that had more gray than brown in it, a pockmarked rawhide face, and shark eyes deadened by Patrón tequila, amyl nitrate, and the realization that total obscurity was probably about five years down the pike.

The last fifteen years had been a mixed bag for Charlie Crawford. As an NYPD homicide detective, he'd put away a lot of killers and made the headlines more than he would have liked. Even made an appearance on "Page Six" of the *New York Post*, but that was another story. After fifteen years, Crawford—burned out and used up —had gone south to the Keys to take it slow, work on his tan, learn how to surf, and just plain chill.

It had taken him about five minutes, stretched out on the Florida sand and sweating profusely, to realize he was not the chilling kind. But he didn't miss shoveling snow and New York winters, so a week later he shotgunned his résumé out to a bunch of police departments in Florida.

Several of them came after him right away, like he was a number-one college draft choice. Panama City talked to him about becoming its police chief. But Crawford knew that would have been a lousy fit. Delegating authority...so not his style. And besides, Panama City? Where the hell was that? He ended up taking a job with the Palm Beach Police Department, even though he would have preferred something just a little more off the beaten path. He was also worried about running across someone from his former life—or worse, someone he was related to. He had heard from his sister that his rich, deadbeat cousin, Anson, was down in Palm Beach somewhere.

The mayor of Palm Beach finally signed him up, offering him autonomy and a decent paycheck. But within a week at Palm Beach PD, Crawford was second-guessing himself again. The cases weren't exactly hard-core. Like a former debutante gone wild—drunk or stoned or just plain crazy—flashing pedestrians and motorists alike at the corner of Worth Avenue and South County. Then right after that, came the highly insured Lhasa apso show dog—complete with four-hundred-dollar haircut—that got snatched at Lazlo Olanders's antique shop. First, it looked like it was a dognapping job, but turned out to be a bungled insurance scam.

Not exactly the kind of cases Crawford had envisioned for the second half of his career. Because, like it or not, he had a big-time homicide jones. The problem, of course, was that murder in Palm Beach was as rare as snow. But finally, about a year after he came down, a high-level hedge fund guy had murdered the brother of a sixteen-year-old girl the man was having an affair with, and Crawford, after a few dead ends, had tracked him down and put him away. But since then—for the last six months—things had gone quiet. Which was not how he liked it.

CAT HAD JUST KICKED IN TO HIS SECOND SET. IT WAS TOUGH FOR the old rocker to summon up freshness when all the audience ever wanted to hear were his quasi-hits: "Love in a Tie-Dyed T" and the one that both put him on the map and became the bane of his existence—"Warren Goes a' Courtin'." It was written after a particularly debauched tour with legendary rock whack-job, Warren Zevon.

Cat, trooper he was, was doing his damnedest up on the cramped stage tonight. But Crawford sadly noted the unmistakable correlation between him trying out his new stuff and his fans' trips to the bathroom.

The Mambo Room was on the second floor of a former warehouse in Lake Worth. Crawford had taken a table down in front with Isabel Hutchins—dark, lithe, exotic-looking—and, as of tonight, a Cat Deville convert. Not as much, though, as a guy in his fifties the next table over. His head was slamming back and forth to the music, like a bobble head doll going over speed bumps. Cat, his fingers dancing over the Stratocaster strings, seemed a million miles away, flashing back to the glorious days of SRO crowds, Crawford guessed.

Crawford kept watching Cat's bottle of Patrón, top off, sitting on the Marshall amp. It would vibrate precariously close to the edge, then Cat would take a step forward, grab it, and take a hefty pull. After that he'd place the bottle farther back on the amp, where it would start wobbling forward again.

"He's incredible," Isabel said, leaning into Crawford's ear.

Crawford, six foot three with piercing blue eyes and a sturdy chin that had taken a few shots over the years, nodded, though he wouldn't have gone quite that far.

At the end of the second set a burst of applause erupted from the ninety-four in attendance. Cat came back for his encore. The tradition was that you did an old favorite, so Cat—gritting his teeth—did "Warren" again. The crowd loved it even more the second go-round.

As they walked out of the Mambo, Isabel reached over for Crawford's hand. He had never been a huge fan of holding hands—except for two notable exceptions—because of how it screamed commitment. He liked Isabel, but a full-time relationship was not in the cards.

They walked down the side street and got into his car. She looked at him like she wouldn't fight it if he leaned across and kissed her. He just turned the key in the ignition, put the car in drive, and flashed to Dominica, one of the few women he had held hands with and actually liked it.

"Feel like a drink somewhere?" she asked.

"Yeah, sure," Crawford said, "but I'm not up on the local hot spots."

Isabel smiled at him and patted his arm.

"Don't worry, you're in good hands, Charlie."

Crawford had been in Palm Beach for about a year and a half but had never been much of a night owl. He and Dominica liked to cook for each other, his specialty being chicken curry à la Crawford.

"How about La Cucina?" Isabel asked.

"Where's that?"

"On Royal Poinciana. This restaurant that turns into a nightclub at around eleven or so."

The old chestnut about not playing where you work muscled its way into his head.

"Okay with you if we go to some place over in West Palm?" he asked. "Clematis or CityPlace, maybe?"

She nodded and said she knew a few good spots there.

Fifteen minutes later they walked into a place Isabel recommended. It looked okay to Crawford. Isabel ordered a Grey Goose and soda, Crawford a Bud.

Isabel reached across the table and ran a finger across his forehead. He had a three-inch scar in the shape of a tiny lightning bolt above his right eyebrow. "I never saw that before," she said. "It's very sexy, you know."

He had no clue how an odd-shaped scar could possibly be sexy.

It came from a barroom brawl in college, though he didn't

discourage New York cops from thinking it was from some dicey takedown gone bad.

As he was just about to take a pull on his Bud, his cell phone rang. He fished it out of his pocket and looked at the number.

"Sorry," he said to Isabel, "gotta take this one. It's my partner... yeah, Mort?"

"Charlie, we got a bad one," Mort Ott said.

Crawford listened, got the address, then hung up.

His date with Isabel had just come to a screeching halt.

FOUR

It was one of the most chilling crime scenes Crawford had ever seen, which was saying something, since he had seen some brutally horrific ones over the years. Snakes—though he was trying to not let it show—scared the hell out of him. Even the little green, harmless ones.

After getting the call, the first uniform on scene had come through the unlocked front door of Churchill Ames's house and had seen the girl's body, along with several writhing snakes through the back French doors. No way was the uniform going to be a hero and try to rescue the girl. He did, however, have the presence of mind to call in an immediate request for lights, the kind they use on highway-construction night jobs; looked like big klieg lights. He told the dispatcher to get as many as they could round up. A police tow truck drove up to a construction site on I-95 near Blue Heron and took away as many as he could.

"Get some snake guys over here too," was the second thing the uniform said to the dispatcher as he gave her the address.

"Some what?" the dispatcher asked.

"Guys who handle snakes," the uniform said, "They're all over the place, a body right in the middle of 'em."

The dispatcher was clearly having difficulty processing the image.

"Where do I find—" the dispatcher started.

But the uniform had already hung up.

The dispatcher had never dealt with a request like this before. She called her supervisor at home in a panic. Eventually the word reached Mort Ott, who had called Crawford. Ott told Crawford he had to wrap up something he was doing and would get there as quick as he could.

When Crawford showed up at the house on Barton Avenue fifteen minutes later, it looked like a Dolphins night game. Lights were positioned all around the outside of the wall on three sides. Two guys in jeans and boots, who looked calmer than the grisly situation seemed to warrant, were walking around with long poles that had wire loops at the ends of them. They were picking the snakes up one at a time and dropping them into two tall metal boxes they had positioned near the deep end of the pool.

Crawford's solution would have been simpler: He would have waded in with a shotgun and started blasting.

A CPR team had arrived about twelve minutes after the neighbor called the police. But because of the snakes, they couldn't get to the woman. Finally, a brave one had raced over to the victim, who was lying on her stomach. He felt for a pulse as he glanced around to make sure no snakes were coming toward him.

Then the CPR guy put the vic's hand down and ran back into the house. There was nothing more he could do. The woman was dead.

Twenty-five minutes after the snake handlers got there, all the snakes were locked up in the boxes and the tops were latched.

The ME and Crawford went straight to the woman's body. Right away Crawford could see two bites: One on her right shoulder and the other on the palm of her right hand, which was twisted back at an unnatural angle. There were two holes a half-inch apart with a trickle of blood that had dried up and was now a burgundy color.

A tech was taking pictures with a digital camera and videotaping the scene. The two snake guys were just hanging around now, their job done. Nobody was saying much. The scene was way too grisly for the usual lame, tension-breaking jokes.

Crawford knew the ME, a guy by the name of Bob Hawes. Their first case together had turned acrimonious.

Hawes had a bulbous nose that was purplish red and veiny. He had dark, gnarly hair with several thick barbed-wire strands that sprouted out from the sides, and a deftly orchestrated comb-over. He reminded Crawford of an old radical lawyer he used to run across when he first started out in New York.

"I'm turning her over," the ME said, looking up at Crawford.

Crawford crouched down to get a closer look as Hawes rolled her.

"Jesus fucking Christ," Hawes said, recoiling.

Crawford tried hard not to let it show how freaked out he was as he took in the four-foot water moccasin, which seemed locked onto the woman's body. It was dead too. Its fangs remained embedded above the bare breasts of the woman. It looked like its skull had been crushed.

Crawford looked over at the ME, whose Adam's apple was bobbing like a yo-yo.

"Thought I'd fuckin' seen everything," the ME said.

Crawford examined the hardened blood where the snake's mouth was stuck to the woman. He didn't know whether the blood was hers or the snake's. Then he noticed two separate red-brown streams that joined together in between the woman's breasts.

Crawford felt queasy.

"I got a feeling what killed her was more the shock than poison," the ME said.

Crawford nodded as he theorized how the snake had died. Had

the woman—in her last, desperate act—killed it with her bare hands? Or maybe it happened when she fell on it.

"Someone brought 'em in here." Hawes said.

"Well, no shit," Crawford said, irritated with the guy's nervous chatter. "I didn't figure they were from the neighborhood."

One of the snake guys looked over at Crawford and stifled a smile.

Crawford heard footsteps on the pool deck and saw the ME turn his head.

"Hey, Bob," said a man.

It was Mort Ott.

Bald, lumpy, and politically incorrect, Ott was a first-rate detective, even though at age fifty-one, he looked ten years older. Part of it was being thirty pounds overweight. At five seven he weighed in at over two thirty, but despite not holding back on the doughnuts or Checkerburgers, he was in shape. He spent an hour a day in the gym before work and could bench three hundred pounds. He had no problem chasing a mutt up a chain-link fence, either.

Ott looked down at the dead woman and the crushed snake.

"Jesus," he said, wincing. "Don't see that every day."

"Yeah, someone dumped twenty of 'em over the wall," Crawford said.

"More than that," said one of the snake guys.

"Who else was here?" Ott asked Crawford.

"I don't know," Crawford said. "A guy named Churchill Ames owns the place."

"But he's not around?"

Crawford shook his head. "No, but I'm guessing he was when it happened."

"Why you say that?"

"'Cause there's two glasses over there, ice cubes still in 'em," Crawford said, pointing. "I'm gonna go check inside the house."

Ott nodded as he watched his partner walk toward the house and go up the steps.

"Your partner," Hawes said, taking a swab from inside the girl's mouth, "why's he always such a testy bastard?"

"Charlie? He's not testy." Ott wasn't too crazy about Hawes, either. "Where you get that?"

"I don't know...just—"

"Maybe not the most patient guy around," Ott said, staring at the victim's contorted face, "but no better homicide cop."

"If you say so," Hawes said, leaning over to examine the bite on the girl's hand.

Ott crouched down close to him and just observed for a few moments.

A little while later, Ott heard footsteps and swung around. Crawford was back.

"Find anything?" Ott asked.

"Nothing much," Crawford said. "Let's go have a chat with the neighbors."

"Okay." Ott's knees crackled as he got to his feet.

"I just can't fucking imagine being in her shoes," Ott said as they walked toward the house.

Ott's eyes suddenly widened. In a blur, his right hand went to his shoulder holster. He yanked out his Glock and fired twice.

Crawford looked down and saw a writhing water moccasin five feet away.

Ott fired a third time. It stopped writhing.

"Jesus Christ," Crawford said, turning to the snake guys. "Thought you assholes got 'em all."

One of them shrugged, the other looked down at his shoes.

Crawford tried to act like it was all in a day's work. But his heart was slamming away like a jackhammer. He shook his head and Ott smiled.

"So, how's this compare with shit up in the Apple, Charlie?"

Crawford thought for a second and slowly shook his head.

"Mutts up there just use guns and knives," he said. "Guys down here...way more creative."

FIVE

CRAWFORD AND OTT WALKED OUT TO THE STREET. CRAWFORD unlocked his car and reached into the back seat for his Maglite.

"Brought 'em in through the neighbor's backyard, I'm guessing," Crawford said, pointing at the house to the right of Churchill Ames's house. "I'll check out that one."

Ott nodded.

"You take the one on the other side," Crawford said. "We're definitely gonna find something. A footprint, maybe. If we're lucky, one of the neighbors'll give us a tip." Crawford shined his Mag back at Ames's house. "Let's see what we find out about Churchill Ames. Like where the hell he is, for starters."

Ott nodded. He went right and Crawford left.

Crawford couldn't get the image of the dead woman out of his head. He knew it would be a while before he could. He imagined being her, the pure, primal terror of the snakes all around her, their heads raised, then lunging and striking. But the worst part was that one hanging off of her, locked onto her in a savagely tenacious death grip.

He hit the buzzer of the house next door. A few seconds later he saw a man looking out through the sidelight to the right of the front door. The man didn't seem eager to open up.

Crawford held up his ID and badge.

The man opened the door, let Crawford in, then closed it fast.

"Sir, my name is Detect—"

"You get 'em all?"

"Yeah, every single one. I'm Detective Crawford."

"John Randall," the man said. "My wife's upstairs locked in the bathroom."

"Can't say I blame her," Crawford said. "So you're the one who called?"

"Uh-huh. At first I just thought it was Churchill up to his usual."

"Which was?" Crawford asked, taking out his notebook.

"Well, just...Churchill likes to 'entertain.' He has a number of lady friends over. I'm kind of an early-to-bed guy and—"

"So Mr. Ames wasn't married?"

"Ohhh, nooo. Well, he was, but...got divorced a year ago. Used to be pretty quiet next door. Not since his divorce, though," Randall said, maybe a little enviously.

"Do you know where he went?"

"What do you mean?"

"He's nowhere around."

"Well, he was. He's the one who yelled at me to call you."

"And you have no idea where he went?"

Randall shook his head.

"What does he do, Mr. Randall?"

"He's a lawyer, a pretty prominent one."

"Which firm?"

"I forget the name; it's over on Philips Point."

"Okay if I look around your backyard?" Crawford asked, putting his notebook in his jacket pocket.

"Help yourself. Those guys with the lights went back there... how'd the snakes get in, anyway?"

"That's what we're trying to figure out."

He walked through Randall's house, went out the slider in back, and then over to the wall. It had ficus and awabuki plants all along it. He walked beside the wall, aiming his Maglite at the wall first, then down at the ground. He had to step around the big lights, but didn't see anything that looked out of place.

Randall trailed close behind, like a kid afraid of the dark.

"Did you hear anything before Ames yelled?" Crawford asked.

"Well, yeah, that woman screaming. Never heard a scream like that in my whole life," Randall said. "I mean, worse than a horror movie."

Crawford wrote something down in his murder book.

"How is she, anyway?" Randall asked. "The girl."

Crawford looked at Randall and gave a quick shake of the head.

"Oh, Jesus."

"Anything else you remember, Mr. Randall?"

Randall scratched his forehead.

"No, sorry, that's all I can think of," he said. "Jesus, she's dead?"

Crawford nodded as he reached the end of the wall. Then he started back, his Maglite scanning the grass farther away from the wall.

He walked back up to the porch of Randall's house.

"Thanks for your help, Mr. Randall. I might need to call you. What's your phone number?"

Randall gave him his number. Crawford wrote it down, put his book back in his pocket, shook Randall's hand, and thanked him again.

He walked outside onto the sidewalk, past Churchill Ames's house to the house on the other side.

He noticed a small, discreet FOR SALE sign to the right of the house's expensive-looking mailbox.

He walked up the few steps of a large, two-story British Colonial. Barton Avenue was one of the more prestigious streets in Palm Beach, with predominantly Mediterranean, Bermuda, and British

Colonial-style houses that started at around five million. For the ocean and lake blocks you could add another couple of million.

The house was dark except for one light. He pressed the buzzer, heard some footsteps, then the door opened.

It was Rose Clarke, a real-estate broker he knew.

"Oh, God, hi Charlie," she said, obviously relieved.

She hugged him and held on a little too long.

Rose was five-ten, had long, lean runner's legs, breasts on the small, but perfectly proportioned side, and a face dominated by flashing blue eyes and steeply angled cheekbones. Her lips, though, were what you remembered most. Mick Jagger had nothing on her.

Rose Clarke had it, and liked to flaunt it.

"What are you doing here, Rose?" Crawford asked.

"This is one of my listings," she said. "The owner called me, said he got a call from one of your guys who told him what happened next door. He asked me to come over, make sure everything was okay here."

Of course it would be her listing, seeing how she sold half the houses in Palm Beach.

"I was at a dinner party," she said, raising a wineglass. "Brought along a roadie."

"That'll be our little secret. Drinking and driving, we kinda frown on that," Crawford said. "You see my partner, Mort?"

"Yeah, doing his thing out back," Rose said.

Crawford walked toward the back door. "Well, I'm gonna see if he found anything."

"Be my guest," she said. "Think I'll stay here, if you don't mind. Not real big on snakes."

Ditto that, thought Crawford, pushing the heavy glass slider. He saw Ott fifty feet down the wall. He was on his knees, vinyl gloves on, like some nocturnal gardener.

Crawford walked over to him.

"This is where it went down," Ott said, pointing.

Crawford got down in a crouch and looked to where Ott was pointing at a mark in the grass.

"A ladder, huh?" Crawford said.

"Yeah," Ott said, shining his flashlight at a three-inch vertical scuffmark on the wall.

"It's fresh, definitely," Crawford said, examining it.

"I couldn't find any shoe-print impressions," Ott said. "Whoever it was, brought 'em in and dumped 'em over."

"Two-man job, probably?" Crawford said.

Ott nodded.

"I'm gonna ask Hawes to send a tech over," Crawford said.

Ott nodded again.

A few moments later they went inside. Rose was standing in the kitchen in her five-thousand-dollar spaghetti-strap dress. She had helped herself to a bottle of expensive wine.

"Rose," Crawford said, "you know anything about the next-door neighbor, Churchill Ames?"

Ott pulled out his notebook.

"He's a big-time attorney," Rose said. "Not to mention way up the social chain. President of the Poinciana, for starters."

Crawford nodded.

"Anything else?"

She moved closer and dropped her voice.

"You didn't hear this from me, okay?"

Crawford nodded.

"You promise?" she said.

"I promise."

"Well...he's had a lot of wives, blown a small fortune on exes. His last divorce, Celia, was a real nasty one," she said. "He comes off as a little arrogant, kind of high and mighty, but, like I said, you didn't hear that from me."

"What's the name of his law firm?" Crawford asked.

"They call it 'four WASPs and a token'...Swiggett, Kirk, Ames, Timpson and Weinberg."

"What kind of lawyers are they?"

"Litigators; a pretty hard-nosed bunch."

"His last divorce," Ott asked, "the 'real nasty' one...what was so nasty about it?"

Rose poured another glass of wine and looked up at Ott.

"Some people think Churchill hid assets," she said. "That was the story making the rounds, anyway. His ex tried to prove it, but couldn't. She ended up getting next to nothing, I heard."

"And, we can assume, wasn't too pleased about that?" Crawford said.

"Are you kidding? How 'bout wanted to kill the bastard?" Rose said. "Wait, are you thinking she—"

"Just asking questions, Rose," Crawford said. "Anything else?"

Rose blinked, then shook her head. "No, I don't think so."

"Well, thanks, that's very helpful," Crawford said. "I'll call you if I have any other questions."

She gave him a toast with her wineglass and smiled. "Call me anyway, will you, Charlie?"

She walked over to Crawford and gave him a kiss. "Well, I guess you boys got everything under control, so I'll be on my way." She nodded at Ott and walked out the front door.

Ott smiled at Crawford.

"What?" Crawford said.

"You know damn well what," Ott said. "Chick's got a hard-on for you."

"Bullshit, I hardly know her."

"Whatever you say, Charlie."

"Let's go," Crawford said.

"Where to?"

"Good Sam," Crawford said, referring to Good Samaritan Hospital in West Palm. "See if that's where this guy Ames ended up. Then I want to head back to the station and brush up on my poisonous reptiles."

SIX

CRAWFORD HAD CALLED IT.

Churchill Ames was at Good Samaritan Hospital, but the people there wouldn't let them in to see him. Crawford told them it was critical police business and involved a fatality, but the doctor in charge insisted that they come back first thing the next morning.

IT WAS 1:30 IN THE MORNING AND CRAWFORD HAD BEEN ON Google for an hour and a half. He now knew a lot about the snake species known as *Agkistrodon piscivorus*, aka water moccasins.

He'd found more than 1,080 entries with the words water moccasin in them. In just about every description of the snake, the word aggressive had been used to describe them. There were plenty of references, also, to how bad they smelled. Several mentioned the musky odor of a skunk.

One site called flyanglers.com breezily described a man's account of a fishing trip on a Louisiana bayou. "When I was a kid," the man wrote, "my father and I got run out of Cotton Canal (so named because of the abundance of cottonmouth snakes) after several water moccasins decided they wanted the fish we had in our boat. Dad killed two with his paddle, but they started coming at the boat from all directions. We fled under power, the outboard tapping and bashing logs as we went."

Then he came across something that helped explain the nightmarish sight he had witnessed in Churchill Ames's backyard. The site described a water moccasin's "habit of latching on during a bite rather than the quick strike-and-release pattern of its cousin, the copperhead."

He had just found an article out of a Jacksonville newspaper. The headline was WOMAN BITTEN BY POISONOUS SNAKE HIDING IN TOILET.

The article began: In one Florida household, a whole family is afraid of the toilet after a poisonous snake used it as a hiding place. Tuesday night, Alicia Bailey was bitten by what appeared to have been a large water moccasin that had been hiding in the bowl in the middle of the night. The snake bit her thigh after she lifted the lid, sending her to the hospital for three days. No one knows how the snake got into the toilet or where it went from there.

Crawford decided to call it a night a little before two a.m. He shut down his computer, walked out of the station house on County Road, and headed over to his condo in West Palm.

He took the elevator to the sixth floor. Ten minutes later, he was in bed, ready for a night of vivid snake dreams in high-def and Technicolor.

SURE ENOUGH, HE WAS IN THE MIDDLE OF A DONNYBROOK between water moccasins and rattlesnakes when his alarm clock mercifully rescued him from the hair-raising dream. He got up, showered, and hit the Dunkin' Donuts around the corner. Then he made the ten-minute drive to Good Samaritan Hospital.

Ott was waiting for him outside the room on the third floor of Good Sam.

"Nurse told me Ames just woke up," he said as Crawford walked up to him.

Crawford took a sip of his extra-dark coffee.

"So let's go talk to him," said Crawford. "Still no ID on the girl yet?"

"Not yet, no purse or ID at the scene."

They walked into the hospital room. Churchill Ames was hooked up to an IV, reading the *Wall Street Journal*, and looking like a mussed-up patrician. He was unshaven, his hair in no discernible pattern, his blue eyes watery.

On a dresser across from him stood a huge bouquet of flowers.

Ames showed little surprise when Crawford and Ott walked in.

"Mr. Ames, I'm Detective Crawford, this is Detective Ott, Palm Beach Police," Crawford said, stopping at the foot of Ames's bed.

Ames nodded as if he was already supremely bored.

"How are you feeling?" Crawford asked.

"Fine. Just a little snakebite."

Crawford nodded back. Given Ames's profile, he'd been expecting the macho act.

"They gonna let you out today?" Crawford asked.

Ames shook his head. "Tomorrow, they tell me."

Crawford nodded. "So tell us what happened, please."

"Well," Ames said, putting his paper down, "I was making drinks in my pool house and I heard a noise—"

"What kind of noise, Mr. Ames?" Ott asked.

Ames shot Ott a look of irritation. Like he was used to interrupting, not being interrupted.

"I don't know, just a noise."

"It's important, Mr. Ames. Can you describe what it sounded like?" Ott asked.

Ames sighed theatrically.

"I don't know, kind of a scraping sound. Like something hard and heavy."

Ott scribbled it down.

"So I took the drinks back to the pool," Ames said, "then heard another noise. Louder."

"Can you describe—" Ott started.

"I'm getting to it," Ames said. "Like a big thump."

Crawford edged closer to Ames's bed.

"Mr. Ames, the woman with you...who was she?"

Ames's eyes started batting.

"Ah... her name's Jessie," he said. "She's a...friend."

His tense was off by twelve hours.

"She was a friend, Mr. Ames." Crawford said. "She's dead."

"Oh, my God," Ames said. "I had no idea."

Crawford eyed him for a full five seconds without saying anything.

"You didn't ask about her," Crawford said, letting a sliver of contempt show. "If she was a friend, I guess I'd expect you to ask how she was."

"I—I ...I've been in shock," Ames said.

Crawford's expression didn't change. "What's Jessie's last name?"

"I didn't know her that long," Ames answered.

"Wait a minute," Ott said, his eyes squinty, "you don't know her last name?"

Ames looked like he wanted to bitch-slap Ott. Instead, he sighed theatrically again, as if reaching the end of his patience.

"No, I don't know her name. She was a friend of a friend."

"Who's your friend?" Crawford asked.

"Name is David Balfour."

Palm Beach was a small town. Crawford knew Balfour from a past case.

"So what exactly happened?" Crawford asked.

"She went into the pool; then all of a sudden they were every-where. One of 'em got in the pool and came toward her," Ames said.

"I think she saw that one. I started to go help her. But by the time I got there, there were two more, one on the pool's edge, right next to her. It bit her as she was getting out." Ames looked away and shook his head slowly.

Crawford felt he was watching a mediocre actor do his version of anguish. Something that might work on a rookie judge or a gullible jury.

"So what did you do?" Ott asked.

"I went back to the pool house," Ames said. "They were all around me. No way I could get to her."

Ott snuck Crawford a look.

Ames intercepted it.

"Listen, whatever-the-hell your name is," Ames said. "I'm sick of your attitude. I could have gotten killed."

"My name is Ott."

"Lose the hostility, please, Mr. Ames," Crawford said. "We're just trying to get a handle on what happened."

"And I'm trying to tell you," Ames said. "I went around my pool house and made a run to the back wall to try to get help. I saw a snake, dodged it, and got bit by another one. Then I climbed up over the wall."

"Did it occur to you to go around, come back through the house and try to help the woman?" Crawford asked.

"Let me ask you a question, Officer: Were you at my house? Did you see how many snakes were there?"

Crawford nodded.

Ames shrugged, as if the answer to Crawford's prior question was obvious.

"Still haven't told us: Why you didn't call the police?" Ott asked.

Ames's face reddened.

"'Cause I'd been bitten by a goddamn poisonous snake. I yelled to my neighbor to call you and went straight to the hospital. Got a problem with that?"

A nurse came in with a huge bouquet of flowers in a glass vase.

"Here you go, Mr. Ames," the nurse said, oblivious to the heat around her. "More flowers. How are you feeling?"

"Fine," he said.

Ames opened the card that came with the flowers, then quickly put it down on the hospital table.

"Nice flowers." Crawford looked over at the big bouquet on the dresser, then the one Ames had just gotten. "Who are they all from, if you don't mind me asking?"

"Just...people at work," Ames said.

Crawford nodded slowly. "Okay, Mr. Ames," he said, "before we leave, how about helping us out a little. Like, for starters, who do you think did this?"

"I have absolutely no idea," Ames said, glaring at Crawford.

"No idea?" Crawford said. "Someone dumps a bunch of snakes in your backyard and you have no idea who could have done it? Really?"

"Clearly a message," Ott said.

"What the hell's that supposed to mean?" Ames snapped.

"What my partner's saying," Crawford said, "is that for someone to go out and round up a bunch of snakes, bring them all the way from God knows where, then carry them up to the top of a six-foot wall and dump 'em...well, wouldn't it be easier just to shoot you in the head?"

"See, Mr. Ames," Ott said, "snakes as a weapon, are a little more hit or miss."

They both eyed Ames for a response. None came.

"No idea who could have done it, huh?" Crawford said. "Not even a wild guess."

Ames shook his head.

"Someone from a past trial, maybe?" Crawford asked.

"No," Ames said.

"A past relationship, a marriage maybe?" Ott asked.

Ames shook his head emphatically.

Crawford glanced over at Ott.

"Okay, Mr. Ames, we're done here," he said. "I'd like to be able to say thanks for all your help, but..."

He took a step closer to Ames and glanced down at the card that came with the flowers.

"Anyway, we'll be in touch," Crawford said as he led Ott out of the room and into the corridor.

———

"NICE JOB, MORT," CRAWFORD SAID, WALKING UP TO A WATER fountain, "your usual bulldog self."

He bent over and took a drink.

"Thanks," Ott said. "Looked like at one point he was gonna jump out of bed and cold-cock me."

Crawford patted him on the shoulder.

"Okay, here's what we gotta do. I need you to look into the girl, Jessie," Crawford said. "I'll see if I can get her last name from that guy Ames mentioned, David Balfour. I know him. It's pretty clear she's a working girl. See what you can find out about how one goes about getting their hands on snakes like that too."

Ott nodded.

"What are you gonna do, Charlie?"

"First, go see a florist."

"See who sent those flowers?" Ott said.

Crawford nodded. "I know who sent the last bunch," he said, "'cause I'm an expert upside-down reader. It was signed Celia. That ring a bell?"

"Oh, yeah," Ott said, watching a nurse walk past. "The broad the realtor mentioned. Wife number two, right?"

"No, actually, number three," Crawford said. "Way I remember it, she didn't think she got a real good shake of the marital spoils."

Ott nodded, then bent over and took a long, slurpy sip from the water fountain.

"Seems like she's got motive," Crawford said. "Even though it's kind of a reach, some society babe rounding up a bunch of deadly snakes."

"That's why people have accomplices, Charlie."

Crawford nodded. "Another thing: Those flowers she sent were lilies. I remember reading something about lilies once."

"What about 'em?" Ott asked.

"They represent death."

Ott cocked his head to one side.

"You're kidding," he said, skeptically. "Where the hell'd you get that?"

"I don't know," Crawford said. "Somewhere. That big bouquet on the dresser-card said Maximus Flower Shop. I've been there—back in my courting days."

"Dominica?"

Crawford ignored the question. "Something doesn't add up. If Ames didn't get here 'til ten last night and—I can pretty much guarantee you—wasn't up to making any calls last night or this morning, then how'd Celia and whoever sent the other bouquet know he was here?"

"That's a damn good question, Charlie," Ott said. "Want to go back in, put the question to our new buddy?"

Crawford rolled his eyes. "Hell, no. I've had more than enough of that jack-off for one day."

SEVEN

CRAWFORD LOVED THE SMELL OF FLOWER SHOPS, PARTICULARLY this one. He had been to Maximus buying flowers for Dominica McCarthy, who was a crime scene tech at the Palm Beach Police Department. It was right after the Ward Jaynes murder case. He had dragged her into the case and given her a starring role in trying to solve it. At one point, it looked like getting her involved could get her killed, but she got through it in one piece, and with her help, Crawford went on to solve it. At any rate, it seemed that the least he could do to show his appreciation was spring for a couple-hundred bucks' worth of flowers for her. And dinner. And, as it turned out, one thing led to another and damned if they didn't end up in bed together. It was good while it lasted, but it only lasted four-and-a-half months.

The woman at the shop remembered him. "I've got some really beautiful roses today," she said, pointing to a display.

"Thanks," he said. "It's Julia, right?"

She nodded and smiled. "Good memory."

He showed her his ID.

"Actually, I just stopped by to ask you a few questions, if that's okay?"

"A detective?" she said. "Wow, that's about the last thing I would have figured you for."

He had heard that before and hadn't yet figured out how to respond to it. Was it a compliment? An insult? He opted to just smile.

"Two bouquets of flowers were delivered this morning to a man named Churchill Ames at Good Samaritan Hospital," he said. "Do you know who sent them?"

"Two?"

"Yes."

"Only one came from here," she said. "A man with an accent called, charged it to a credit card."

Then she went over to a stack of receipts.

"Was it a really big bouquet?" Crawford asked.

"Oh, yes, our best one," she said, going through the stack and stopping at one. "Here it is. The man who sent it was"—she paused to grapple with the pronunciation—"Aleksandr Zinoviev."

"You mind if I look at that?" Crawford asked.

"No, not at all, here you go," she said, handing him the invoice. "Oh, that's right, he ordered two bouquets, one for Mr. Ames and the other one for someone up on the north end."

Crawford wrote down the man's name and address.

"Here you go," she said. "Here's the address for the other one he sent."

Crawford looked down and saw the address: 210 Queens Lane.

It was an address he was very familiar with and had been to many times. The same place he had sent his bouquet of roses to. It was Dominica McCarthy's address.

"Thank you very much," he said, sniffing a bouquet of roses. "You know, you could make a fortune in perfume if you could bottle up the smell of this place."

"What a great idea," she said.

"Well, thank you very much for all the help, Julia," Crawford said. "Time to get back to my musty-smelling office now."

HE WENT BACK TO THE STATION, LOOKED UP CELIA AMES' address, and he and Ott headed over there. She lived just past the bridge in West Palm Beach.

Westminster Street wasn't actually in El Cid. It was on the cusp. El Cid was one of the nicest neighborhoods in West Palm. It was the step before you moved across the bridge to a house in Palm Beach. Or the step after you got stiffed by a guy who came up short on alimony. The streets in El Cid were almost all fancy-sounding Spanish names like Valencia, Barcelona, and Cordova. Westminster Street, though a fancy-sounding English name, was a more modest street with houses ranging in price from two hundred thousand dollars to half a million for something bigger and in mint condition.

It was about 12:30 when Crawford and Ott got to Celia Ames's house. They had called from the station but had only gotten a recording. Celia Ames answered their knock with a caramel-colored drink in her hand. From the look of her eyes, Crawford guessed it was not iced tea.

They showed her ID and she told them to come in. They sat down in her somewhat threadbare living room. Crawford detected the smell of a cat or dog, something from the domesticated animal kingdom. But the only living thing he saw was a cockroach skitter across the dull parquet floor.

Crawford smiled at the wary-looking woman. She had tiny lines all over her face that reminded Crawford of a cranky, old-maid aunt of his. He guessed too much sun and not enough money from her ex were contributing factors to Celia's rhino hide.

"Mrs. Ames, do you know what happened at your ex-husband's house last night?"

Crawford's sense was that everybody within a twenty-mile radius knew, even though it hadn't hit the papers yet.

"Of course," Celia said. "I was sorry to hear about that poor girl... should have been old shithead instead."

Ott maintained a straight face with difficulty.

Celia smiled and took a double pull on her drink.

"Why do you say that?" Crawford asked.

"'Cause the man's a goddamn bum. Fraud too."

Crawford liked direct people.

"All his 'to the manner born' crap," Celia went on. "Guy was born in Wheeling, West Virginia, for Chrissakes. Father was a coal miner; changed his name from Elmer to Churchill."

Another guy who reinvented himself in Palm Beach, thought Crawford. Not an unusual occurrence.

"But you sent him a bouquet of flowers?" Ott said.

Celia scowled.

"Yeah, so? It was a fifty-dollar way of saying, 'Awww, so sorry about your little snakebite, Churchie. Sorry it wasn't lethal, that is.'"

"How'd you find out about it, Mrs. Ames?" Ott asked.

Celia shifted around in her chair, like she had fleas up her dress.

"First of all, it's not Mrs. Ames. I went back to my maiden name: It's Ms. Senior. And second, my old neighbor, Judy Randall, called me. Told me she was locked up in her bathroom, petrified to go outside. She heard a girl screaming. And Churchill? He was nowhere to be found, she said."

"So how'd you know he was at the hospital?" Ott asked.

"'Cause I was magna cum laude at Radcliffe...I mean, where else would he go? Unless maybe to one of his strip joints. Get one of his pole-dancer friends to suck the poison out."

Crawford leaned forward, but Ott spoke first.

"Would you be willing to take a polygraph test to prove you had nothing to do with what happened?" Ott asked.

Celia almost lost her mouthful.

"It could help clear your name," Ott said.

"My name is clear," Celia said.

"So you had nothing to do with it. Is that what you're saying, Ms. Senior?" Ott asked.

"If I planned to kill him, my little friend, I'd make damn sure I did."

Ott smiled. To Crawford's knowledge, Ott had never been called "my little friend" before.

"So, that would be a no?" Ott said.

Celia threw back the last of the amber liquid and wiped her lips.

"That would be a king-size no," Celia said. "What are you talking to me for? Go talk to Maddy Sorenson or Buzz Cox. They're big fans of my beloved ex."

"Who are they?" Ott asked.

"Like I said, two people who have the same high regard for Church as I do," Celia said. "Maddy's a slutty little cock-tease at Church's law firm who's in a big hurry to screw her way to the top. And Buzz is Churchill's former best friend, now biggest enemy."

Ott wrote down the names.

"So you're saying those two had motives to kill your ex-husband?" Crawford asked. "As opposed to, in your case, just hoping for the worst?"

Celia chuckled. "You have a clever way with words, Detective."

"So what would be their motives, Ms. Senior?"

"In Buzz's case, Church lost all his money," Celia said. "Maddy— it's a little more complicated. You'll have to ask her."

"But your ex-husband was a lawyer," Crawford said. "Not a money manager."

"True," Celia said. "Just talk to Buzz. He'll tell you all about the whole debacle. I doubt either one would ever kill him, but they might hire someone." Then she locked eyes with Crawford. "All clear?"

"Crystal," Crawford said.

Celia pushed out of her Salvation Army-looking love seat and got up.

"Can I get either of you something to drink? Got a nice bottle of rotgut over there."

Ott shook his head.

"No thanks, not a big rotgut man," Crawford said as he watched

Celia shamble over to her bar and pour another four fingers of bourbon. "Anybody else you can think of?"

"Hmm, anybody else?" Celia pondered Crawford's question as she walked back to the love seat. "Well, actually, yes; plenty of people. I mean, he used to come home after a trial and boast about screwing over so-and-so. To quote the great barrister—'ream 'em a new asshole'—was how he always put it. Charming, huh?"

Crawford was having difficulty squaring this Ames with the one who was president of the most prominent, blue blood club in town.

Crawford decided to go for a long shot. "Did those flowers you sent him have any special meaning?"

Celia Senior looked at him quizzically.

"The lilies, you mean?"

He nodded.

"Why, what did you think their secret meaning might be?"

Crawford shrugged. "Oh, I don't know."

"Sometimes, Detective, a lily is just a lily."

Crawford stood up. Ott followed his lead.

"Well, thank you, Ms. Senior," Crawford said. "We'll be in touch."

But Ott wasn't quite done.

"Just curious: Do you live alone here, Ms. Senior?" he asked.

Celia hesitated. "Yes, yes I do."

"No pets or anything?" Ott asked.

"No, just me and all my happy memories."

"Thank you, Ms. Senior," Ott said, shaking hands with her. "Appreciate your help."

———————————

INSIDE THE CROWN VIC, CRAWFORD TURNED TO OTT. "KIND OF a bitter woman, wouldn't you say?"

"Yeah, with good reason, I'd say," Ott said.

Crawford nodded.

"You notice her reaction when I asked if she was living alone?" Ott asked.

"Sure did. My bullshit-o-meter went through the roof," Crawford said. "And what the hell was that smell?"

The place could definitely use a douse of Maximus Flower Shop, he was thinking.

"Guarantee you," Ott said, "at least one of God's creatures is hanging its hat at Celia's roach motel."

"I agree."

Ott cocked his head. "Hey, what about those lilies?"

"What about 'em?"

"Well, like the girl said...sometimes a lily is just a lil—"

"Yeah, yeah, put a sock in it."

EIGHT

CRAWFORD DIALED ROSE CLARKE IN THE CAR. HE KNEW ROSE A little better than he had let on. And Rose knew everybody who was anybody in Palm Beach. That was probably what made her the most successful real-estate broker there. That and the fact that she also knew all their little secrets—dirty and otherwise.

Crawford heard she averaged over five million a year in commissions. Last year, a few years after the recession, when things were still pretty soft, someone told him she still made a very respectable three million dollars.

"Hello," Rose answered.

"Hey Rose, it's Charlie Crawford," he said. "Got a question for you."

"Of course you do," Rose said. "About one of your cases—the girl who got killed probably. Surprise me just once, Charlie, and make the question, 'How 'bout dinner tonight?'"

His other option was a turkey burger and four-month-old frozen broccoli florets at his apartment overlooking the Publix parking lot.

"How 'bout dinner tonight?"

"I thought you'd never ask," she said. "I accept. What was your question anyway, Charlie?"

"Do you know a man named Aleksandr Zinoviev?" he asked.

ROSE, WHO WAS IN THE MIDDLE OF PRIMPING A TIRED-LOOKING house at 1290 South Ocean for her 12:30–2:00 open house, pondered how best to answer the question. She always invested in her listings and open houses. Why wouldn't she? When she stood to make somewhere north of a four-hundred-thousand-dollar commission on a dog of a house like this one? What was a thousand bucks in orchids, a cleaning crew, and getting that sweet old black man, Raymond, to make sure all the windows facing the ocean were spotless? Rose always brought along a stack of fashionable coffee-table books, which she stored in a large Bergdorf bag in the trunk of her Jag. Today she had replaced the owner's dusty bargello needlepoint book and the dog-eared Peter Arno cartoon collection from a million years ago on the living-room coffee table with Slim Aarons's *Once Upon a Time, Island Life* by India Hicks, and *The Most Beautiful Houses of Tuscany*. It went a long way to bringing the house out of the Marimekko seventies and into the early twenty-first century.

She was now carefully positioning several magazines, which she'd brought from home, on the night table next to the master bed. The bland but necessary *Town & Country*; *Vanity Fair*, of course, featuring its inevitable starlet-in-a-bathing-suit cover, the ultra-high-gloss, house-worshipping *Architectural Digest*, and—to intellectually class up the whole presentation—*The New Yorker*.

Last came Rose's olfactory transformation, which was crucial since, in many cases, that's exactly what houses that had recently been died in smelled like: old factories. Rose brought in the miracle ionization machine from Sharper Image that sucked away all the decayed, desiccated smells of various body dysfunctions. It had miraculously purged the air of forty years' worth of Chesterfield cigarettes too. Another cardinal rule of Rose's was to remove all walkers, respirators, hospital beds, bathtub grab bars, and yellowed toilet booster seats from her listings.

Then she had her cleaning lady, Herminia, shampoo the living-room carpet using a few drops of expensive lavender oil, which Rose had bought in Paris. After that she lit scented candles and placed a bar of L'Occitane in each soap dish. Rose had arm-twisted the heirs of the estate into springing for a one-coat paint job and a land-scaping face-lift, but they had nixed her request for new kitchen cabinets.

All in all, Rose could have authored the definitive manual on how to prep a house, but why share her secrets with the competition?

Instead, she kept them to herself and reaped the rewards. She had a seven percent open-house hit rate—her term for getting a signed contract from an open-house attendee—while the average for other brokers fell somewhere between one and two percent.

As she finished off her remaining tasks at the South Ocean prop-erty—like nipping a bud off of a Confederate jasmine—Rose, Blue-tooth clamped to her ear, answered Crawford's question about Aleksandr Zinoviev.

"Aleksandr is one of two Russian brothers who live up on the north end," she said. "Why?"

"What can you tell me about him?"

A pause. Then she turned all business.

"Our usual deal, right?" she asked.

She and Charlie had worked out a little arrangement. He liked to ask questions and get answers, but wasn't so good the other way around. After all, as he was quick to point out, he was a detective and asked questions for a living. Rose, however, had made it clear from the start that this particular equation didn't work for her. If she was going to feed him valuable information, then she expected something in return.

"You scratch my back, Charlie," she had said a couple months back, "and I'll...dig my nails into yours."

"Okay, the usual deal," he replied. "But this conversation is totally off the rec—"

"Yeah, yeah, I know," Rose said. "So what do you want to know?"

"Aleksandr Zinoviev's name came up in the course of one of my investigations," Crawford said. "What do you know about him? And what about his brother?"

"Well, Aleksandr's the cute one. His brother, Vasily, um, not so much," she said. "I don't know that much about them except clearly they're very rich. They bought the Schwartzreich house up near where the Bloviator lives."

"Who?"

"El Rushbo."

"Oh, gotcha," said Crawford.

"They didn't buy it through me, though," Rose added. "Right after they closed, they tore the house down."

"Why'd they do that?"

"You'll appreciate this," she said. "Somehow they managed to get their hands on Hugh Hefner's old plans for the Playboy Mansion and copied it brick for brick."

"The exact same house?"

"Identical."

"What did you mean...I'll appreciate it?"

"Just that you probably went through a Playboy fantasy period in your youth." Rose said. "You know, dreaming about all those bunnies with the twenty-pound boobs swimming around naked in the grotto with the Hef-ster."

"Just for the record, Rose, I was a Penthouse guy," Crawford said. "So just the two brothers live there?"

"Oh, no-oo," Rose said. "Word is, they have a harem of Russian women."

"Why?"

Rose, a multitasker before the word was invented, was thumbing through the pages of *Island Life* with one hand, fluffing up a pillow with the other and carrying on the conversation.

"Why? Oh, I don't know, Charlie. Sex would be one reason that would occur to me," she said. "But then, it occurs to me quite often."

Crawford wasn't going there. "So what do these guys do, anyway?"

"No clue," she said. "Aleksandr seems to spend most of his time chasing women. Hasn't gotten around to me yet."

Rose heard someone walk in.

"Sorry, I've got to run, Charlie," she said. "I'm at an open house and someone just showed up."

"Thanks, Rose."

"You're welcome. Do I ever disappoint you?"

"Never."

"Ha. Wish I could say the same for you."

NINE

It was 1:15 on Saturday and Crawford and Ott had just briefed Norm Rutledge, Chief of Detectives of the Palm Beach Police Department, about what had happened after they arrived at the murder scene the night before. They talked about the investigation and what they had observed at the scene. Then Crawford described their meeting with Churchill Ames that morning: the flowers, the card he had read upside down, and what he had just heard about the Russian brothers. Given what Rose had told him about Aleksandr's woman-chasing ways, Crawford had a pretty good idea why the other bouquet had been sent to Dominica.

Next, Ott laid out what he had found out about Ames's three divorces: He had dug around and confirmed that Celia Senior was indeed very unhappy, not so much that the marriage had gone south, but about her paltry cut of the Ames assets. Crawford said he was still nosing around, seeing if there might be someone out to kill Ames because of the outcome of a trial and, per Celia Senior's recommendation, told him that he planned to meet with Buzz Cox and Maddy Sorenson right away.

Rutledge commended them for the thorough report, then got in their faces.

"Guess what? I just got a call from Ames," Rutledge said, spit starting to fly. "I never met the man, but I sure know who he is."

"Yeah...and?"

"He complained you two were 'unprofessional and confrontational.'"

Ott shook his head and rolled his eyes. "Is that a fact? Well, my complaint is he was an arrogant, uncooperative asshole."

Crawford laughed.

"You think that's funny?" Rutledge said. "This is not the first time I've gotten complaints about your attitudes."

"Christ, Norm," Crawford said. "The guy leaves a woman to die at his pool. Doesn't even tell anyone about her. So now, you're busting our balls for asking him tough questions and doing our jobs?"

"No, not for that, just the way he said you treated him," Rutledge said. "Like he was some kind of Riviera Beach street thug."

"First of all, that's not what we did," Crawford said, "and second of all, you're making the guy out to be some kinda choirboy."

It was Ott's turn. "And third of all, the guy had a hooker at his house."

"How do you know that?" Rutledge asked.

"Well, for one thing," Ott said, "when a guy has a normal date, he usually knows her name."

Rutledge looked like he needed to chew on that a bit. "All right," he said at last. "Not like I'm taking this guy's side here. All I'm saying is, use some discretion, especially when the guy's a victim. All right?"

Crawford looked at Ott and fought an urge to shake his head. Rutledge's message was old hat. As usual, he expected them to tiptoe gingerly around the rich and powerful and do things the Rutledge way. As usual, that was not going to happen.

"Hey, Norm, we're all about crime victims," Crawford said, calmly. "But get your head around the fact that a woman who was with Churchill Ames died in a pretty horrible way and it was like he just didn't give a shit."

"Okay, I hear you," Rutledge said, "and I get it. I feel bad for the girl. But the way Ames tells it, you two were making it seem like he killed her."

Ott shot a look at Crawford, who was far from done.

"No, Norm, all I'm saying is that this girl—whose name is Jessie, if anyone gives a shit—would have been alive if she never ran across Churchill Ames." Crawford raised his eyebrows, making sure the point had sunk in. "Girl was an innocent victim and somebody's gotta give a damn about her. 'Cause I can guarantee you, old fish-lips Ames sure as hell didn't."

TEN

CRAWFORD WAS STILL SEETHING ABOUT RUTLEDGE'S REACTION. He was mumbling "fuckin' idiot" a lot in his office with Ott.

Then Ott left, and Crawford still couldn't get it out of his head. Wondering whether Rutledge was chief of detectives or ambassador in charge of making sure there were no ruffled feathers in Palm Beach? What got him really crazy was how Rutledge's reaction was as much about keeping a big player like Churchill Ames happy as about tracking down the killer of a bit player like Jessie.

CRAWFORD WAS AT THE STATION THE NEXT MORNING. IT WAS Sunday. He was waiting for Ott. The two of them had a particularly unwanted job scheduled for a little later.

Two on-duty detectives at the station were going through a Sunday ritual with the Glossy. The Glossy was the nickname for the *Palm Beach Daily Reporter*, which—particularly on Sunday—featured pages and pages of real-estate ads mixed in with pictures of people attending society functions. On extremely rare occasions, you'd find a few paragraphs devoted to actual news.

The drill was they'd peruse the Glossy and examine pictures taken at charity benefits and fundraisers. Then a vote would be taken to determine which tightly stretched and unsmiling face—accentuated by trademark "just been goosed" eyes—would be proclaimed the winner of the worst face-lift of the week award. The hands-down favorite was always Fanny Kluge, of the lockset and sliding-bolt fortune Kluges.

After watching a new winner be proclaimed, Crawford walked back to his office flashing back to his conversation the night before with Churchill Ames's friend, David Balfour. Balfour, after first playing dumb about Jessie, finally told Crawford her last name was Kammerer. Last thing Balfour wanted was to be connected to the victim in any way. Crawford had to assure him that there wouldn't be any leak to the press and that his name wouldn't show up in any police blotter. Balfour said all he had done, after all, was given Ames a name and a phone number. Then he added how he was truly sorry about what happened to her, that she was a real sweet kid, and yada-yada-yada.

Next, Crawford had gotten the number of Aleksandr Zinoviev from an Internet directory. It was listed simply as E. A. Zinoviev and the phone number, but no address. Crawford had called the number twice. No one answered and he had left two messages. If he didn't hear back in the next few hours, he was going to get the address from Rose Clarke and go straight to the house.

After that, Crawford had logged onto the public database Lexis-Nexis and then had gone onto FCIS, the Florida Crime and Information System. He found that Jessie had a minor criminal record. She had been arrested in November 2006 for a DUI in Boca Raton that had been pled down to a moving violation. A second criminal case showed that Jessie had also done a stint onstage—the stage of a West Palm Beach strip club—and had been arrested coming out of there one night with a couple of other girls possessing high-grade marijuana, ecstasy, and Quaaludes.

After a series of calls, Crawford had tracked down the name and address of Jessie's parents. He and Ott were about to go do the job cops hated the most.

CRAWFORD, FOLLOWING OTT'S DIRECTIONS, TURNED RIGHT onto the crushed clamshell driveway. They were in Palmsville, a nothing little town about an hour and fifteen minutes north of Palm Beach. It was just after 9:30. There was no good time to deliver a death notification, though Crawford hated doing it early in the morning. It was a terrible way to start a day for a victim's loved ones. Because there you were—the face of doom—on the porch of someone's house. Just like a military guy showing up at the parents' house of some poor kid who was suicide-bombed in Afghanistan. Whoever answers, they know right away. The tall guy in a suit with the short, uneasy-looking bald guy behind him aren't there to hand out Jehovah's Witnesses' brochures.

A woman came to the door, wearing a simple, conservative dress with white piping on the lapels. She was smiling. But it faded fast.

"Mrs. Kammerer?"

"Yes. Who are you?" she asked, then turned back into the house. "Leo."

"I'm Detective Crawford, this is Detective Ott," Crawford said, feeling like the grim reaper.

A large man in a blue collared shirt came up behind Mrs. Kammerer. "What's wrong?"

"Is Jessica Kammerer your daughter?" Crawford asked.

"Yes," said the mother, her expression wide with dread.

"What happened?" asked the father, suddenly breathing faster.

"I'm sorry to have to tell you," Crawford said solemnly, "but your daughter died night before last."

The woman turned to the man, threw her arms around him, and started sobbing.

"What—what—?" was all Leo Kammerer was able to get out.

He looked disbelieving, shocked, and utterly destroyed.

Crawford explained what had happened.

It took a while for them to grasp the full horror of it. As it sank in, Mrs. Kammerer found a moment's composure and invited Crawford and Ott inside.

She asked if they wanted something to drink. No one did. Crawford told them what happened. The only way to do a death notification was to just keep slogging along, not slow down no matter how emotional the loved ones got. The natural thing was to let them react, but you needed to get all the facts out first. Otherwise, the process could go on forever.

"Who was the man our daughter was with?" Mrs. Kammerer asked.

"His name is Churchill Ames. He was bitten too, but he survived. He was released from the West Palm hospital," Crawford said.

"Where is our daughter now?" Leo Kammerer asked.

Crawford told them.

Mrs. Kammerer nodded slowly, tears running down her cheeks.

"Did she suffer?" she asked in almost a whisper.

"No, we're pretty sure she went into shock immediately," Crawford improvised.

At that, Mrs. Kammerer rose suddenly and walked away without a word. Crawford glanced at Ott, then at Mr. Kammerer, who had lapsed into a thousand-yard stare. It was not focused, and Crawford had a sense he was maybe replaying a childhood scene featuring his daughter. A moment or two later, Mrs. Kammerer returned. She had several pictures of Jessie. One was of her, nine or ten maybe, wearing a cowboy hat and an ear-to-ear smile. A big sheriff's star was pinned on a white shirt in the middle of her chest.

"She was the cutest kid," said her mother. "She wanted to be a paralegal. But we couldn't afford college."

Mrs. Kammerer was showing them another picture of Jessie now, maybe sixteen, on the back of a motorcycle. The boy driving had mutton chop sideburns and looked kind of sketchy.

Mr. Kammerer opened his mouth, stopped, then spoke.

"I was out of work for a couple of years," he said.

Crawford detected guilt in his voice.

Ott shot Crawford a look. He recognized it as Ott's maybe-we-should-get-going look.

"You got any others?" Crawford asked Mrs. Kammerer. "Pictures, I mean."

She got up and a few moments later came back with a photo album.

She came up to Crawford and opened it up to the first page.

Fifteen minutes later, they got to the last page. Leo Kammerer occasionally glanced down at the old pictures but seemed to be seeing through them.

Ott caught Crawford's eye again. His look said he didn't think hanging around any longer was doing anybody any good.

"When was the last time you saw Jessie?" Crawford asked.

Mrs. Kammerer closed the photo album and stared away.

"It's been probably a year and a half since we last heard from her."

The answer made Crawford profoundly sad. No Christmas check-in. No happy birthday call.

"Thank you," he said. "I think it's time for us to go."

He and Ott shook the Kammerers' hands, then they walked to the door.

Crawford turned.

"I just want you to know how truly sorry we are," Crawford said, handing her a card. "Anything you need, or any questions you might have, just call. I'll check with you when we know more."

"Thank you very much, Detective," Mrs. Kammerer said.

Mr. Kammerer nodded.

"Anything you can think of that might be helpful, please call," Ott added.

Mrs. Kammerer nodded and they walked to the car.

They both got in. Crawford sighed.

"Christ," he said, "sometimes I really hate this job."

ELEVEN

CHURCHILL AMES HAD GONE HOME FROM THE HOSPITAL AT around 3:00. He went right upstairs and into his voluminous walk-in closet. He pulled out the largest suitcase from the top shelf. He packed it full, then called the limo service. On his way to the airport he phoned his partner, Chris Kirk, at the office. He told Kirk in a measured, businesslike tone that he was going to take the rest of the month off and, for that matter, maybe the month of June too.

His next calls were to the nine members of the Poinciana Board of Governors. Because while Ames had regarded the presidency of the Poinciana as a huge feather in his cap—not to mention how it had landed him a few big clients and got him laid once or twice—the job hardly seemed worth it anymore. Let some other poor bastard face down the next Russian snake invasion.

———

CRAWFORD WAS IN HIS OFFICE AFTER HE AND OTT RETURNED from the Kammerers, reading more stories about water moccasins on his computer. He had a story of his own: His first experience with the slimy little bastards. His father had bought some land in Florida one time when he and his family were there on vacation. Crawford's brother and he were in his father's Mustang convertible, his father at the wheel, going to check out the land. Crawford looked out his window when his father came to a stop in a swampy area just off the Intracoastal. The place looked like prime snake and alligator territory to young Charlie.

His father and his brother hopped out of the car, eager to explore their new property. His father grabbed a golf club out of the trunk.

Crawford stayed put in the back seat.

"Come on, Charlie," his father said, looking back at him. "What are you waiting for?"

His brother knew. "He hates snakes."

"Come on, buddy," his father said, "they're more scared of you than you are of them."

Crawford had heard that one before and it didn't make him any less scared.

"I—I'm just gonna wait here for you."

His father shrugged his shoulders.

"Suit yourself," he said.

Five minutes later Crawford heard some thrashing noises from the swamp. He looked up at the car's dashboard, trying to figure out how to put up the convertible top. Then, through the rearview mirror, he saw his father and brother coming toward the car. His father had something at the end of the golf club.

They got closer and Crawford saw it was a dead snake. Its white mouth was open. It was a water moccasin.

Aside from snakes, Crawford regarded himself as—for the most part—fearless.

Well, there was his fear of heights.

And needles.

But that was about it.

Oh, yeah, and being underwater.

And probably a few others he couldn't remember at the moment.

THEN HE CHANGED THE CHANNEL AND FLASHED TO DOMINICA McCarthy. He wondered what the best way to play it with her was. Her cubicle down in CSEU—which stood for Crime Scene Evidence Unit— was exactly sixty-one steps from his office.

Yes, he had counted.

She'd be in. Working on a Sunday even if she wasn't on duty. She was a workaholic but nowhere near as bad as him. That was a big part of why they weren't going out anymore.

He walked the sixty-one steps. She was in her cubicle.

Dominica was an incredible natural beauty, with the most devastating eyes in Palm Beach. And the rest of her was hard to beat: big prominent cheekbones, long legs, and a killer body. He used to love how she kept the makeup to a minimum too, especially with Palm Beach being the makeup capital of America. Possibly the world. Not to mention the face-lift, Restylane, chin implant, eyelift, and porcelain veneer capital too. There was more damn rouge, eye shadow, and fake-tan stuff per square inch here than anywhere. That made no sense to Crawford—the fake-tan stuff, anyway—since all you had to do was go outside and get the real thing. But then he realized—oh, yeah, wrinkles.

But he digressed.

"Hey, Mac," he said, as he approached her cubicle.

"Well, well, Charlie Crawford," she said. "What brings you down to the slums of PBPD?"

"I missed your snappy banter."

She cocked her head.

"Cut the shit, Charlie, it's me," she said. "I know you cold, remember? Tell me what you want."

Crawford shook his head slowly. "Okay, but do you always have to be so damn suspicious?"

She smiled her killer smile. He realized how much he had missed it.

"Who's suspicious?" Dominica said. "I'm just asking you what you're after. Something tells me it has something to do with that murder on Barton."

He started to sigh, but knew she'd call him on it.

"What can you tell me about Aleksandr Zinoviev?"

She didn't show much reaction.

"Well, he's a man with impeccable manners," she said, "and has a cute little scar on his face, just like you. Why do you ask?"

"Let's just say he's a person of interest." Crawford shifted from one foot to the other.

"The murder?"

Crawford nodded.

"My first reaction is," Dominica said, "you got the wrong guy. How do you know I know him?"

"A little birdie."

"Come on, Charlie."

"I found out he sent you some flowers."

She smiled. "Something you never did."

"That is so not true. How can you possibly forget that big monster bouquet of roses?"

"Yeah, 'cause you were feeling guilty about almost getting me killed," Dominica said, tapping her computer. "Aleksandr hardly strikes me as a guy who would dump a bunch of snakes over a wall."

"What about his brother?"

"Um...I don't really know Vasily."

Crawford shrugged.

"What does he do? Your friend Aleksandr?"

Dominica shrugged.

"I don't really know," she said. "International man of mystery."

"What about Vasily?"

"No clue," said Dominica. "I just met him once and I wasn't too crazy about him."

"Why do you say that?"

"He just struck me as having thug tendencies," she said. "Like he could be hooked up with one of those oligarchs you hear about. Or maybe even be one."

"But Aleksandr's what...a choirboy?"

Dominica laughed. "I just met him a little while ago. He sure doesn't put out the scary vibe that Vasily does."

"Doesn't sound like the two have much in common."

Dominica thought for a second.

"That's true, all you have to do is look at them. Total opposites," she said. "Aleksandr kind of reminds me of that cute actor who played Dr. Zhivago. Vasily kinda like a bald Barney Rubble."

Crawford smiled. "Just so happens Barney's a personal hero of mine."

Dominica laughed.

"So," Crawford probed, "if you don't mind me asking, how many times have you and Dr. Zhivago gone out together?"

Dominica twisted a strand of her long, dark hair.

"Exactly twice. Last time was on his boat," she said. "Along with six other people."

Crawford eyed her, wondering about the flowers.

She leaned forward and lowered her voice. "Just for the record," she said, "the first time was right after you dumped me."

Crawford leaned closer.

"Just for the record," he said, "I didn't dump you. You told me not to call you until I had quote, 'more than forty-five minutes to spend on a date,' unquote."

"Yeah, exactly, and you never called."

"Well, 'cause it was right in the middle of that kidnapping," Crawford sighed.

He hadn't planned to get this far off course. "So anyway...a guy by the name of Churchill Ames wasn't on Aleksandr's boat, by any chance?"

"No," she said. "Ames was the guy with the girl who got killed, right?"

"Yeah, a real sweetheart too," Crawford said, taking a step toward the door. "Well, Mac, it's been real, but I gotta run. So, I just want to say, thanks. Thanks for nothing."

She laughed.

"Anytime, Charlie," she said. "You got a hot date you gotta get to or something?"

He turned back to her and smiled.

"Or something."

TWELVE

"So, I got some good info on the Russian brothers," Rose said, leaning across the white tablecloth of their table at Scalamandre's. "'Cause I know that's the real reason you asked me out."

"Come on, Rose," Crawford said. "I asked you out because I can't get enough of your fun-loving personality."

Rose leaned forward in her chair.

"Thank you, Charlie. Before you pump me"—Rose faked a blush—"before you ask me a million questions, that is, I have to tell you about this open house of mine I just had. You'll get a kick out of it."

"I love your real-estate stories," Crawford said. "They get me fantasizing about living in one of your big ol' houses, instead of my dump."

"You'll have to ask me over to your 'dump' one of these days; I'll fluff it up for you," she said. "So anyway, it was earlier this afternoon and I had been there for about an hour. It had been pretty slow, then out of the blue I hear this shuffling sound coming from the living room. I looked up and saw this really, really old guy wearing these shiny black socks, hair sticking out through them, hiked up almost to his knees, wearing brown wingtip shoes and these canary yellow shorts. Ve-ry sexy, let me tell you. So, the man's shuffling toward me and I see this sparkle in his rheumy old eyes that kinda creeps me out."

The girl could paint a picture.

"And I have the music system in the house turned down low," Rose went on, "coming out of these speakers in the ceiling and the old guy asks me right after he signs in my register if the place has an elevator. So I look down at the register, see his name, and go, 'Oh, yes, Mr. Burke, right over there.' And he says, 'Call me Dirk, Mr. Burke makes me feel ancient,' then he asks, 'By the way, how old are you, honey?'"

"Wait, his name was Dirk Burke?"

"Yup, and he's asking me how old I am—"

"—and calling you 'honey'."

"Exactly. So now I'm like, 'Christ, get me out of here.' Like the early-warning alert for horny old geezers trying to hit on me was wailing away. So, I told him I'm thirty-two and add quickly, 'Notice the butler's pantry over there...extraordinary space, isn't it?' And he goes: 'Who cares? I either go out for dinner or order in Chinese.' Then he tells me he's ninety-four and I look him over—no walker, no hearing aid—and I think: Not bad for ninety-four. So, I steered him out to the porch, 'cause I figured it was safer out in the open, and I say, 'Beautiful pool, isn't it...Dirk?' And he goes, 'I'm a hot-tub guy myself.' I do my damnedest not to picture that and he goes back inside. Then he says out of the blue, 'That's Frank, isn't it?' and he was looking up at the ceiling. And I hear doobie-doobie-do and it clicked. So I say, 'Oh, yeah, Old Blue Eyes.' And I see him get this look and suddenly it's like he turns into this courtly old gent and asks, 'Would you care to have a dance, my dear?'"

"Come on seriously?" Crawford said. "So what did you do?"

"What could I do? We twirled around the floor a while," she said. "He stepped on my toes a few times with those wingtips."

"So...did he buy the place?"

"He made an offer, at least," she said.

"Yeah, I'll bet he did."

Rose laughed. "You know what I mean," she said. "I just need to get him up another million or so."

Only in Palm Beach, Crawford thought.

He couldn't wait any longer. "Okay, Rose …so talk to me about the Zinoviev brothers."

She nodded and scratched her head.

"So in between people at my open house, I called a friend in New York who writes for one of the newspapers up there," Rose said. "I had heard Aleksandr and Vasily spend a bunch of time somewhere in the city."

"Where, like Brighton Beach or something?" Crawford asked.

Rose shrugged. "I have no idea, I just heard New York. So, anyway, Vasily—"

"The short, beefy one?"

Rose nodded.

"The short, beefy, dangerous one, it turns out."

"What do you mean?"

"Well, supposedly he's a really bad actor," she said. "My friend told me he was given a life sentence back in Russia."

"For what?"

"Murder."

Crawford leaned forward. "Keep going."

"For killing two guys."

"You're kidding," Crawford said.

"Not only that," Rose said, "he was fourteen years old when he did it."

"Jesus."

"And, get this: with a pitchfork."

Crawford tried to picture that. First time he'd ever heard of murder by pitchfork.

It wasn't much of a leap, Crawford thought, to see the Russian using snakes as murder weapons.

"What about the other one? Aleksandr?"

"The cute one?" Rose said. "My friend didn't really know much about him. I..."

Rose stopped and looked away, then started nervously tapping her fingers on the table.

"What?" said Crawford.

She looked back at him. "What do you mean, what?"

"You started to say something."

"Just..."

"Come on, Rose, out with it. What were you gonna say?" Then it clicked. "Oh, I know. You were gonna say something about Aleksandr seeing Dominica...that's what it was, right?"

She nodded sheepishly.

"I know about them, Rose. Just for the record, Dominica and I stopped going out quite a while ago," he said. "But, as Dominica's friend, you might want to tell her about what you just told me."

"It was about Vasily," Rose said.

"I know, but—"

"Can we change the subject, Charlie?"

He didn't really want to, but figured he could circle back.

"Sure," he said. "What do you want to talk about?"

She put her hand on Crawford's hand and fluttered her eyelashes. "I was just wondering...did you maybe want me to come over? Fluff up your place a little after dinner?"

Crawford smiled. "Yeah, sure," he said. "Is that—is that, by any chance, some kind of a double entendre?"

She leaned across the table and kissed him on the cheek. "It is, if you want it to be."

THIRTEEN

Crawford went into Ott's cubicle a little past ten the next morning.

"Come on," he said, waving his hand for Ott to follow him.

Ott looked up.

"Where to?"

"The Russian section of Palm Beach."

"What?" said Ott.

"I'll fill you in on the way up there."

Driving up, Crawford put in a call to Buzz Cox, the man who Celia Senior described as formerly being Churchill Ames's best friend, now worst enemy. He didn't get him, but left a message.

He and Ott drove down the long driveway of the Russians' house up on the north end. From the outside, the house didn't look much different from any other twenty-thousand-square-foot, sixteen-million-dollar house in Palm Beach. Long driveway, lushly land-scaped, and that, "oh, wow" moment when the house's facade popped in to view, the ocean stretched out majestically behind it on both sides.

"So this is what the Playboy Mansion looks like," Ott said. "Pretty fuckin' ugly."

Crawford nodded in agreement.

He was going through a mental slideshow of his preconceived notions of Russian women as he parked and walked toward the house. There were two distinct types in his mind: the older peasant woman with a potato face and babushka, wearing clunky, espadrille-like shoes. At the other end of the spectrum was the drop-dead gorgeous fashion model, invariably six feet tall with razor-sharp cheekbones and beautiful hard, cold, unsmiling eyes.

The woman who answered the door was neither. She was a petite Asian-looking woman wearing boxy black sunglasses with Dior in big metal letters on both sides, flashing like a Las Vegas hotel sign. She had shiny black hair, no makeup, and red wine colored lipstick. She was stunning, but about as un-Russian as you could get.

"Can I help you?" she asked.

"I'm Detective Crawford," he said. "This is Detective Ott, Palm Beach Police. Are the Zinovievs here?"

"I am not sure," she said.

"Why don't you go see," Ott said impatiently.

"I am not sure they are available," she said.

"Tell 'em it's important," Ott said forcefully, and the woman turned and walked away.

A minute later, a tall blonde man in dark pants, a green short-sleeve silk shirt, and Gucci loafers with no socks came to the door.

"Mr. Zinoviev?" Crawford said

"Yes, I'm Aleksandr," he said with a big, toothpaste-ad smile.

"I'm Detective Crawford. This is my partner, Detective Ott."

"Please come in," Aleksandr said. "Can I offer you something to drink?"

They both thanked him, but declined his offer.

"Follow me, then," Aleksandr said. "I'll be glad to help you in any way I possibly can. But what is it you'd like to know?"

They followed him down a wide hallway and into the living room.

The room was loud. Bright colors everywhere. Flashy fabrics. Screaming yellow carpet. An Andy Warhol painting of Campbell soup cans.

Aleksandr sat in the red-leather club chair. Crawford and Ott sat in a burnt-orange sofa facing him.

"So, what did you come here about?" Aleksandr asked solicitously.

"You sent some flowers to Churchill Ames at Good Samaritan Hospital," Crawford said.

"Oh, yes," he said, "my brother and I did."

"Why?" Crawford asked.

"Because we heard what happened at his house," Aleksandr said. "Those snakes. Poor Mr. Ames, he is a friend of ours."

Crawford's eyes got steely. "Poor Mr. Ames? What about the woman with him?"

Aleksandr nodded. "Well, yes, of course. That was a very terrible thing that happened to her."

He brushed something off his pants that was invisible to Crawford.

"How did you find out about what happened?" Crawford asked.

Aleksandr glanced away.

"I do not know," he said. "My brother found out."

"And where is your brother?"

"He is on a business trip. He left this morning."

"Where to?"

"Philadelphia, Pennsylvania."

Crawford nodded slowly.

"And how is it that you know Mr. Ames?"

Aleksandr patted the arm of the red-leather chair distractedly.

"We have a business relationship," he said. "As a matter of fact, my brother and I had a business lunch with Mr. Ames a few days ago."

"What kind of business, Mr. Zinoviev?"

Aleksandr smoothed back his thick blonde hair.

"We are interested in buying some land for a new golf course or possibly an existing golf course in the western part of West Palm Beach or Wellington," Aleksandr said. "We thought Mr. Ames, because he is president of the Poinciana Club, might know of something."

"Did he?" Crawford asked.

"No, unfortunately, he did not," Aleksandr answered. "So we had a most pleasant lunch. Mr. Ames is a fascinating man. A great sense of humor too."

Crawford snuck a look at Ott.

"And your brother and Mr. Ames, how did they hit it off?" asked Ott.

Aleksandr cocked his head. "Hit it off?"

"Get along." Ott said. "You know, like each other."

"Oh, absolutely. My brother confided in me after our lunch what great respect he had for Mr. Ames. He is a highly respected attorney, you know."

Ott nodded. "So they say," he said, light on conviction.

"So is that what you do?" Crawford asked. "Develop golf courses?"

"Well, actually, we wear many hats, detective. Oil and gas, real estate, commodities."

Crawford nodded.

"But you're not sure how your brother found out about what happened at Mr. Ames's house?"

Aleksandr shook his head.

Crawford and Ott just stared at him for a few seconds.

Aleksandr smiled his movie-star smile back.

Crawford got to his feet. "Well, thank you, Mr. Zinoviev, for your help." He pulled a card out of his wallet. "Do me a favor: When your brother gets back, have him call me."

"Absolutely, Detective, I will," said Aleksandr, flashing his pearly whites again.

Crawford started toward the front door, looking around the room. "So I understand this house is exactly like Hugh Hefner's house in California."

Aleksandr beamed.

"Yes, Detective, my brother and I are very big fans of Hef," he said. "You might say he's an inspiration of ours."

He said Hef like they were childhood buddies. Like they had grown up in some Moscow suburb together.

"Very nice," said Ott, eyeing Warhol's soup cans as they walked to the front door.

"Well, thanks again," said Crawford.

"It was all my pleasure," Akeksandr said. "Let me know if I can be of any further assistance."

"We will," Ott responded as he opened the door and walked out.

At the bottom of the steps, Ott stopped and turned to Crawford. "That sense of humor of Churchill Ames's he was talking about," Ott said. "Can't say I picked up on that."

"Yeah," Crawford said, "me neither."

"Friendly enough guy," Ott said, "but the word unctuous comes to mind."

"Unctuous, huh?" Crawford said. "I'm gonna have to look that one up."

"Don't gimme that shit, Dartmouth, you know exactly what it means," Ott said.

Crawford chuckled.

"Plus," continued Ott, "guy was a little slick too. All smarmy and fawning and smooth-talking."

Crawford nodded, but he definitely could see the guy's appeal to women.

FOURTEEN

CRAWFORD FIGURED WHILE HE WAS IN DROP-IN MODE, HE'D PAY an unannounced visit to Churchill Ames. He dropped Ott back at the station, then drove over to Ames's house. A woman in a light-blue dress the color of hospital scrubs answered the door.

"Yes, sir, can I help you?" she asked in a heavy Spanish accent.

"I'm Detective Crawford, Palm Beach Police. Is Mr. Ames here?"

"No, he went away."

"Went away? Where?"

"To the airport."

"Do you know where he was going?"

"I'm sorry, he did not tell me."

Crawford thanked her and walked back to his car. Something told him Ames's tough-guy act might have crumbled. That maybe he thought it wise to a put a few states between himself and the snake people.

He called information and asked for the number of the law firm where Ames worked, then got the number and dialed it.

The receptionist who answered confirmed Ames was not there,

but that was all she knew. She connected Crawford to Chris Kirk, the managing partner.

"Hello, Chris Kirk," a high-pitched voice said.

"Mr. Kirk, my name is Detective Crawford, Palm Beach Police. I'm trying to locate Churchill Ames. It seems he left town. Do you know how I can get in touch with him?"

"I have no idea where he went," Kirk said.

Crawford thought for a second.

"Does he have another house somewhere?"

"Yeah, little place up in Maine," Kirk said.

"Where in Maine?"

"Place called Northeast Harbor."

Crawford wrote it down.

"I've got to go," Kirk said, like he wanted to click over to a five-hundred-dollar-an-hour client instead of wasting his time on Crawford.

"Wait, you don't have the number up in Maine, do you?" Crawford asked.

"Sorry," Kirk said. "Goodbye, Detective."

Crawford was able to stop Kirk before he clicked off. He asked him to switch him over to Maddy Sorenson.

He waited a few rings, then a woman's voice picked up.

"Hello?"

"Ms. Sorenson?"

"Yes."

"My name's Detective Crawford, Palm Beach Police. I'd like to ask you a few questions about the homicide at Churchill Ames's house."

"I don't know anything except what I read in the paper—but sure, ask away."

"Do you have a few minutes right now?" he asked. "I'd like to come see you in person."

"Yeah, sure, come on over."

Waiting in the reception area of Maddy Sorenson's law offices, Crawford looked up at the name of the firm on a brass plaque behind the receptionist. Swiggett, Kirk, Ames, Timpson and Weinberg. If this had been New York, there'd be at least one Italian on the masthead and more than just one Jew. Maybe throw in someone whose name ended in *ski* too. Even for down here, he thought, Swiggett, Ames, Kirk, Timpson and Weinberg hardly represented the disparate South Florida population.

Maddy Sorenson let him cool his heels for fifteen minutes. She apologized when she came out.

She was around five-five, wide-set, bright brown eyes, and auburn hair tied up on top in a casually appealing way. She had on plain-Jane glasses and reminded Crawford of an actress in a movie who wore glasses so people wouldn't think she was too good-looking to be smart.

They walked back to her exterior office that had a view looking up the Intracoastal. Crawford sat down opposite her desk.

She smiled and grabbed a pencil from its holder.

"So, Detective, I've heard about you. From up north, right?"

"Uh-huh, New York."

She nodded. "And what can I do for you?"

"Well, for starters, Ms. Sorenson," he said, "it would be really helpful if I knew where to find Churchill Ames."

Ms. Sorenson scratched her cheek.

"For you and me both," she said, then smiled. "I've gotten a lot of his cases dumped on me."

"That quick, huh?"

She shrugged. "Yeah, we've got some very demanding clients."

"So nobody knows where he went?"

"Not that I know of."

Crawford nodded slowly. "Second question: As far as you know, did Ames have any clients who were—"

"Disgruntled? Pissed off?" she said. "Wanted to kill him?"

"Let's go with the latter," Crawford said.

Sorenson got up, walked over to the door, and closed it. Then, she walked back to her chair.

"Churchill can be stubborn and prickly, sometimes even a total ball-buster," she said. "But maybe that's what makes him a good lawyer. Did he always get everything his clients wanted for them? No, course not, but...who does? Plus, I wouldn't say he had a lot of killers for clients."

"His ex-wife had a few interesting things to say about him," Crawford said.

"Don't they always," she said. "Did she also say I was sleeping with him?"

"Um... she had her suspicions."

Maddy shook her head and sighed.

"Bitch is a complete head case," she said. "Not that Churchill didn't hit on me. I just had absolutely no interest. When I first heard about what happened, I figured it had to be Celia. She's still my leading contender."

"Really," Crawford said. "You mean, you think she might have hired someone to do it?"

"I wouldn't say hired." She started tapping her pencil. "All she had to do was get that nasty-piece-of-work boyfriend of hers on it."

"Who?"

"Jesus, Charlie, do I have to do all your work for you?" Maddy said, her eyes twinkling. "You haven't run across Lanny yet?"

He shook his head.

"His name is Lanny Krew—I think that's his last name, anyway. The diametric opposite of Churchill. Rides a Harley, black jeans, Fu Manchu, getting the picture? Moved in with Celia before the divorce was final."

"How do you know that?"

"Churchill told me," Maddy said. "It was a little tidbit he was only too happy to share with the judge too."

Celia Senior had catapulted to the top of Crawford's re-interview list.

Maddy tapped her pencil on her desk a few more times. "Because I'm such a public-spirited citizen and because you'll hear it from someone else anyway," she said, "I've got another clue for you."

Crawford leaned closer. "I'm all ears."

"Ames does almost all trial work now," she said, "but he started out in T and E."

"Trust and estates, right?"

"Yes, and he's still got a few old clients. And when I say old, we're talking one foot in," she said. "Anyway, one of them is named Maggie Shattuck, actually, Margaret Johnston Cox Ireland Shattuck, to be exact. Has the name Buzz Cox come up?"

"Yes, he sure has," Crawford said.

"So Buzz is Maggie's son. And Buzz and Churchill used to be good friends. Until about a month ago, that is, when Buzz came charging into the office and started going at it with Churchill. Accused him of all kinds of stuff, mismanaging his mother's account, embezzling, looting the trust, you name it. Long story short, the money that Buzz was counting on to live happily ever after on was history."

"Thanks to Ames."

"Yes, and the way I heard it, Buzz claimed Ames was day-trading, doing really speculative stuff with the money."

"So we have a pissed-off heir, who isn't one anymore," Crawford said. "But it doesn't sound like Cox is really the type to kill somebody."

"Yes, normally I would agree," Maddy said, "except that's exactly what he threatened to do."

"You're kidding? To kill Ames?"

"Yep. And half the office heard it," Maddy said. "The two of them were screaming at the top of their lungs."

They spoke for a few more minutes, then Maddy gave him her cell number. Crawford thanked her and left her office.

It had been a worthwhile interview. He didn't know who to go see first: Celia Senior or Buzz Cox.

By the time he got to his car he'd decided to make a return trip to the roach motel on Westminster Street.

FIFTEEN

OTT CALLED WHILE CRAWFORD WAS ON HIS WAY TO CELIA'S. HE
told Crawford that he had found out Churchill Ames had flown business-
class to Portland, Maine and then rented a Honda Accord at Avis. As for
where the snakes could have come from, he was still working on that. He
had located a number of Internet sites that sold them, from Snakeman
Jack to one called Exotic & Venomous Snakes, LLC, both of which were
based in some backwater town outside of the Okefenokee Swamp.

"You should take a ride up there," Crawford said, flashing to his
father coming out of the bushes with the cottonmouth at the end of
his nine-iron. "See if someone placed a large order of water moccasins
recently."

"You don't want to come along, Charlie?" Ott asked, knowing
about Crawford's love of snakes.

"Thanks, Mort, it's very tempting, but I got my hands full,"
Crawford said. "I'm headed back to Celia Senior's house. Gonna
introduce myself to her boyfriend."

"Boyfriend?"

"Yeah, s'posed to be a real beauty."

As Crawford crossed the bridge over to West Palm Beach, he thought about Churchill Ames flying up to Maine. It reminded him of going up there every summer when he was a little kid. He, his parents and brother and sister, always used to pile into their SUV, fill it up with their stuff, and drive up from their place in Connecticut. The name of the town in Maine where they went was called Cabot's Point, but it was nicknamed Bellsville because so many people named Bell lived there. His mother was a Bell; so were his uncles. Crawford remembered that some famous artist like Homer or Hopper had a studio on the craggy rocks overlooking the ocean at Cabot's Point. He remembered how the ocean was always freezing and the black flies weighed about five pounds each. His great-grandfather bought a house there in the early 1900s. A "cottage," they called it. Some cottage: twenty-six rooms and about as many porches. Last he knew, his Uncle Henry still owned it. A stone's throw from a little beach club that had three clay tennis courts with lines he always tripped over.

Most of the people in Bellsville came from Boston and the houses there were their summer homes. He was related to a lot of them. They all seemed to have a thing about dowdy, threadbare houses with heavy wooden furniture, even though most of them were rich. He remembered an aunt of his saying, "If it was good enough for Grandmère, it's good enough for me." He didn't figure out what grandmère meant until he was about twelve.

Crawford took a right onto Westminster Street. He spotted a green Volvo station wagon and a five-year-old silver Corvette in Celia Senior's driveway. He parked on the street across from her house, walked up to the porch, and pressed the buzzer.

"Who is it?" He could hear Celia's petulance through the thick, moldy four-paneled oak door.

"Detective Crawford," he said, then heard two sets of footsteps.

"Just a second," she said.

He turned the knob and pushed open the door.

Celia Senior, walking toward the door, glared at him.

"It's common etiquette, Detective, not to just barge in—"

"It's common etiquette, Ms. Senior, not to lie to a police officer," he said, surveying the room. The smell he had noticed the first time was even stronger now.

"What are you talking about?" Celia said, hands on her hips.

"That man who just beat it out of here. I thought you told me you lived here alone," Crawford said, then raised his voice. "Come on out, Lanny, or I'll come back there and drag you out."

After a few seconds Crawford heard footsteps, much slower this time, and a man appeared. It was like he had figured it was better than having Crawford yank him out from under a bed.

The man looked like Elvis, if the King had made it to sixty. But it was the accoutrement around his neck and shoulders that made Crawford do a double take. It was a waxy-skinned boa constrictor as thick as Crawford's neck that seemed to be sound asleep.

"Lanny's just an occasional guest," Celia said.

"Oh, really," Crawford said skeptically. "How 'bout putting your little friend back in its cage, Lanny. Then I got some questions for you."

"Sorry, he doesn't have a cage, Detective," Krew said.

"Well, how 'bout a guest bedroom?" The snake was beginning to seriously freak him out.

Krew started to walk out, then turned.

"You don't like snakes?"

"I only like rattlers," Crawford said.

Lanny nodded and walked out. He was back a few moments later.

"So where'd you get that thing?" Crawford asked.

Krew sat down in a peach-colored love seat and put his filthy Crocs up on the coffee table.

"A place down in the Everglades. Why?"

"They sell water moccasins there too?" Crawford asked.

Celia shook her head and waved her arms. "Wait a minute—"

"What's the name of the place, Lanny?" Crawford insisted.

"Place called Billy Fortune's," Lanny said. "What difference does it make? It was three years ago."

"And you haven't been back since?"

"No."

"Where were you around ten o'clock last Saturday night?"

Celia jumped in.

"Right here with me," she said, like she didn't trust Lanny's answer.

"I asked him," Crawford said, not taking his eyes off Krew.

Krew scratched behind his ear. "Like the lady said. Right here."

"What were you doing?"

Celia smirked. "That's a little personal, isn't it, Detective?"

"Where exactly is this place, Billy Fortune's, Lanny?" Crawford said, shooting a look at Celia. "Let him answer."

"Outside a town called Mangrove City."

Crawford wrote it down, then looked up at Celia. "The way I see it," he said, his eyes drilling into hers, "there are two ways this could have gone down. One: You two did it to scare Ames into giving you the money you think he owes you. Or two: You had nothing to do with it. Convince me of the latter."

Celia slouched down into her chair. "How would Churchill be able to give me the money he owes me if he got killed by snakes?"

"My guess is you took a calculated risk that chances were slim they'd actually kill him," Crawford said.

"Come on," Celia said, shaking her head, "you really think we'd go to all that trouble just to put the fear of God in him?"

"No way in hell," Krew piped in. "Besides, I don't go anywhere near poisonous snakes. They scare the hell out of me."

Crawford eyed him. "You work, Lanny?"

Lanny shook his head. "Nah. Well, except on my car."

"Mr. Krew is independently wealthy," Celia said. "Heir to the Krew used car fortune."

Lanny laughed.

"Is that right?" Crawford said, getting up. "By the way, I want you two sticking around, keeping it local for a while. No trips or anything. I'm sure I'll have more questions for you."

Crawford saw something skitter across the floor between them. Celia stomped on it.

"So you saying I need a permission slip if I want to go down to Boca and shop?" she asked.

"Don't push it," Crawford said. "You're both suspects."

He walked to the door and let himself out.

Happy to breathe fresh air again.

SIXTEEN

ON THE WAY TO THE STATION, CRAWFORD GOT A CALL BACK from a friend in the New York FBI office. He had called him a few hours before and left a message asking if the bureau had anything on the Zinoviev brothers. It turned into a long conversation. He ended up talking to his friend for a half an hour while he was in the parking lot behind the station house.

After he hung up, he went straight to Ott's office and barged in.

"Hey, Mort, I gotta tell you about—"

Ott looked up, startled.

"Jesus, Charlie," he said, "they got this thing called knocking. I mean, Christ, what if I was picking my nose or something?"

"Sorry," Crawford said. "So I just got the lowdown on our Russian friends. Thought you might want to hear."

Ott motioned to the chair opposite him. "Hell, yeah. Tell me all about 'em."

Crawford sat down.

Ott had a leather-framed picture of Bruce Lee, his martial arts idol, on his desk. On one of the walls was a full-length poster of a race-car driver in a white leather suit with vertical blue-and-red stripes and a white racing helmet, giving the camera a thumbs-up sign.

It was Ott. One of his hobbies a few years back had been to learn how to be a stock-car driver. He took lessons about how to drive in circles at a hundred and eighty miles an hour at a place out west of West Palm called Moroso Speedway. And except for one other picture of him with a forlorn-looking dog in his lap, that was it for decorative flourishes in Ott's office. But still, it was more than Crawford had in his.

Crawford said, "Okay, so after Vasily pitchforked those two guys, he got put in the jug in Siberia or wherever they go. Then after communism went down, he got a pardon. Bribed someone, is the feds' theory. After that, he hooked up with this outfit called Ohshina, a big Chechen gang."

"Slow down a minute," Ott said. "Where'd you get all this?"

"FBI guy I know up in New York."

"So you saying they're Russian mafia?" Ott asked.

"I don't know exactly what they are," Crawford said. "The Russian mafia's got a million loosely allied groups over there, my buddy told me, a lot of 'em over here now. Anyway, after Vasily got out of jail, he and his brother came here and made a specialty of extorting Russian hockey players."

"Extorting them? How?" Ott asked, tilting his chair back and putting his hands behind his head.

"What happened was they'd pick guys who'd just signed big NHL contracts," Crawford said. "Then find out where they were from in Russia, after that track down their parents or their brother or sister, then call the hockey player and say, 'Hey, Yuri, I got your sister, Svetlana, here. I'm gonna chop her head off unless you send me a hundred large in three days.'"

Ott was shaking his head. "Now that's a business model I've never heard of before."

"No kidding," Crawford said. "So they worked that racket for a while—supposedly cut the hands off the mother of one guy on the

Bruins—then went and stepped up in class."

"To what?" Ott said. "I'm afraid to ask."

"High finance," Crawford answered, "but not exactly as you know it."

Ott leaned forward. "Keep going."

"Back in '98, close to seven billion dollars was laundered through Bank of New York accounts. The brothers apparently were the ringleaders." Crawford tapped his knuckles on Ott's desk. "Then, after that, they really hit the big time. Hooked up with a bunch of badass Mexicans. Sinaloa cartel supposedly. That guy El Chapo."

Ott raised an eyebrow. "No shit. Wait a sec." He slid open a drawer and pulled out a bottle of Clan MacGregor whiskey.

Crawford shook his head. "Doin' your Philip Marlowe thing?"

Ott laughed and poured a few ounces into two paper cups.

"Except Sam Spade would never drink that shit," Crawford said.

Ott handed Crawford a cup. Crawford downed it.

"But it's good enough for you," Ott said, refilling Crawford's cup.

"So when they joined forces with the Mexicans was when they really hit the FBI's radar screen," said Crawford.

"Jesus, what took so long?" Ott asked, heaving back another shot of the Clan.

"What do you expect? It's the FBI," Crawford said. "Then— you'll love this—the Russians put a deal together to sell an old Soviet sub to the cartel. The Mexicans loaded it up with coke, brought it in somewhere off the Keys."

"You're kidding," Ott said. "And they got through?"

Crawford nodded.

"FBI got there right after they unloaded," Crawford said. "Busted 'em all. But Vasily and Aleksandr were history."

"You got good intel from this guy. So is that how the brothers ended up in the Sunshine State?"

"I guess," Crawford said. "Must have liked the weather and decided to stick around."

Ott started to pour Crawford another one, but Crawford waved him off.

"So when Aleksandr told us they were in commodities," Ott said, "I guess he musta meant coke."

"Yeah," Crawford said, his eyes falling on a distant point on the other side of the room. "We're dealing with some big-time, brutal players here."

"So the snake thing—"

"—Kids' stuff," Crawford said. "Like they put the JV on the field for that one."

SEVENTEEN

CRAWFORD WANTED TO TALK TO VASILY ZINOVIEV—YESTERDAY.

Based on what his brother had told them about Vasily's business trip, Crawford had gotten Ott to check all domestic flights from Philadelphia to West Palm for the next week to see if Vasily had a reservation. Despite Aleksandr's explanation that the flowers sent to Churchill Ames were simply a gesture of consolation, Crawford wasn't buying it.

But in checking return flights, Ott hadn't come up with anything. Then it dawned on Crawford that Vasily would travel like every other rich capitalist who owned a few expensive Warhols and a sixteen-million-dollar house inspired by Hugh Hefner. He'd have his own metal. And if he didn't own it outright, he'd at least have a NetJets or Wheels Up share.

Sure enough, a flight plan had been filed for Vasily Zinoviev and five passengers to arrive at West Palm at 10:00 the next morning. On a Citation X, no less. Ott did some digging and found out that the brothers had bought it last year. Fourteen-and-a-half million, all cash. So, between the crib and the ride, the brothers had plunked down just north of thirty million in the last two years to live very high on the hog.

No doubt about it, crime paid.

Based on the brothers' criminal history, Crawford had convinced a judge to issue a warrant. Then he requisitioned three bags— uniformed cops—to accompany Ott on a search of the Russians' house up on the north end. He recommended they take along an interpreter.

It was going to be done at the same time that Crawford and another detective would serve as the welcoming committee for Vasily Zinoviev and company at the West Palm airport.

Crawford watched Zinoviev's Citation taxi up. He was at the counter of the private aviation company, along with Detective Gus Wilmer. Two men in pink and green were talking next to them.

"No way I'd ever go back," one of them said to the other.

"Are you kidding?" the other guy said. "Babies crying, fat guys in tank tops, fags passing around drinks; life's too short."

Crawford rolled his eyes at Wilmer. Oh, the indignities of flying Delta instead of Ego Air.

They had just met with the private airport's manager, a short, gray-haired woman in her sixties named Mary Ann Walling, who had an American flag on her lapel. Crawford showed her the warrant, which covered the Zinovievs' jet, while Wilmer, carrying a camera, snapped a few shots of the Citation through a window. Crawford asked Walling what she knew about the Russians and she said the short one was rude and arrogant and the handsome one polite and friendly. Then she volunteered how they always seemed to travel with what she described as "a harem." Crawford gave her a card and asked her to call him if she ever saw anything that looked suspicious.

Then Crawford and Wilmer, warrant in hand, thanked her and walked out of the office onto the tarmac.

Right after the Citation stopped, they went up to the sleek, gleaming jet and waited for someone to open up the hatch. After a few seconds, a uniformed flight attendant slid it open and looked surprised to see them standing there.

"I'm Detective Crawford, this is Detective Wilmer," Crawford shouted up to her. "We have a warrant to search the plane."

She looked frazzled, like she needed a higher authority.

"Let me get the captain."

Crawford saw a man suddenly loom up behind her.

"Who are you?" the man said in a thick Russian accent. He had a three-day stubble and a prominent tattoo on his neck. Right behind him was a skinny guy with bad acne scars.

"Palm Beach Police. We've got a warrant to search the plane," Crawford said.

He and Wilmer charged up the steps. The tattooed man took a step forward, blocking them.

"Get out of my way," Crawford said as Wilmer clicked off a few shots of the tattooed man and the skinny guy.

But the tattooed man didn't move.

Crawford heard a loud voice from inside the plane say something in Russian.

The tattooed man took a step to one side. Crawford gave him a slight nudge with his shoulder and elbow as he went past him. The man drew back his arm, then seemed to think better of it.

Crawford looked past the tattooed man and the guy with acne and saw a short, stocky man with a shaved head and no shirt walking toward him. He was buckling a skinny brown alligator belt. Behind him, Crawford saw an open door to a bedroom. On a king-size bed with a lavish headboard, he saw two women, more undressed than dressed. One was standing beside the bed, hastily putting on a skimpy black bra. The other one was in the bed. When she saw Crawford and Wilmer, she pulled the covers up over her head.

"Who the hell are you?" said the stocky man.

Crawford flashed him his ID.

"Palm Beach Detectives Crawford and Wilmer. You Mr. Zinoviev?"

"Yeah," Vasily said.

"This is a warrant to search your plane," Crawford said, holding up the warrant.

Vasily ignored it.

"The fuck is the reason for this...in-fasion of my privacy?" Vasily said.

"We're investigating the murder of a woman at your friend Churchill Ames's house," Crawford said.

"Who?" Vasily asked.

"The man your brother said was a 'dear' friend of yours. Churchill Ames."

Vasily didn't change his expression.

"Oh, yeah," Vasily grunted. "My buddy."

Crawford took a step closer and could smell Vasily. It was nothing like the Maximus Flower Shop.

He had a gold chain around his neck that looked like it weighed a couple of pounds.

"Tell me what you know about what happened at Ames's house," Crawford said.

Vasily glanced at the captain, who had come out of the cockpit, then back at Crawford.

"I don't know what you're talking about," Vasily said. "You can't harass me, I'm American citizen."

Wilmer inched up to Crawford's side.

"Nobody's harassing you," Crawford said. "You're welcome to talk about this down at the police station. Oh, and just so you know, another search is being conducted at your house up on North Lake Way, as we speak."

"Are you fugkink kiddink me?" A few beads of sweat had popped up on Vasily's shaved head. On his forehead was a long, protruding vein that slalomed down to just above his left eyebrow.

"No, I'm not," Crawford said. "So it's your call: Stay here, go to the station or go home. But before you go, we need to search you and go through your luggage."

Nobody moved.

The tattooed man looked at his boss. Vasily, almost imperceptibly, nodded his head. Then he turned back toward the cabin behind him and said something in Russian to the girls. One of them gave him a one-word answer.

Vasily flashed a malevolent look at Crawford as he started toward the exit door. Crawford returned it.

"So, tell me," Crawford called after him, "what were you doing up in Philadelphia?"

Vasily glowered at him. "Seeing the bell with the big crack in it."

A Russian David Letterman.

"Put your arms up, please, Mr. Zinoviev," Crawford said. "I need to search you."

Vasily rolled his eyes and put his arms up just over his shoulders. Like barely complying was the best they were going to get out of him.

Crawford patted him down. Nothing, except for a very large wallet.

Then Vasily walked off the plane muttering something in Russian to the tattooed man.

Crawford and Wilmer spent the next hour finding nothing that connected the Russians to the Jessie Kammerer homicide.

Unfortunately, it was the same with the house up on the north end, where Crawford went next to join up with Ott. No smoking gun in either place. In fact, Crawford was surprised about how little they came up with, considering Vasily's résumé.

Ott and the uniform cops, who had been at the house for over two hours, had completely struck out at finding anything that could link the Russians to Kammerer. The bust was... a bust.

But not entirely.

Because before Crawford got to the house, Ott had discovered a shiny new file cabinet in a locked closet. The entire cabinet had a single theme: the Chechen separatist movement in Russia. After

Crawford arrived, Ott showed him the contents of the file cabinet and for the next half hour they snapped pictures of documents, memoranda, and newspaper articles with their cell-phone cameras.

Crawford's other discovery, while even less pertinent to the case, had to do with the Zinovievs' houseguests, who seemed to be there on a more or less permanent basis. There were fourteen women, to be exact. All of them were young and beautiful and had proper papers.

Aleksandr was hovering around at the end of the search, while Vasily was nowhere to be seen. As Crawford and Ott wrapped it up and headed to the door, Aleksandr followed them.

"As you can see, Detective, we are nothing more than business-men," Aleksandr said to Crawford, then with a wink, "Who like what you Americans call our creature comforts."

EIGHTEEN

THEY WERE AT MOOKIE'S AT JUST PAST SEVEN THAT NIGHT. Mookie's Tap-a-Keg was a little dive across the bridge in West Palm where the beer was cold and Norm Rutledge didn't hang out.

"So sum it up, Mort," Crawford said, leaning back in his chair. "I want to hear what you think we got so far."

"Well, Charlie, it's simple," Ott said, taking a long pull of his Yuengling. "We ain't got shit."

"Short and pithy," Crawford said. "Just like you."

"But the Russkies are definitely the leading contenders."

Crawford nodded. "Yeah, but you haven't met Celia's boyfriend yet. This mutt, Lanny. Check him out on the computer, will ya. No way in hell he ain't got a sheet."

Ott took another sip and ended up with froth on his upper lip. "Yeah, I will. And motive, that they sure got."

Crawford nodded. "I could even see old Celia cookin' up the whole scheme, being Magna Cum Laude from Radcliffe and all," he said. "But I got a hard time seeing 'em actually pulling it off."

"Why's that?"

Crawford eyes scanned the no-frills bar. "Well, for starters, it requires a lot of work," he said. "And my take on Lanny is he's not capable of much more than changing the oil on his T-Bird."

"Thought you said it was a Stingray?" Ott said.

"Whatever," Crawford said. "I mean, think about it. First, he's gotta go buy the snakes somewhere, then transport them without anybody knowing, then make sure Ames is gonna be out by the pool when he gets there, then chuck 'em over into Ames's yard. I mean, this thing's got a lotta moving parts."

Ott nodded. "Yeah, I hear ya," he said. "But Celia definitely coulda come up with it. And talk about packin' a lot of ill will for her ex. Question is: Why not just have Lanny go break Ames's knees?"

"Yeah, I can see him doin' that," Crawford said, putting his Bud down on the coaster. "Okay, then, suspect number three, Buzz Cox. Based on what I told you that lawyer Maddy Sorenson told me about him threatening to kill Ames, he's a possible."

"I know, but is anyone with the name of Buzz capable of anything other than jaywalking?" Ott paused to watch a couple walk in. "I mean, maybe...maybe spitting on the sidewalk."

Crawford laughed. "Yeah, but he did threaten to kill Ames, so we gotta take that seriously. I've left three messages on his phone, went to his house twice and left my card."

"Maybe he's out of town," Ott said.

"Maybe he skipped town," Crawford said.

Ott thought for a second. "My money's still on the Russians."

"Yeah," said Crawford. "Time to crank up the thermostat at the Playboy Mansion south."

NINETEEN

CRAWFORD WAS SHOVING RED PUSHPINS INTO THE WALL BEHIND his desk, putting up another yellow-lined piece of paper. It was an extension of his progress chart and timeline on the Kammerer case.

At the moment, however, progress was minimal.

Earlier, Crawford had skimmed through the photos they'd taken of the contents of the Zinovievs' filing cabinet at their house. Most showed newspaper clippings about violent clashes provoked by Chechens eager to unhitch themselves from the Russian wagon. While none of it seemed particularly relevant to his case, Crawford looked at it as a bargaining chip for extracting more information from his FBI friend.

Ott, sitting in a chair opposite his desk, was watching him work on his chart.

Norm Rutledge walked in, a third-degree scowl on his face.

"Hello, Norm," Ott said.

Rutledge didn't say anything, just stared at Crawford.

"Hel-lo, Norm," Ott said again.

"I heard you the first time," he said. "We need to talk."

Crawford motioned for Rutledge to have a seat, then sat down himself.

"Go ahead, Norm, you got the floor."

Rutledge held up a one-page typed letter.

"This is from a lawyer named Chris Kirk at a firm called—"

"—Swiggett, Kirk, Ames, Timpson and Weinberg," Crawford said.

"How do you know that?" Rutledge asked.

"Because the third guy on the totem pole is none other than Churchill Ames."

Rutledge's scowl remained.

"So anyway, this guy Kirk is the lawyer for a Russian by the name of Vasily—"

"Zinoviev," Ott said.

"Okay, both of you, just shut the fuck up and listen," Rutledge said. "Zinoviev claims you assaulted a guy who works for him."

Crawford looked over at Ott and shook his head.

"Are you kidding me?" Crawford said. "All I did was bump into a guy on Zinoviev's plane who wouldn't get out of my way."

Rutledge waved the letter.

"His lawyer calls it a 'forcible assault' and cc'ed the mayor on it."

Crawford's shook his head and his eyes dropped to the floor.

He looked up and started shaking his head. "I don't care whether he cc'ed fuckin' Trump," Crawford said. "Why don't you surprise us just once, believe us instead of some asshole lawyer. I mean, you'd probably believe this guy if he said we waterboarded his client after pistol-whipping his wife."

Ott laughed as Rutledge fumed.

"Here's the thing, Crawford. You two got a history," Rutledge said. "That brawl in the bar in West Palm last year, for starters."

Crawford's eyes met Ott's. They both knew that defending their position was pointless.

"Okay, Norm, whatever," Crawford said.

"Yeah, that about sums up your whole attitude, Crawford. Whatever."

"Whatever," Crawford said again, getting up. "Now if you'll excuse us, we've got a case to solve and I got a suspect to interview."

They walked out of the office, leaving Rutledge fuming more than before.

At the elevator, Crawford turned to Ott. "Is it just me," he said, "or is his head up his ass so far you can't even see his lips?"

"Yeah, just his neck," Ott said. "Where you headed, anyway?"

"Track down Buzz Cox," Crawford replied. "The more he avoids me, the more suspicious I get. You're gonna look into Celia's boyfriend, right?"

Ott nodded. "Oh, yeah, that's what I was gonna tell you," he said. "I checked him out already."

"And?"

"As you predicted, dude's got a sheet."

"No shocker. For what?" Crawford asked as they walked out the back door of the station.

"Assault. Two domestic-abuse charges," Ott said, getting his car keys out of his pocket. "Also, concealed weapon back about six years ago."

Crawford opened the door to his Caprice parked next to Ott's Crown Vic.

"That Celia sure can pick 'em. I'll pay 'em another visit after I break Cox's door down," Crawford said, hoping Lanny Krew wouldn't be sporting his boa necklace.

Crawford drove out of the parking lot and dialed Buzz Cox's number once more. He got the same annoying recording he'd gotten three times before: Hi, this is Buzz— raspy male voice—and Francie— a squeaky female voice chimed in, then their way-too-cute tandem request to leave a message.

This time he really did feel like busting down the door. But he was pretty used to it—the fact that not many people in Palm Beach treated getting back to him as a high priority.

Cox's house at 2 1 3 La Puerta was pretty far up on the north end of Palm Beach and Crawford's reaction to the white stucco house with green shutters was that—by Poinciana standards, anyway—it was somewhat modest. Which meant that by the standards of the rest of the world, it was palatial. Just the "dirt" alone—that's what Rose Clarke called the land a house sat on—had to be worth a million dollars.

This time a woman answered the doorbell. She looked like a Francie. Togged out in Lilly Pulitzer and needlepoint slippers from Stubbs & Wootton, her expression indicated she wasn't too thrilled to see a police officer leaning on her buzzer. She scurried away to get her husband.

Buzz Cox had bloodshot blue eyes and looked like he had been born bald. Instead of opting for the more fashionable shaved-head look, though, Cox had an old-fashioned Friar Tuck fringe.

The main thing, Crawford noticed, was how pale and washed out he was. No sign of a tan, like he lived in Seattle instead of Florida. And his slug-colored skin hung like sheets on a clothesline. When he turned his head, the skin under his chin swayed as if a gentle breeze had just wafted through.

"I was just about to call you back," Cox said.

Sure you were, thought Crawford.

"Come on in." Cox put his hand out to shake Crawford's.

The voice and the handshake didn't go with the face. Cox's voice was husky and deep, his handshake firm.

"Where can we talk, Mr. Cox?"

"Come on back to my library."

The library doubled as a home office. Cox explained he was in the reinsurance business. Crawford looked around and saw lots of pictures of Cox fishing: strapped into a captain's chair at the back of a boat, his rod bent like a U-turn, then another picture of him on a dock standing proudly beside a six-foot sailfish and another one of him casting. Crawford wondered again how the man could be so damn pale. Probably wore one of those big, goofy hats with the earflaps, Crawford figured, whenever he was out fishing.

Crawford sat down in a bamboo chair and launched right in. "Mr. Cox, I want to talk about Churchill Ames."

Cox's expression darkened and he shook his head slowly.

"My old pal Church," he said, almost under his breath. "Go ahead, ask away."

"I get the impression there might be bad blood between you two," Crawford said.

"It can't get any badder, Detective," Cox responded, then he blinked a few times. "Hang on—you're not thinking I had something to do with what happened at his house?"

Crawford gave him his stock answer. "I'm just going around asking a lot of questions."

"Well, I can promise you, I most assuredly had nothing to do with that."

Crawford bet he tossed around the phrase 'most assuredly' a lot.

"Tell me about the relationship between you and Ames."

Cox made a face like the name alone caused a stiff jolt of physical pain.

"I don't know what you heard, but basically Churchill took a small fortune of mine and shrank it down to almost nothing."

"What's a small fortune, if you don't mind me asking?"

"Ten million dollars...that's now worth about a hundred thousand."

"What exactly happened?"

"We're trying to figure out whether he actually embezzled it or just invested it in a lot of bad deals. My guess is a combination of both. I hired a forensic accountant to get to the bottom of it. 'Course, now Ames has disappeared and maybe we'll never know."

"Mr. Cox, would you be prepared to take a polygraph test to say you had nothing to do with what happened at Ames's house?" Crawford asked, like it was nothing out of the ordinary.

Cox looked like he had just been kneed in the groin.

"I'd say that's a little extreme, wouldn't you, Detective?"

"Not really. I thought maybe you'd want to get your name off my suspect list," Crawford said. "By the way, that 'small fortune,' wasn't that, in fact, your mother's money?"

"Yes, well, I'm her only child." Cox got a cranky look on his wan face. "And that's totally ridiculous, me being on your suspect list in the first place."

Crawford looked around the room, then his eyes drifted back to Cox.

"Did you ever threaten Ames, Mr. Cox?" he asked.

"No, I most assuredly—" Cox stopped himself. "I guess you must have spoken to someone at his office...Okay, I lost it that one time, I admit it. But I didn't mean a word of it."

Crawford nodded.

He had ninety-five percent ruled out Cox.

"Here's the thing, Mr. Cox. When someone threatens to kill someone, and then something happens like what happened at Ames's house, you can be sure I'm gonna be taking your threat very seriously."

"I understand, but I can assure you—"

"I'm sure you can assure me all day long, but do you make a habit of going around and threatening to kill people?"

Cox exhaled.

"Detective, it was a big mistake. I regret it. I just lost my cool."

Crawford looked into his eyes. He was one hundred percent sure now. No way this mousey little guy with the clammy skin did it. Plus, he would have absolutely no clue how to go about hiring some lowlife to do the job in the first place.

"Okay, Mr. Cox," Crawford said, getting to his feet. "Try counting to ten or something next time."

"Don't worry, Detective. I can guarantee you, there definitely won't be a next time."

TWENTY

As Crawford crossed the middle bridge to West Palm to drop in on Celia Senior and Lanny Krew again, he thought about Buzz Cox's claim that Churchill Ames had shrunk his family fortune from ten million dollars down to a hundred thousand. The story had an aching resonance. It was like the Crawford family saga.

When the parents of Lucius Crawford, Jr. died within a year of each other in 1926, Crawford's grandfather had inherited roughly eighteen million dollars, which would translate today to over a hundred million. Lucius Crawford, Jr. was in his early twenties when three years later the market crashed and cut his inherited net worth by two thirds. But back then, one could survive on six million just fine.

Precocious in the pursuit of pleasure, Lucius quickly developed a healthy appetite for sailing yachts and shooting quail on his newly acquired, ten-thousand-acre plantation in Georgia. Not to mention, keeping the company of extravagant women, seven of whom he married. Though a Bostonian of the highest pedigree, Crawford lived a lifestyle that not even the most self-indulgent of Boston blue bloods could keep pace with. It was decadent to the max.

After his second marriage fell apart at age twenty-eight, Lucius moved to New York, where to his delight, he found a plethora of like-minded hedonists. His fast, reckless life left little time for work, even though he met many people along the way who guaranteed him they could multiply his fortune. But Lucius chose investment advisors the way he chose wives: Badly. In 1938 he married wife number three and two years later his first son, Lucius III—Charlie's father—was born. That same year he moved his family out of New York to Greenwich, Connecticut.

The problem turned out to be that Lucius, Jr. was incapable of passing along any knowledge to his son except how to pursue a dissolute lifestyle. So, Lucius III struggled at first, having no role model. But he was sure of one thing: He would never emulate any of his father's self-indulgent ways. By the time Lucius III was eight, his father was on to wife number four and living in a house in Newport that he bought from a Vanderbilt heir who had a fondness for cocaine.

Lucius III's mother had sole custody of him and from then on he only saw his father on holidays and whenever his boat sailed up Long Island Sound. The best thing that ever happened to Lucius III was when he met Mary Quinn in 1968. Lucius III, at that time, was a stockbroker at Kidder Peabody and Mary Quinn was what was known, back in that pre-assistant age, as a secretary. She came from a big Irish family of cops, firemen, bartenders, and one state assembly-man. They married and had their first son in 1977, deciding, mercifully, to put an end to the Lucius first-name legacy. Their second son had been Charles.

Crawford's father slowly rose through the ranks at Kidder Peabody by working twelve-hour days, dispensing well-researched financial advice and finally got wooed away to J.P. Morgan, where he became a managing director. While Lucius, Jr. squandered most of the Crawford fortune on decadent pursuits as well as wives four, five, six, and seven, Lucius III was a striver and a saver. Lucius, Jr. ending up dying in a second-rate nursing home in Providence, Rhode Island, while Lucius III moved his family into a six-bedroom brick colonial in New Canaan.

But Lucius III was dogged with what one shrink called the "Crawford curse." His uncle and grandmother had committed suicide. Back when his grandmother slit her wrists, it was called "melancholia." When his uncle hung himself, it was known as depression.

Charlie found his father one day when he opened the garage door looking for a hockey stick. The medical examiner estimated his father's Lincoln Continental had been running for at least an hour.

CRAWFORD LOOKED DOWN AT HIS OLD BLACKBERRY AND READ an e-mail that he had asked Ott to send him. It was Lanny Krew's sheet. The man knew his way around petty crime and violence. Krew had never killed anyone, or at least had never been charged with it, but seemed very adept at knocking people around until they bled profusely. Crawford thought about Krew a little more and came to the conclusion that you never could know when someone might ratchet it up to the next level and kill someone. In any case, it was definitely too early to rule him out as a murderer. But also too early to charge him with anything.

This time, Lanny's Corvette was not in Celia Senior's driveway.

Celia opened the front door, wearing a dark green skirt and a tight collarless buttoned shirt. The second button down was in the wrong hole, which gave her a lopsided look. The misplaced button probably had something to do with the ever-present, half-filled glass of amber liquid in her right hand.

"Ah, the return of the hunk," she said.

"Ms. Senior, I need to ask you a few more questions."

"Sure, come on in," she slurred.

"Where's your friend, Lanny?" he asked.

"Damned if I know."

She sat down, showing way too much leg and thigh for a woman in her mid-fifties.

"Ms. Senior—"

"Please, Celia."

"I want to go over this whole thing again," Crawford said. "You think your ex-husband hid assets from you at the time of your divorce, right?"

"Think? Of course, he did. Everyone knows that."

"Okay, so then it would stand to reason that you'd want to get your rightful share. Correct?"

"Yes, of course I would," she said, itching the side of her head, "but I had a lousy lawyer."

"I'm not talking about through the courts," he said, hardening his tone.

She shifted in her chair and was now showing even more leg and thigh. "Listen, sweet thing, it might not have occurred to you, but I have absolutely no leverage over Churchill."

For a Radcliffe College girl, she was proving slow on the uptake.

"Come on, Ms. Senior, your friend, Lanny, could have provided that leverage," Crawford said. "I discovered a few convictions for crimes of a violent nature in his past."

"Lanny?"

"Yes, two for assault."

"Must have been a long time ago," Celia said, taking a healthy sip. "Lanny's a pussycat these days."

Crawford studied her buttons again. He wasn't hearing resounding conviction in her last statement.

She swiveled in the chair and threw one leg over one of the arms. Crawford could see practically up to her hip-bone. It was not pretty and he glanced away quickly.

"I need a cell number for Lanny, please."

"Sorry, I don't ever call—"

"Come on, Ms. Senior," Crawford said. "You know his number."

She shot him a spiteful look. "561-329-6397."

Crawford scribbled it down. "Thank you. When you speak to him, tell him to call me right away, please."

She nodded earnestly, but he wasn't going to hold his breath.

CRAWFORD HAD BARELY DRIVEN AROUND THE CORNER IN HIS car when Lanny walked out of Celia's garage, where his Corvette was parked. He had been working on his Harley Fatboy, which seemed to have more chrome on it than the Chrysler Building. When, through the garage window, he saw Crawford pull up, Lanny had put his wrench down and kept quiet.

He walked into the living room.

"You were very friendly with the Detective, sweetheart," Lanny said.

"I'm very friendly in general," said Celia, still with one leg over the chair's arm.

She got to her feet and her skirt dropped down to a more respectable level, just below her knees.

"I liked it when you called me a pussycat," he said.

She smiled and came over and started to put her arms around him.

He shoved her away and backhanded her.

"What the hell was that for?" she shouted, holding her mouth.

"I heard you come on to that guy...calling him sweet thing."

Lanny looked as though he was about to slap her again.

She rubbed her face.

"Goddamn jerk," she said. "I was just answering his questions."

"Oh, really? And flashing him your cooter."

Celia's mouth dropped. "Cooter? Jesus, what century are you from?" She shook her head. "And stop with the goddamn jealousy, will you?"

Lanny took a step toward her.

Celia shrank back.

"Relax, baby, I'm your pussycat, remember?" He slapped her hard across the face. She staggered backwards and fell into the ratty brown couch.

TWENTY-ONE

IF JOHN CALHOUN-JONES HAD BEEN ABLE TO DO CARTWHEELS, he would have. But Calhoun-Jones was forty pounds overweight, had a suspect ticker, and wasn't all that coordinated to begin with. He was, however, on top of the world.

John Calhoun-Jones had just been made the new president of the Poinciana Club. And though he'd never admit it to anyone, even his wife, this was the fulfillment of a lifelong dream. It was his personal validation. Calhoun-Jones had been born sixty-four years ago in Columbus, Ohio, the son of a dentist, but not the dentist favored by the rich, successful businessmen and industrialists of Columbus. No, his father's patients were from the families of men who worked on production lines. His birth certificate read John Calhoun Jones, which is how it remained until Jones graduated from Creighton Business School and was about to set off into the world of banking.

He decided that John Jones was utterly lacking in gravitas. Nothing to capture the public's imagination like John David Rockefeller or John Jacob Astor. So he added a hyphen and made Calhoun-Jones his last name. It puzzled his mother and outraged his father. But they got over it.

They'd probably be very proud of their son now, especially since the Poinciana Club had to be in the top twenty of all clubs in the United States. Not that there was any kind of official ranking for fancy clubs, but unofficial was good enough for Calhoun-Jones. He had come up with a roster of the top clubs in his head: two in Greenwich, Connecticut, one or two on the North Shore of Long Island. New York City had a few, of course; there were a couple out in Southampton and East Hampton, and then Lake Forest, Grosse Pointe, Newport, Far Hills, and Brookline each had one or two. There were also some out in California, but he didn't know any of them by name.

Churchill Ames's call to him, a few days ago, had been a little cryptic. Of course, Calhoun-Jones knew all about the incident at Ames's house. "The snakes that bit the snake" was how one wag, who was not a big Churchill Ames fan, described it. Ames had simply said that he was going on a "long-overdue vacation" and that he wouldn't be able to "give the Poinciana the attention it deserved" and blah-blah-blah. What did Calhoun-Jones care? He was being handed the high-status—albeit, unpaid—job of a lifetime. Ames told him that he had dictated a letter of resignation, and that copies of it would be hand-delivered to each member of the executive committee. In response, Calhoun-Jones tried to suppress his joy and solemnly thanked Ames for his dedication and for a job well done. Ames said, "You're welcome and sorry I didn't give you more notice, but sometimes that's just the way it is."

So, that was that. Short and sweet. The cherished presidency was now his.

One of John Calhoun-Jones's first congratulatory calls was from a man he had never heard of before. Vasily Zinoviev, his name was. Calhoun-Jones played back the message: I understand congratulations are in order because of your election to the presidency of the Poinciana Club. Would you please give me a call on my cell phone at your earliest convenience? Mr. Rush Limbaugh suggested that I speak of you.

Okay, the man's English wasn't all that great, but—more out of curiosity than anything—Calhoun-Jones decided to call him back.

VASILY ZINOVIEV WAS EATING LUNCH AT A LITTLE RESTAURANT in Riviera Beach that was at the opposite end of the Zagat spectrum from Delbasso's in Palm Beach. He punched the green button on his cell.

"Hello?"

"Mr. Zinoviev, this is John Calhoun-Jones returning your phone call."

"Hello, Mr. Calhoun-Jones," said Vasily, who had a full report on Calhoun-Jones's more humble beginnings as John Jones, son of a second-string dentist. "I was wondering if it would be possible to meet with you. I have an interesting business proposal which I'd like to discuss with you."

"Well, thank you, Mr. Zinoviev, but I'm not really active in business anymore. I'm pretty much retired," Calhoun-Jones said.

"This matter, I believe, will interest you in your new capacity as president of the Poinciana Club," Vasily explained.

"Well," said the new president of the Poinciana. "Okay. Sure. Why not?"

TWENTY-TWO

IT WAS EASY TO SAY YOU WERE GOING TO TURN UP THE HEAT ON the Russians; quite another thing to actually do it.

Crawford decided to pay a visit to David Balfour, the man who had given Jessie Kammerer's name to Churchill Ames. Balfour was kind of the male equivalent of the real-estate broker Rose Clarke. A guy who knew everyone in Palm Beach and had a handle on practically everything going on there. The difference was, he didn't work. Never really had. Never really had to. There were quite a few men like that in Palm Beach.

Crawford had been to Balfour's house on Eden Way several times before for help with cases. Crawford had discovered, quite by accident, that if he showed up just after lunch—after Balfour had his three poolside Bull Shots—the information flowed freely.

Balfour met him at his front door, clutching his signature Bull Shot. Balfour was an easygoing, devil-may-care guy. The problems of the world never seemed to register on his boyish face. He and Crawford had actually gotten quite friendly, as in a two-guys-shootin'-the-breeze kind of way.

"Hey, Charlie, welcome back, come on in," Balfour said. "Can I get you a drink?"

Balfour always asked him that and Crawford always politely declined.

"Thanks, David, I'm—"

"'On the job,' right?"

"Exactly." Crawford followed him inside.

"Let's go into the library." Which is where they always went.

Balfour's library had a comfortable feel to it. On the shelves were trophies, silver cups and bowls from athletic triumphs. Photos showed Balfour swinging a golf club, presumably at the Poinciana, and shooting birds while he was dressed up in well-shined boots and a Barbour jacket. The only thing missing in Balfour's library were books. Except for the one shelf, which contained the complete, unexpurgated works of Clive Cussler.

They sat down in a corner of the room in two fat leather club chairs and caught up for a few minutes.

Then Crawford cut to the chase.

"David, I'm sure you've given it some thought why someone dumped those snakes into Churchill Ames's backyard?"

Balfour set his Bull Shot down on top of a *Vanity Fair* magazine on a side table.

"Yeah, you're right," Balfour said. "I sure have."

Balfour liked to play slightly hard to get and have Crawford coax things out of him.

"So tell me what your thinking is."

Balfour looked from side to side, like someone might have snuck in, poised to eavesdrop on them.

"Okay, Charlie," he said, "you know the drill, right?"

"Of course," Crawford said, "same as always; nothing goes out of this room. You're my C.I."

Crawford knew that gave Balfour purpose and pride, being declared his unofficial confidential informer.

"Okay," Balfour said, "so I'd say you should put down Vasily and Aleksandr Zinoviev as persons of interest."

Crawford leaned forward and played dumb.

"Who are they?"

"These two Russian brothers who approached Churchill about buying the Poinciana."

Crawford's heartbeat kicked up a notch.

"You're kidding. Since when is the Poinciana up for sale?"

Balfour laughed. "Since never," he said. "It's not now and never will be, but that didn't stop these guys from approaching Church."

He watched Balfour take a pull of his Bull Shot.

"So what were they going to do with it—these Russian guys—if they bought it?" Crawford asked.

"Build a million high-end condos or something," Balfour said. "That's what Church told me."

"Could they actually do that?"

"No, not the way the zoning laws are," Balfour replied. "Maybe they planned to bribe someone to work around the laws or something. Whole thing's kind of fishy."

Crawford was dying to fill in Ott.

"Church said they were fixing to pay us over three-hundred million for it," Balfour said.

"That's incredible. And you guys wouldn't take it?"

Balfour laughed.

"Nah, half the guys in the club are worth more than that already."

Crawford flashed to his Camry and his condo overlooking the Publix parking lot and felt quite insignificant.

The cordless phone on an end table rang. Balfour picked it up and looked down to see who the caller was.

"Oh, Christ, I gotta take this. Just two minutes," said Balfour, holding up a hand.

Crawford nodded.

"Hey, P.D.," Balfour said.

Crawford pondered his poverty and thought about shelling out a few bucks for lottery tickets, as he heard the caller's voice buzz unintelligibly from the phone five feet away.

"All I'm asking is you tell me what you got me invested in," Balfour said. "I mean, shit, it's a pretty basic question, P.D. For Chrissakes, for all I know it's pork bellies or goddamn orange-juice futures or something."

Balfour listened. The voice was loud and didn't slow down.

"All right, all right," Balfour said, evidently frustrated. "I guess it doesn't really matter. Whatever it is, it's making me thirty percent a year. Okay, P.D., yeah, talk to you later."

He hung up and looked up at Crawford.

"Christ, it's so damn frustrating," he said, shaking his head. "You know who P.D. Miller is?"

Crawford shook his head.

"I've got this account with him, in one of his offshore funds," Balfour said. "The thing does great, but I have no clue what I'm invested in. Guy keeps his cards real close to the vest."

Crawford nodded, wanting to get back to Churchill Ames and the attempted Poinciana buyout.

"So what do you think," Crawford asked, "the snakes might have been to convince Ames to get the other members to sell?"

"Yeah, that's what I think."

"And why Ames left town?" Crawford said. "'Cause he was scared what the Russians would do next?"

Balfour nodded and polished off the last of his Bull Shot. "Yeah, that's what I would have done. Gotten the hell out of Dodge. The whole condo story's pretty dubious, though."

"Why?" Crawford asked.

"I don't know," Balfour said. "It just doesn't seem to add up. Something's missing."

They talked for a few more minutes, then Crawford thanked Balfour and left.

He called Ott just as soon as he got out of Balfour's house.

Ott said "ho-ly shit" seven times in the course of a two-minute conversation, which might have been his personal record.

TWENTY-THREE

KIMBERLY COLEMAN, THE SOCIAL SECRETARY OF THE Poinciana, led the two Russians into the pecky-cypress-paneled room. It was an odd procession. Kimberly was tall and angular, no softness or curves to her at all, just an extraordinarily efficient woman dedicated to making things go smoothly at her beloved Poinciana. Behind her came Vasily Zinoviev, a five-six block of granite with a huge head. He was clean-shaven, having dispensed with his trademark three-day facial growth in deference to what he predicted would be the conservative tastes of John Calhoun-Jones and his fellow board members.

A step behind Vasily came his brother, Aleksandr, decked out in a double-breasted blue blazer, yellow silk tie, and gray flannels. He looked as though he was there to be interviewed to become a member of the Poinciana. Aleksandr appeared as relaxed as his brother was wound tight.

To their surprise, the brothers had learned that instead of taking a meeting with Calhoun-Jones alone, they'd won an audience with the entire executive committee. The official reason Calhoun-Jones had called them all in was because he felt this might be a matter that needed the whole committee's consideration. But the real reason was that Calhoun-Jones was an exceedingly cautious man who preferred that if he had to make a tough call his first week on the job, he'd like to make it with the support of all twelve committeemen. That way no one could ever point the finger at him and say he'd screwed up the first thing he got his hands on.

Calhoun-Jones had put out a memo, the day after being named president of the Poinciana, which said that two Russian friends of Rush Limbaugh's had a proposal of some kind to present.

Buzz Cox, a long-standing member of the executive committee, caught Calhoun-Jones's eye as the odd Zinoviev duo was led in. His look said, *this should be interesting*. Calhoun-Jones simply smiled and nodded.

"Gentlemen," Calhoun-Jones said, standing up to shake hands with the brothers, "I welcome you to the Poinciana Club" —then getting right to it— "Now, if you would, please tell us what it is you are proposing."

Vasily stood up. "My brother and I would first like to thank you for allowing us the opportunity of coming to your extraordinary club. Ever since we first visited Palm Beach, we have greatly admired your beautiful golf course and magnisifent buildings."

Aleksandr cringed for a split second, but quickly replaced the look with his movie-star smile.

"And," Vasily continued, "of course, we hope you will entertain and accept our generous offer."

Calhoun-Jones reacted with a quizzical look. "Your generous offer," he said. "I don't understand...for what?"

Vasily frowned and his head seemed to swell even larger.

"Oh, I assumed Mr. Ames told you," Vasily said. "Our generous offer to buy the Poinciana Club."

Several members burst out laughing.

Another one gasped.

Others reactions ran the gamut, from 'Did I hear that correctly?' to amused chuckles at the brazen cheek of these oafish foreigners. As for John Calhoun-Jones, his jaw went into free fall.

"Mr. Zinoviev," Calhoun-Jones began slowly, realizing the need to show how much of a take-charge guy he was. Having just landed the plum job of a lifetime, he wasn't about to give it up anytime soon. "I know I can speak for the collective membership of the executive committee: The Poinciana Club has been here for seventy-five years and we fully expect it to be here seventy-five years from now."

Vasily didn't even have time to react to Calhoun-Jones before a tall, gray-haired man who bore a striking resemblance to Stonewall Jackson rose from his chair and started gesticulating wildly.

"Well said, C.J, well said," the man cried out, then raised his voice to a bellow as he stared at the Russians. "Where do people like you get off? You come to this country—make money God-knows how —and think you can buy anything you damn well please."

A few heads started nodding vigorously.

"You come here—most of the time illegally—and take advantage of our system. Operating your little underground economy, paying no taxes, and making a mockery of everything that we hold so dear and have worked so many generations for. Why don't you just go back to wherever it is you come from? Buy a golf course in...in—"

His geography was failing him.

"Leningrad," a member whispered.

"Yes, Leningrad," the tall, gray-haired man proclaimed righteously.

Aleksandr snuck a glance at his brother. Vasily was starting to breathe faster, his eyes darkened to coal black.

But the man who was speaking had only paused.

"Twenty-five years ago," he went on, "you were our mortal enemy and now you're here, undermining our country and throwing around your filthy, contaminated money."

The man paused again, building to a crescendo: "*Nyet*, I say. That is my answer to you and I'll say it again. *Nyet*. Next thing we know, some goddamn Guatemalan will try to buy the Breakers—"

Vasily had heard enough. Being compared to a Guatemalan was apparently the last straw.

"Lee-sen you fugkink ah-soul," Vasily said, his accent thickening as his temper rose, "you high-and-mighty—"

A few of the younger members of the executive committee stood up and started advancing toward him.

"Gentlemen, gentleman, please," Calhoun-Jones said. If he had a gavel he would have rapped it.

Aleksandr hopped to his feet and looked like he was afraid of being lynched.

The tall, gray-haired man sat down. He looked spent, like he had just delivered a rousing speech to the United Nations General Assembly.

But Vasily wasn't finished. He stood before them, eyes blazing, face blood-red. He turned to a shell-shocked Calhoun-Jones four feet away.

"You and everyone else in this room will regret this," he said. "Trust me—Mr. son-of-a- fugkink-dentist—you will regret this most definitely."

Then he turned and walked away, his brother at his side, not waiting for the social secretary to escort them out.

TWENTY-FOUR

CRAWFORD WALKED OUT TO HIS CAR IN BACK OF THE STATION. IT was Saturday and he and Ott had just had their morning coffee together, as they looked over Lanny Krew's sheet again, then talked over the Russian brothers' possible motives. Crawford's gut told him the real-estate angle had considerable merit and he decided he wanted to talk it over with an expert. A little before nine, he got up and said he was going to go drop in on Rose Clarke.

Ott got a mischievous look on his face and asked, "Business or pleasure?"

Crawford shook his head, looked offended, and asked, "What do you think?"

Ott shrugged and said, "I don't know, Charlie, that's why I asked."

"Wiseass," he said. "She's my expert."

CRAWFORD GLANCED DOWN AT THE CLOCK ON THE DASHBOARD of his car: 9:15. A little early for a drop-in, he decided. He was approaching the roundabout just south of Mar-a-Lago when he saw a green convertible sports car go into the turn. He recognized the man at the wheel, blonde hair and a mouth full of dazzling white teeth. It was Aleksandr Zinoviev, in stylish black wraparounds. Beside him in the passenger seat was a woman. She was wearing a white headband and an ear-to-ear smile.

He did a double take, then realized the woman was Dominica McCarthy.

She hadn't seen Crawford. She'd been too busy smiling and chatting, gesturing with both hands, as they blew past him.

It hit him like a baseball bat to the gut. His old girlfriend, smiling like he had never seen her smile before, like she had just won the Powerball and looking hotter than ever. It was a seriously depressing sight to Crawford. Here he was, a hapless cop in a white Caprice, bird shit all over the back windshield, left in the exhaust fumes of a two-hundred-thousand-dollar English sports car, piloted by a rich, handsome Russian playboy.

He drove north on Ocean Drive in a state of heightened agitation, coming up with at least seven scenarios based on what he had just seen. In one of them, Dominica had just spent the night at the Russians' house up on North Lake Way. Swum in the grotto, quaffed expensive champagne, then spent the night—occasionally sleeping—between thousand-count Egyptian cotton sheets.

Not that that was really like Dominica. She was a far cry from easy. Well, at least with him, anyway. Nevertheless, he ended up being tormented by every single one of the scenarios his fertile imagination came up with. They all made him want to pound his steering wheel and scream at the top of his lungs.

Instead, he speed-dialed Rose Clarke on her cell.

"Hello?"

"Hi, Rose," he said, trying to low-key it.

"Wait a sec, Charlie, hold on," she said, breathing heavily.

"What are you doing?" he asked, not sure he wanted to know.

"Downward dog," she said, puffing.

He wasn't sure he wanted to ask. "What the hell is that?"

"Yoga...and texting a customer on my iPhone."

"And talking to me," he said. "You might just be taking this multi-tasking thing a little too far."

"Yeah, maybe," she said and laughed. "What's up, lover boy?"

"Just checking in."

There was a pause.

"You never just 'check in,'" Rose said. "Come on, Charlie, it's me."

"Okay, okay," He paused a moment, reconsidering what he was about to say, then plunged ahead. "So I saw Dominica five minutes ago with one of those Russians." He made it sound like one of those mass-murderers.

"Yes," she said. "You mean, Aleksandr."

"Yeah, so what's the story?" Crawford said, pulling over to the shoulder of the road. He had to concentrate.

"Calm down," she said, "she's just going out on his boat."

He heard her grunt, like she had just pretzeled herself into some strange new position.

"Sure didn't take her long to get back into circulation," Crawford said.

"You mean, since you two broke up?" Rose said. "Charlie, I got news for you: Your last date with Dominica was three months ago."

"Two and a half."

Rose laughed. "But who's counting? Look, why don't you come over for lunch and a swim? You need to chill out a little."

"Me? Iceberg Crawford?" he said.

"I'm not so sure, Charlie," Rose said. "Come on over. I'll be back here after eleven."

"Where you going?"

"I have a really big showing at ten. My gazillion-dollar listing."

"Well, good luck with it."

"Thanks," she said, breathing heavily again.

"You're still doing it, aren't you?" he asked.

"What?"

"That dog thing."

"Yeah," she said, "but at least I stopped texting."

HE CALLED HIS FRIEND AT THE FBI AGAIN, TRYING TO GET Dominica out of his head. He reached his machine and left a message. The gist of it was that he'd appreciate seeing the dossier, or whatever the guy had, on Vasily and Aleksandr Zinoviev and he'd be happy to reciprocate with some of the shots he'd taken up at the Russians' house.

At a little after eleven, he knocked on Rose's door. She didn't answer, so he turned the knob and walked into her house. Through the French doors in back he saw her in her pool. Doing laps.

Then, as he got closer, he saw that—yes, in fact, she was doing laps—but completely nude. As she made a turn at the deep end, she spotted him out of the corner of her eye, smiled, and gave him a little wave.

She swam a little further, then stopped in the middle of the pool and looked over. Crawford just concentrated on making solid eye contact and not letting his eyes stray. It was about five feet deep where she was. As she stood, Crawford noticed—not for the first time—how gym-trim and tight she was. And, though she wasn't exactly flaunting it, she certainly wasn't hiding what God, and her Romanian trainer, had created.

Squinting a little, her long blonde hair splayed out around her, her breasts just breaking the surface of the water, Rose playfully squirted a jet of water out of her mouth at him.

"Hi, Charlie."

He gave her a little wave. "Maybe I should come back when you find your bikini."

Rose laughed. "Funny boy," she said. "You know, after what happened, I didn't dare go in my pool for a while."

It didn't click right away. Then he got it.

"Oh, yeah, you mean the snakes."

"Yeah, can you imagine? What a horrible way to go."

"I know," he said, having difficulty maintaining eye contact. "Rose, I would really appreciate it if you put something on."

She got up on her tiptoes. "Why don't you just jump in and cool off?"

"Left my bathing suit at home."

"Good place for it."

He shook his head. "I'd get a sunburn in all the wrong places."

"You know, Charlie, you're really no fun," she said. "Oh, hey, that reminds me: Maddy Sorenson told me you came by her office and asked her a million questions."

Crawford shrugged. "Yeah, so? That's my job."

"I really don't see Maddy being your type, Charlie," she said. "You know, she's so aggressive."

Crawford had a feeling Rose saw herself as his type.

"Rose, just for the record," he said, "I didn't go see Maddy Sorenson to ask her out."

Rose laughed and started walking toward the pool steps. She was walking deliberately, almost in slow motion, like a model down a runway. Then suddenly she turned toward him at the top step.

He was peeking.

"Busted," she said as his eyes shot to a nearby gumbo-limbo tree off to her right. He kept his eyes trained on it, like its bark was totally mesmerizing.

"Didn't know you were such a tree lover, Charlie. It's okay to look now."

He glanced back at her. She was wrapped in a white, oversized terry-cloth robe. She went and stretched out on the big teak double chaise near the shallow end. It had a thick foam mattress covered in a soft, pale-green fabric.

She motioned him over with her hand.

"Come on, Charlie, I don't bite," she said, then lowered her voice. "Too hard."

He walked toward her.

"You know anything about her?" Rose asked.

"Who?"

"Maddy Sorenson."

He shook his head. "What's to know? Seems like a competent lawyer, probably got very good personal hygiene."

Rose laughed. "Yeah, but listen to this. She tried to get into the Poinciana and got shot down."

"Really? What happened?" he said, noticing how her tan contrasted nicely with the white terry-cloth robe.

"She got caught cheating in a golf tournament," said Rose.

"Get outta here. You mean like Jordan Baker?"

"Who's Jordan Baker?"

"Daisy Buchanan's friend in *The Great Gatsby*," he said. "That's my one and only literary allusion."

Jesus, how'd he get so far afield? He realized he wasn't within a hundred miles of what he came to talk about.

"A literary allusion. I'm impressed," Rose said. "So what did you want to ask me about, anyway?"

"Real estate," he answered.

She smacked her forehead. "Oh, my God, I forgot to tell you." She shot up into a sitting position. "I got an offer on my gazillion-dollar listing and it was accepted. I Fedexed the contract out a half hour ago."

"Congratulations," he said. "How much?"

"Well, it's kind of tacky to say," she said, "but eighty-eight-million-five."

"What?" said Crawford, thinking maybe he had missed a decimal point somewhere.

"Eighty-eight million, five-hundred thousand dollars, to be exact," Rose said, raising both arms in triumph. "The new record in Palm Beach. More than Nelson Belk's house a few years ago."

"Jesus, Rose, that's incredible. Nice going," said Crawford, wondering why a buyer would even bother with the five hundred thousand dollars.

"Thanks," she said with a little fist pump. "It closes in just forty-five days."

Crawford was doing the math. On, say, a three-percent commission, it was around... holy shit, three million dollars.

"Rose," he said, "I just figured out what you make on that deal and...will you marry me?"

Her face broke into a wide grin. "In a New York second," she said, then turned up her lower lip, "if you really meant it."

"So who's the lucky guy?" he asked.

"The guy who sold it, you mean?" she asked, lying back down on the chaise.

Crawford nodded.

"A guy named P. D. Miller."

Crawford cocked his head to one side. "Second time I've heard that name in the last few days."

"Runs a big vulture fund," Rose said. "Goes into developing countries and buys stuff cheap. He has investments all over the world. One of the first guys into China when they decided capitalism wasn't such a bad thing after all. Russia too, right after communism bit the dust."

"What's P.D. stand for, anyway?" Crawford asked, looking out over the pool.

"I think it's Philip something, but a girlfriend of mine calls him 'Penile Dysfunction.'"

Crawford laughed and held up his hands. "Okay, I really don't want to go there. So back to my real-estate questions."

Rose lay back on the double chaise and beckoned Crawford with her finger. "Come on, Charlie, there's plenty of room here."

Crawford hesitated, but then got down on the chaise and stretched out.

Rose took his arm and put it around her shoulder.

"Make you a deal," she said, her soft, sultry voice kicking in. "You can ask me all the real-estate questions you want, but…"

"But?"

"You have to pay me."

"Only got ten bucks on me."

"Not in money."

Rose slowly reached down and pulled lightly at the sash of her terry-cloth robe. The robe fell open.

"How 'bout pay me first," she said, "ask questions later."

TWENTY-FIVE

On his way back from Rose's house, Crawford called the Zinovievs' number. He recognized the voice of the petite Asian woman. He asked for Aleksandr. A minute later, Aleksandr picked up.

"Mr. Zinoviev, my partner and I would like to come talk to you again about the murder at Churchill Ames's house," Crawford said.

Aleksandr exhaled. Like he had just sucked in all the air around him.

"Okay, Detective, I would be happy to see you," Aleksandr said. "But I'm not sure my brother will be available."

"Why not?"

"I just don't think he will be," Aleksandr said. "What time were you thinking?"

"Two o'clock," Crawford said. "And do whatever you can to make your brother available, please."

THERE WAS A WHITE AUDI PARKED NEAR THE FRONT PORCH when Crawford and Ott pulled up to the Russians' house.

Crawford parked behind it and they both got out.

They walked up the four steps and Ott pressed the buzzer.

The Asian woman came to the door.

"The Zinovievs are expecting us," Crawford said as he and Ott brushed by her.

She caught up and took them down the long hallway to the living room.

Crawford saw the back of a woman's head sitting across from Aleksandr.

The woman turned when she heard their footsteps. It was Maddy Sorenson.

"Welcome back, gentlemen," Aleksandr said, standing up and gesturing toward Maddy, who remained seated. "I believe you know my attorney."

"Sure do," Crawford said. "Hi, Maddy, this is my partner, Mort Ott."

"Hi, Charlie," Maddy said, then turned to Ott. "Detective."

Ott nodded.

"So what exactly are you doing here?" Crawford asked her.

"I should ask you that," Maddy said. "As Aleksandr said, I'm his and his brother's attorney."

"And they wanted you here because?" Crawford asked.

"Is that a serious question?" Maddy asked. "Because this is the third time you've showed up here. For what purpose do you keep coming back?"

"Do you mind if we sit?" Crawford asked Aleksandr. "Being a regular here, I know just how comfortable this couch is."

"Of course," Aleksandr said, gesturing toward the red leather couch.

Crawford sat down and looked at Maddy.

"Comfortable now?" she asked.

"Very," Crawford answered.

"Good," she said, "so let's cut to the chase. What do you want with my client?"

"First of all, where's my friend, Vasily?" Crawford asked.

"I don't think he'll be joining us," Maddy said. "Please answer the question."

"Okay," he said, "Aleksandr and Vasily met with your colleague, Churchill Ames, who now appears to be on an indefinite leave of absence."

Maddy nodded.

"The purpose of their meeting was apparently to buy the Poinciana Club."

Ott leaned forward. "Which was a completely different story than the one Mr. Zinoviev here originally told us," he added.

"Okay," Maddy said, "so is offering to buy the Poinciana Club against the law?"

"Of course not," Crawford said, "but killing Jessie Kammerer is. As you know, we're investigating her homicide."

"Yes, I'm aware of that," Maddy said, "but are you saying that you suspect my clients had something to do with it?"

"Matter of fact, that had crossed our minds," Crawford said.

"Well, that's absurd and you have absolutely no proof," Maddy responded. "The only thing that you've said that is true is that my clients met with Churchill Ames. That's it."

Crawford looked at Aleksandr, then Ott, then back to Maddy. "I've got a math question for your client, Maddy."

Crawford heard steps coming down the hallway. Vasily walked in, wearing black jeans and a purple Hawaiian shirt.

"Hello, Vasily," Maddy said, "thanks for joining us."

Vasily just nodded and sat down in a club chair next to her.

"Detective Crawford here was just saying he had a math question," Maddy said to Vasily. "I have no idea what his question is about."

"About buying the Poinciana," Crawford said to Vasily, who hadn't made eye contact with him yet. "I did a little homework and found out that based on its present zoning that if you knocked down all the Poinciana buildings—which you'd never be able to do because of their historic designation—but, if you did, then built the maximum allowable number of condominiums, you would only get a hundred and twenty-two condos. In terms of total square footage, that's just over a million square feet."

Vasily looked irritable, Maddy looked like she was tracking, and Aleksandr looked disinterested.

"Okay, that's all very interesting," Maddy said. "And your question is?"

"My question is, if you paid three-hundred-and-twelve million for the property and built those units at a cost of two-hundred dollars a square foot—which I'm told is about right—then sell them at today's market price, you'd end up losing your shirt. Somewhere in the neighborhood of a hundred-million-dollar loss, to be exact."

"I still don't hear a question," Maddy said.

"The question is obvious." Crawford said. "That's a really bad real-estate deal, so why would you ever do it? But, turns out, you can't do it anyway, because the buildings are historically designated and you can't tear 'em down."

Maddy shot a look at Vasily, who maintained his scowl and started tapping his pointy-toed shoe on the floor.

"I don't know the answer, Charlie," she said. "But my off-the-cuff response would be to go in for a zoning change. Try to increase the density on the property, i.e., get more units. But the bigger question is: Since when is it the job of the Palm Beach Police Department to evaluate real-estate deals? And where do you get off determining whether private citizens can or cannot make any damn real-estate acquisition they want to?"

"Maddy," Crawford said, leaning back, "what I'm saying is this whole condo thing smells. Like one big, elaborate smoke screen."

Maddy tapped her fingers on the coffee table in front of her.

"Okay," she said, "you two are skating dangerously close to harassment of my clients. I am going to demand that, unless you've got a damn good, legally defensible reason, that you cease and desist from contacting them. That you don't come around here anymore to float your real-estate theories or for any other misguided reason." She glanced at Ott, then gave Crawford a hard, cold stare. "Do you understand me?"

Crawford stood up and Ott followed. Crawford looked over at Vasily, who was now staring intently at him.

"Okay, Maddy, I understand you," Crawford said. "Now it's your turn to understand me. The next time we show up here will be when we come to put your clients away."

They walked out of the house and got into their car.

"Jesus, man, that was pretty impressive," Ott said. "Where'd you get all that 'maximum allowable' and 'historic designation' shit? You sounded like goddamn Trump or somebody."

He turned to Ott and smiled. "My friend Rose Clarke," Crawford said. "Why do you think I went to see her?"

TWENTY-SIX

Pete Nicastro, and Yulena, whose last name Pete didn't catch except that it ended in "kova," were at Applebee's for Sunday brunch. It was twenty miles from another Applebee's in Royal Palm City, where Pete took his wife every Friday. To make sure he wasn't going to get spotted, Pete had his Dolphins cap pulled down low and was wearing his polarized Oakleys. He had met Yulena at the Palm Beach Building Department, where he worked.

Pete was the building inspector for Palm Beach. It was a job with a fair amount of power even though it didn't pay much. Building inspectors were entrusted with the job of interpreting and enforcing the building code. That could mean construing it very strictly, thus causing long delays, untold headaches, and massive cost overruns in building a house. Or it could mean giving someone a pass to make the whole procedure go quick and smooth. Pete Nicastro had the power to make people very appreciative, or want to torture him, slowly and painfully. As he well knew, it was in the best interests of Palm Beach residents to get on and stay on the good side of this otherwise quite unremarkable man.

Yulena had come in with a survey of a house on the north end that she said she was thinking of buying. Pete saw her out at the front desk. The new girl who was working there looked confused, clearly not understanding the pleasant but English-challenged young woman. Pete had stepped in helpfully. Eyeing the ample cleavage on display and her large, sensuous lips, he'd fielded her questions, one of which he never fully understood, then gave her general answers that he was pretty sure she didn't understand at all.

Her main question—he thought, anyway—was whether she could add a second story to an existing one-story house. But then again, maybe it was: Could she add a second house to an oversized lot? He had given her a yes-and-no answer to the first; yes, you could, but you had to abide by a formula based on the total square footage of the lot. That clearly threw her. Her reaction, however, was unusual. Rather than ask another question and seek clarification, she had smiled winsomely and leaned forward for no apparent reason, providing Pete with another eyeful of her round, firm breasts, which appeared unencumbered by any support system. She remained in that position for what seemed like a blissful eternity to Pete.

Then she moved from across the table to the chair next to him and turned the survey around. She asked him another quite incomprehensible question. As he turned to seek clarification to what she was asking, her lips brushed his cheek. Pete knew it was intentional. She was somehow finding him flat-out irresistible, which was odd, since he had been building inspector for seven-and-a-half years and no woman had ever given him a second look. Pete had a lunch date scheduled with a junior zoning official, but chose to let it slip his mind.

Yulena then gave him a smile, tore off a corner of the survey, and wrote down a phone number.

He called the number later that afternoon and asked her to brunch at the Applebee's far from his home.

Yᴜʟᴇɴᴀ ʜᴀᴅ ɴᴇᴠᴇʀ ʜᴀᴅ ᴇɢɢs Bᴇɴᴇᴅɪᴄᴛ ʙᴇғᴏʀᴇ ᴀɴᴅ Pᴇᴛᴇ ʜᴀᴅ never been touched under a table at Applebee's before. Pete paid the check in a hurry because something told him this might be his lucky day. They went out to the parking lot and got into his car. A minute later they were necking like teenagers on prom night.

Pete wasn't worried because his car windows were tinted. He could see out, but nobody could see in. Pete moved his hand along Yulena's back and none-too nimbly undid her bra. The he moved his hands down and cupped her hardening nipples.

"Let's hop in back, honey," he said eagerly.

She didn't seem to understand, so he flicked his head in the direction of the back seat and scurried through the opening between the driver and passenger seat. She got the idea and followed him back.

Pete peeled off his shirt, then did the same with her top.

She pulled her skirt and underpants down in one swift motion and he lowered his khaki trousers.

A few minutes later, he was so absorbed in his passion that he didn't hear the door open. Noticing a sudden intrusion of sunlight inside the car, he turned and saw a man aiming a tiny camera at them.

"Say cheese, cowboy," the man said.

Pete tried to cover his face, but was too late.

TWENTY-SEVEN

"Mr. Calhoun-Jones?"

"Yes."

"Sorry to call you on a Sunday," the voice on the phone said. "It's Dick. Dick Spears." Dick Spears? Who the hell—oh, yeah, the superintendent of the Poinciana golf course.

He could tell by Spears's tone something was wrong.

"What's up, Dick?"

"I'm calling because we've got a big problem with the golf course."

"What do you mean? What's the problem?" Calhoun-Jones figured those voracious chiggers must be at it again.

"It's dying," Spears said as though speaking of a loved one.

"I don't understand? Where?"

"Everywhere. The greens, the fairways, the tees, the whole damn course. Sorry, I—"

"No, I understand. I'm glad you called."

It was time for Calhoun-Jones to swing into action and take charge. This was the second crisis of his nascent reign and he wanted this one to go better than the first. The first had made something of a hero of Reggie Henderson, who had delivered what became known in cocktail circles as the *nyet* speech. Fellow members had come up to Henderson after the meeting with the Russians and thumped him on the back, saying things like, "Way to tell 'em, Reg." He was given the moniker "Give-'em-hell Henderson" and became suddenly lionized in the upper echelon of Palm Beach society. Calhoun-Jones, however, regarded the incident as a personal failure, a meeting that had totally gotten away from him.

"Tell you what, Dick, I'll give Jack Remsen a call." Remsen was head of the golf committee. "We'll meet you at the first tee in an hour."

"Sound good. Thanks, Mr. Calhoun-Jones."

Calhoun-Jones thought Dick Spears sounded impressed with the cool comportment of the new commander-in-chief. He hoped that Spears would get the word out to the Poinciana troops about this decisive new man of action at the helm of the Poinciana.

P.D. MILLER HAD JUST COME FROM HIS ARCHITECT'S OFFICE. Tim Kurchon, the architect, was going to renovate his new place and make it similar to something he had seen in Mustique—except about ten times the size. The place in Mustique was owned by a Greek billionaire, who didn't want anything with columns or pillars because he'd had enough of that in Athens.

Miller's new place—there was absolutely no question about it— was going to be the most phenomenal house in Palm Beach. Hell, maybe even the entire country. The scale was enormous and he knew that only Kurchon could pull off an architectural transformation of this magnitude. The connected guesthouse alone would be twenty-two-thousand square feet of space. He calculated that was almost as big as the Greek's entire Mustique house, which gave him huge satisfaction, since the Greek had such a colossal ego and had gotten the better of him in a deal five years before.

Kurchon was going to adapt the main house in such a way that it had all the standard mega-rich guy's bells and whistles: a thousand-bottle wine cellar, a squash and basketball court, a fifty-car underground garage for his collection of Shelby Cobras. Kurchon was also throwing in the usual Greenwich-mansion toys too. But this was, after all, Palm Beach, and P.D. Miller wanted—as always—to be well ahead of the curve. That desire led to the whole scenario that was in the final stage of being played out. It was, in fact, his coup de grâce, the thing that separated a centi-billionaire like himself from mere billionaires. And, incredibly enough, it was flying below everybody's radar screen. That would all change, of course, but only when he wanted it to.

He was a secretive man because he had to be.

He pulled into the parking lot at John Smith's Subs in Lake Worth in his Bentley GT. There were mostly pickups, Corollas, Civics, and Tauruses in the lot. He had been there about five minutes when he saw the other car pull in. Completely predictable, he thought: James Bond's car.

The car meandered slowly over to where Miller was parked. The passenger-side window rolled down. The car stopped parallel to him.

Miller spat it out. "It's time for you guys to quit screwing around and get the job done."

The one in the passenger seat nodded. The other one, the driver, kept his eyes straight ahead and didn't change his expression.

"Did the girl hook up with the building inspector?" Miller asked.

The driver didn't answer. He just handed Miller a manila envelope.

Miller opened the manila envelope and looked at the pictures of the couple in the back seat of the car in the Applebee's parking lot.

"That's good," he said. "I need this guy Nicastro on my team."

The man in the passenger seat grinned. The driver just kept staring straight ahead.

"We had a little talk with him," the man in the passenger seat said. "He'll approve anything you want to do."

Miller smiled, hit the button for his window, and pressed the accelerator on his Bentley. He cut off a low-riding Honda as he exited and went back over the bridge to Palm Beach.

TWENTY-EIGHT

John Calhoun-Jones, Jack Remsen, and Dick Spears were all in squatting positions on the first green.

"It reminds me of when I was in Nam," Spears was saying.

"What do you mean?" asked Remsen.

"Defoliation," Spears said. "You know, dropping chemicals on the Cong to kill all the trees."

Remsen nodded.

"Somebody poisoned the whole damn course," said Spears, cutting to the chase. "I mean, just look."

He pulled up a dark clump. It looked like it had been through a forest fire. The putting green was somewhere between beige and brown with a few patches of pitch-black.

"I hate to say it, but if I had to guess, the whole thing'll be completely dead in a few days," Spears said, extreme distress in his voice.

"Jesus Christ," said Calhoun-Jones in a panic, "we've got to save it. Can't you flood it with water or fertilizer. Something?"

"Yeah, there's gotta be something you can do," an ashen Remsen chimed in.

Dick Spears just shook his head.

"I'd like to tell you there is, but I don't know what can save it," he said, his voice trailing off. "I got an emergency call in to the PGA rep, but I don't think there's any miracle he can come up with."

Calhoun-Jones stood up and motioned to Remsen to follow him over to the edge of the green.

"This is a flat-out disaster, Jack," said Calhoun-Jones.

"No kidding," said Remsen, looking at Calhoun-Jones for direction, a contingency plan. Something. Anything.

"Got any ideas?" asked Calhoun-Jones, handing the ball back to Remsen.

"Fuck no, I don't know anything about—"

Calhoun-Jones threw up his hands. "That's all right, man," he said, steely command in his voice. "I'm going to call an emergency session of the executive committee."

Remsen looked at him blankly, like he was not a man who had much faith in groupthink solutions.

When Calhoun-Jones got home an hour later, his wife told him he had gotten a call from a Mr. Zinoviev and also one from Dick Spears. He called Spears first.

"It's John Calhoun-Jones, Dick," he said. "You called?"

"I just thought you'd want to know," Spears said. "We have a couple of security cameras on the course—"

"Yes, yes," Calhoun-Jones said impatiently. "I'm aware of that."

"Well, the ones on the eighteenth green and ninth fairway picked up something pretty scary," Spears said.

"What?"

"A drone."

"What do you mean, a drone?"

"Whoever did this," Spears explained, "apparently used a drone to dump the napalm or Roundup or whatever it was on the course."

Wow, thought Calhoun-Jones, this was so far out of his league. His heart was pounding hard now as he tried to pull himself together.

"Thanks, Dick," he said finally. "Thanks for getting me up to speed."

Calhoun-Jones went into his den, closed the door, and called his secretary. That's what he called her. He couldn't bring himself to use the modern term assistant any more than he could call stewardesses "flight attendants." As far as secretaries went, Liz Burns was a hell of a good one, especially when Calhoun-Jones took into consideration the other personal services she so generously provided.

"Hi, John," she said, sounding surprised.

He rarely called her on weekends. She probably assumed he was in the mood for a good Sunday tumble.

Or from her standpoint, a fair-to-medium one.

"I got a huge problem and need a favor from you," he said. "Call all the members of the executive committee and tell them there's an emergency session at six today."

Liz didn't hesitate.

"Sure, John," she said. "I'll take care of it. I thought maybe you were calling about—"

"No, Liz," he lowered his voice, "not today. I've got a major crisis on my hands."

"What's wrong?"

"Tell you later," he said. "Insist that all of them be there. You have that list of cell-phone numbers, right?"

Calhoun-Jones, anal-retentive that he was, had insisted a few days ago that she bring home the work, cell, and home phone numbers of all the members. Just in case.

"Yes, I have all of them."

"Good. Start right now, please."

"Okay, John, I will."

"Thanks a million, Liz. You're a doll."

And you, Liz thought, are a major pain in the ass.

———

NEXT, CALHOUN-JONES CALLED BACK VASILY ZINOVIEV, WHO
had called and suggested they have a serious talk. Just the two of
them. No loudmouth Reggie Henderson. No executive committee.
Calhoun-Jones agreed, thinking he had to do something and maybe a
conversation with the guy might actually go somewhere. Zinoviev's
choice of venues was unusual: the Checkerburger joint in West
Palm.

———

VASILY WAS WEARING A STRANGE BLACK MESH SHIRT, ALONG
with charcoal-gray cargo shorts and flip-flops. Calhoun-Jones noticed
that his toes were dirty and wasn't surprised.

The Russian was waiting for him at a table in a corner. He had
insisted they meet in person because he didn't trust phones. He was
eating a double Checkerburger. As Calhoun-Jones approached, he
saw juice—which looked more like motor oil—gush out of the burger
as Vasily chomped down on it.

Vasily put the burger down and stood up as Calhoun-Jones
approached. "I need to check you for bugs."

"Oh, for Chrissakes, I don't have—"

Vasily patted him down, including his genital area.

Two black girls at the counter started tittering.

"Okay," said Vasily, satisfied, and he sat down.

"Jesus, that was ridiculous," Calhoun-Jones said, smoothing his
shirt. "I came here at your request. I'd expect a little respect in return.
So, what do you want to talk about, Mr. Zinoviev?"

"I heard you had a problem with your golf course." Vasily sank
his teeth into the Checkerburger again.

The juice oozed down his fingers, and Calhoun-Jones noticed
Vasily's long pinkie fingernail for the first time. It looked like something a hooker might be sporting.

"I'm deducing you know all about the problem with my golf course," Calhoun-Jones said, "since you're responsible for it."

Vasily licked the Checkerburger juice off his lips.

"Churchill Ames made a big fugkink mistake and you made an even bigger one." Vasily reached for an undercooked French fry.

Calhoun-Jones watched him jam the fry down his throat.

"I offered Mr. Ames a very generous amount of money—three-hundred-twelve million, to be exact," Vasily said. "He should have taken it."

"He couldn't possibly," Calhoun-Jones said. "As I told you, the Poinciana was not, and never will be, for sale."

Suddenly Zinoviev leaned forward into Calhoun-Jones's space.

Calhoun-Jones pulled back a few inches.

"I made an incredible offer to you and your committee and look what happened?" Vasily said. "First, I was insulted, then my country was, then I was compared to a fugkink Guatemalan."

Vasily picked up his Checkerburger and took another bite that squished noisily. He started talking with his mouth full. "And now your precious Poinciana is worth much less—"

Calhoun-Jones was furious. "Yes, because you poisoned it."

Vasily held up his hand.

"My offer is now three-hundred million," he said. "Don't be a fool again, Mr. Calhoun-Jones, take it this time."

Calhoun-Jones flashed to his legacy. His place in Poinciana history. How he would be known as the president under whose watch the golf course had been destroyed. Or as the president who was in charge when it was sold at a fire-sale price. Way, way worse than Tommy Simpson who, ten years before, was the president who had raised club dues twenty percent and instituted the odious food minimum, which resulted in a tumultuous membership revolt.

Calhoun-Jones was wondering why he had ever wanted this thankless job in the first place. He glanced over at the counter. The two black girls were looking over again. Their expressions seemed to say, What are these jive-ass white dudes gonna do next?

Zinoviev stood up, grabbed a few fries, and said, "I would strongly suggest you convince your people to take my offer. Before anything else happens to your club, its members or to you yourself, Mr. son-uva-fugink dentist."

Vasily fixed him with a flinty stare and held it until Calhoun-Jones turned, got up, and slumped toward the door.

TWENTY-NINE

ONE MEMBER OF THE POINCIANA, WHOSE FAVORITE SPORTS pastime had just been snatched away from him, decided to do something about it.

Crawford's cell phone rang.

"Hello?"

"Charlie, hi, it's David Balfour. I've got to speak to you."

"Sure, David, what's up?"

"I mean, in person," Balfour said.

"You want to come down here, to the station?" Crawford asked.

"No way," Balfour said. "Can you come back here again?"

"Sure. Give me fifteen minutes."

BALFOUR MET CRAWFORD AT THE DOOR. HE DIDN'T HAVE HIS trademark Bull Shot in his hand and looked uncharacteristically solemn. Balfour was typically a free-and-easy, mellow guy, but not at this moment. The problems of the world never seemed to register on his boyish face. But today was different. For the first time Crawford could remember, Balfour actually looked his age.

"Thanks for coming," said Balfour, then he shook Crawford's hand. "Let's go into the library."

They sat down in a corner of the room in the two fat club chairs, Balfour's back to his complete, unexpurgated Clive Cussler collection.

"I want to tell you about something that might help with your investigation," Balfour said, "but before I do, you have to promise me—"

Crawford held up his hands. "Not outside these four walls," he said. "Full C.I. treatment. As always, you have my word."

"I mean, this is an incredibly dangerous situation," Balfour said, smoothing out a crease in his linen pants. "I'd be in big trouble if certain parties heard I told you this."

"I said, you have my word."

He leaned forward.

"Have you heard anything about what happened to the Poinciana golf course?"

"No. What?" Crawford said, looking over Balfour's shoulder at a picture of Balfour in a bathing suit next to a blonde.

"Well, trust me, the whole town's about to hear about it," Balfour told him.

For the next forty-five minutes, he told Crawford all about what happened, drone and all, then about the meeting that the executive committee had with the Zinovievs and finally about John Calhoun-Jones's private meeting with Vasily, which Calhoun-Jones had recently leaked to a few friends.

Crawford took notes and asked a lot of questions. Twenty minutes later, he thanked Balfour for filling him in and drove back to the station.

Forty-five minutes after that, Crawford and Ott walked into Rutledge's office. Then Crawford told the two of them what Balfour had just told him.

"Holy shit," said Ott, turning to Rutledge, "that's a crime you don't hear about every day. What would be the charge for something like that, Norm?"

"Well, you got criminal trespass, destruction of property, for starters," said Rutledge. Then he turned to Crawford. "But that's kids' stuff. I mean, these are the guys who did the snakes, right? Killed the girl?"

Crawford and Ott nodded in unison.

"Got any doubt at all?" Rutledge asked.

"Nope, not any more," Crawford said. "What I want to do is find out what chemical was used on the course and where it came from. My guess is for a job like that you don't go to Home Depot and clean out the weed-killer shelf. If there's a way to connect the defoliant to the Russians, that's a start."

"Yeah, we gotta get something on these guys," Ott said. "Get some traction somewhere."

"Right after here, I'm gonna go talk to the Poinciana president, this guy John Calhoun-Jones," Crawford said.

Ott turned to Crawford. "Hope he's not a dick like Churchill Ames."

Crawford nodded. "Yeah, me too."

"How 'bout being nice, for a change," Rutledge said, "'stead of your usual testy self."

THIRTY

It was a chaotic scene in the Palmetto Room at the Poinciana that Sunday afternoon. Calhoun-Jones had gotten there at a quarter of six to prepare for the meeting. At five before six they started straggling in. Zack Baylor and Buzz Cox, in tennis whites, had come directly from one of the six clay tennis courts, beads of sweat still rolling off Baylor's cheeks and forehead. Then came Roddy Milne in a blue suit. He was known as a prodigious churchgoer who sometimes caught the service at Bethesda, then would pop over to either Wellington, where he liked the politics of the minister, or Lake Park, where a singer in the choir had caught his eye.

After Milne came Walter Berry, clearly in the bag. Despite being thought of as an affable drunk, there had once been a movement to remove him from the prestigious executive committee and throw him a bone by letting him head Entertainment. But Berry had some powerful friends on the executive who felt that the obvious demotion and resultant humiliation might drive him even deeper into the bottle. Berry slumped down next to Calhoun-Jones, who was at the head of the long table.

"Hey, C.J." Berry greeted him with a lopsided smile.

Calhoun-Jones nodded stiffly. "Thanks for coming, Walt. I know you have better things to do." He had no clue what they might be.

"I checked my drink at the door," said Berry, as if to say 'the sacrifices I make.'

Calhoun-Jones nodded.

At 6:07, all twelve members of the executive committee were assembled. Calhoun-Jones began.

"Gentlemen, thanks for coming on short notice, and giving up part of your weekend. Obviously, you're all aware of the condition of the golf course, having seen it firsthand."

That was the beginning. At 7:32, an hour and twenty-five minutes later, the meeting came to a rancorous close.

Kimberly Coleman's notes recorded what took place at the meeting best (she opted for both shorthand summaries and, at other times, direct quotes):

C-J: Options—Sell to Zinoviev. Or redo course. Expensive. Plus, problem doesn't go away.

Dave Broxall: Could buy cheap land out west nr. Powerline Road. Build new course.

Cox: No way. Half-hour drive away.

Berry: Besides, that would be rolling over to these Commie bastards.

Broxall: Yeah, but at least no one else gets killed.

Hollingsworth: Should seriously think about bringing in police.

C-J: Don't think we're at that point yet. Can still resolve it ourselves.

Berry: Yeah, we've done such a bang-up job so far.

Baylor: How much to fix course?

Remsen: Six to seven million. Twenty-five-thousand assessment per member.

Final outcome: No conclusion. C-J called for another emergency session tomorrow.

Kim Coleman's final note said it best: In other words, kick the can down the road again!

THIRTY-ONE

P.D. Miller was in his Bentley waiting in the far corner of the parking lot at John Smith's Subs. The two men pulled up in the green sports car. It was a short conversation.

"Time's a-wasting," Miller said.

"We have one more day," the driver of the sports car replied.

"Exactly. And after that I'm paying you twenty-five percent less. That was our deal."

"Don't worry," said the driver. "We'll take care of it."

"Trust me, I'm not worried. You're the one who stands to lose a million and a quarter," Miller said, rolling up his window, stepping on the gas, and speeding out of the parking lot.

———

John Calhoun-Jones decided the best thing to do was meet with Vasily Zinoviev again. Then report back to the executive committee with a solution, even if it wasn't perfect. Show them he was a fearless, proactive negotiator. In the meantime, it would at least stall Vasily from taking further actions. So, he called Vasily and suggested they meet again. Vasily agreed, and as he had before, came up with the meeting place.

On the way to the meeting, after carefully weighing all the options, Calhoun-Jones decided to do something that didn't come natural to him: He decided it was time to grow a backbone—take a bold stand and play hardball with Vasily Zinoviev. After all, what more could Vasily do? He wasn't going to drop a bomb, nuke the Poinciana buildings...was he? Bottom line, Calhoun-Jones just couldn't live with the legacy of being the chump in charge when the Poinciana got sold to a guy who could barely speak English. Besides, his stand wasn't irreversible. He could always back down if his bluff didn't work.

Calhoun-Jones drove south on Flagler off the middle bridge. He looked up at the ghostlike 1515 S. Flagler building. Twenty-four stories and nobody living in it since the second hurricane back in 2004, when it was found to have major structural problems. Reminded him of the Poinciana golf course. Once stately, now crippled and incapacitated.

The Norton was an art museum in West Palm Beach. Skimpy by the standards of most museums, but no one ever accused West Palm Beach or Palm Beach—its pretty little sister across the Intracoastal—of being cultural meccas. Calhoun-Jones was examining the Norton's one Rothko right next to its one Jasper Johns when he smelled Vasily.

"Call that art?" Vasily hissed.

Calhoun-Jones gave him a look that said *like you'd know.*

"I need a decision now," said Vasily, eyeing the Rothko as if it was a framed turd instead of the artistic labor of one who sprang from his motherland.

"Oh, do you now?" said Calhoun-Jones.

"Yeah," said Vasily, not turning.

"Tell you what," whispered Calhoun-Jones, which was unnecessary because there was no one else, not even a security guard, in the large room, "why don't I just give it to you right now?"

"All right," said Vasily, still eyeing the painting disapprovingly.

"First of all, if you threaten me ever again, or any member of my club," Calhoun-Jones said, jabbing with his index finger in a newfound tone of bravado, "I'll go straight to the Palm Beach Police, the Attorney General of Florida, who I know personally...and the FBI."

Vasily looked at him for a few seconds and then started snickering. It got throatier and then became a full roar. An older couple in matching khaki cargo shorts and sandals came into the room and frowned at the offending sight and sound of Vasily.

He just kept laughing. "You just don't understand who you're fugkink dealing with, do you?"

The couple shushed him loudly.

Vasily shook his head and bolted away from Calhoun-Jones. On his way out, he veered slightly off course and crashed through the couple, sharp elbows out. He clipped the woman in the ribs. She spun, lost her balance, and fell hard on the unforgiving floor. Vasily didn't look back.

Calhoun-Jones rushed over and, along with the woman's shell-shocked husband, helped the woman up. But then the woman flung his helping hands away and glowered at him.

"Your friend is a monster!" she shrieked.

"He isn't my—" but he decided it was just easier to leave it alone and walk away.

CALHOUN-JONES DROVE OVER THE BRIDGE AND BEMOANED THE fact that as a bluffer he left a lot to be desired. He thought about calling Zinoviev right away and backing down from his position. But what was he going to say: I was just kiddink?

THIRTY-TWO

CALHOUN-JONES KNEW HE WAS IN WAY OVER HIS HEAD. HE WAS just a banker, after all. Had been, anyway. From the Norton Museum, he had gone over the Southern Bridge, then driven down south to the cluster of high-rise condominiums whose official address was Palm Beach, but was referred to as the Gaza Strip by a few local wags. He got as far south as the Ritz-Carlton, then turned around and took the long, slow twenty-mile drive up to the north end of Palm Beach.

Calhoun-Jones knew he had a serious problem. He drove all the way up to East Inlet Road, then turned around and headed back down south again. Then he retraced his way to the bottom of the island. This time he turned around a mile short of the Ritz-Carlton, opposite the bridge over to Lake Worth. In the past, this had always been his problem-solving ritual, working things out at thirty miles per hour, AC to the max.

But after this particular turtle-paced drive-and-ponder session, the only solution he could come up with was to accept Vasily's offer. Somehow talk the members of the executive committee into it. Explain how all their lives might be in jeopardy unless they accepted his offer. And soon. There was no compromising with the man. He headed back up to his house on Dunbar, pulled into his driveway and got out of his car. He needed a stiff drink.

———————————

CRAWFORD HAD GOTTEN JOHN CALHOUN-JONES'S NUMBER from David Balfour. It was time for them to talk. Crawford didn't see how calling him directly would in any way implicate David Balfour as the man who had told him about the Poinciana golf-course nuke job. If Calhoun-Jones asked, he'd just say he heard about it from some unnamed employee of the Poinciana. He needed to find out what Calhoun-Jones could add to what Balfour had told him. He dialed the phone number.

Susan Calhoun-Jones answered the phone and went and got her husband. He had a glass of clear liquid in his hand. It was unheard of for him to have his first Ketel One before six at night. But Susan knew there was no way it was water. Not with the big hunk of lime floating in it.

"Hello," Calhoun-Jones said, taking the phone from his wife.

"Mr. Calhoun-Jones, this is Detective Crawford, Palm Beach Pol—"

"I know who you are, Detective," said Calhoun-Jones, tilting the glass up to his mouth.

"I'd like to talk to you, sir. In person," Crawford said. "I need to meet you as soon as possible and ask you a few questions."

Crawford grabbed a pen to take down the address.

Calhoun-Jones made a snap decision. Yes, it was time to get the police involved. Before it was too late. He was just not equipped to handle this whole thing anymore.

"Sure, Detective, absolutely," he said congenially. "Why don't—it's almost five-thirty now—why don't we make it, say, six-thirty?"

"That's good. What's your address?" Crawford asked.

Calhoun-Jones gave it to him.

"See you in an hour," he said.

THE FERAL MAN TOOK THE BLACK TALONS OUT OF THE BOX IN his closet and loaded two into the chamber. That was all he'd need. Two for two.

Then he went to the garage and got into the Mercedes. He looked admiringly at the red leather upholstery and the ultra-high-tech instrumentation on the dashboard. He didn't know what half the gizmos did. He started up the car, loving the sound the engine made. A quiet, but powerful growl. He backed out of the garage. Damn nice wheels for a hit man.

"JOHN, ARE YOU DRINKING?" SUSAN CALHOUN-JONES ASKED HER husband.

"Sipping," he said.

"That's so unlike you, before six o'clock," she said, sitting down across from him in the library.

"Hard day at the office," he said.

"What happened now?" she asked.

She knew about the golf course. He gave her a brief summary of his latest meeting with the Russian troglodyte.

"Good God, John," she said, "you can't behave that way with a man like that."

"I know, I know," he answered. "Don't worry, I'll take care of it."

"But—"

"I said, I'll take care of it," he said forcefully, then finished his Ketel.

Susan looked at her watch. She picked up the TV remote off a table and clicked it on. *Jeopardy!* was on now, *Wheel of Fortune* next. Susan had a thing for Pat Sajak.

THE FERAL MAN PARKED THE CAR A BLOCK AWAY FROM THE house, pulled down the brim of his baseball cap, and walked up to the porch. Then he looked around, reached into his pocket, yanked out the nylon stocking, took the hat off, and pulled the stocking down over his face. He had used ski masks before, but they were itchy. Especially in the Florida heat and humidity.

John Calhoun-Jones and his wife looked like a privileged, middle-aged couple on their first cocktail of the night, even though it was his third. He was in a wingback chair reading the *Wall Street Journal* and she was watching *Wheel* in a love seat, smiling adoringly at Pat Sajak.

Gloves in place, the man crept in without the couple seeing him until he had zeroed in on Calhoun-Jones with his Glock from no more than ten feet away. He took out Calhoun-Jones in a single, muffled pop. Then, before Susan Calhoun-Jones even had a chance to beg for mercy, he pivoted and fired at her.

He picked up the two empty shell casings, turned, walked out, and was back in his car a minute and forty-five seconds after he got there. He was sure it was his personal best.

CRAWFORD PUSHED THE DOORBELL TO THE LEFT OF THE RED door. After a few moments, when nobody answered, he pushed the doorbell again. Finally, he decided to see if the door was open. He turned the knob and it opened.

The only voice Crawford heard was Pat Sajak's off in the distance.

"Hello?"

Nothing.

"Mr. Calhoun-Jones?"

Nothing.

He knew something was wrong.

He walked through the foyer into the living room. The scene reminded him of a murder-suicide up in the West Nineties and Amsterdam ten years ago in New York. Except, of course, this was no murder-suicide. Not only that, it had gone down very recently. He could still smell the sharp tang of cordite in the air. Instinctively, he drew his Sig Sauer semi and—carefully as possible—proceeded to clear the sizable house, room by room. Satisfied no one was there, he went and felt for a pulse on the woman's wrist. Nothing. He took two steps over to John Calhoun-Jones's body and squatted down. Same thing.

Then he called in the murders.

Whoever did it could shoot. It was one of the cleanest hits he had ever seen. The bullet holes were equidistant between the hairline and bridge of the nose on both of them. The shooter had probably just snuck in, aimed and fired before John Calhoun-Jones knew what hit him. But Crawford didn't get how the second shot could be so perfect. He assumed that was the one that took out Mrs. Calhoun-Jones, since the shooter would always take out the primary first. But it almost seemed as though the wife hadn't even reacted. No apparent fight-or-flight response. Then, he theorized, maybe it was two hitters. They snuck in, aimed.

Boom. Boom. Simultaneously.

Or maybe it was just one and the woman simply froze.

He pulled a pair of vinyl gloves out of his jacket pocket, walked over to the body of Calhoun-Jones, and squatted down next to him again. The entry wound was wide. Usually guys who did close-up jobs like this used small-caliber guns—a .22 or maybe a .25. Not much firepower, but .22's and .25's were easy to conceal and lacked a kick. And if you went for a headshot, the tiny hollow-point bullet would ricochet around in the vic's head for maximum damage. The back of Calhoun-Jones's head was blown away, though, which ruled out a .22 or a .25. No, this killer had used a hand-cannon.

Blood was in two separate pools. One large pool was in the

middle of the Marketplace section of the *Wall Street Journal* on the floor. The other was on an expensive rug.

He got Ott on his cell, gave him a quick summary, and told him to meet him up at the Russians' house in twenty minutes. Then, without disturbing the crime scene, he searched the area for bullet jackets or any other evidence, but found nothing.

There was no more he could do. It was time for the ME and the techs to take over. He doubted they'd come up with much.

A few minutes later, a young uniform named Harry Grace showed up. He nodded to Crawford and looked down at the bodies. Then he looked up at the TV that was still on.

"Jesus, that Vanna, she's put on a few pounds," he said casually. It was his way of telling Crawford he'd been around; he was no stranger to dead bodies and grisly crime scenes.

Crawford walked over to the TV, punched the off button, and walked out to his car.

He went north on Lake Way, doing seventy all the way.

THIRTY-THREE

CRAWFORD KNEW HE HAD GROUNDS FOR PROBABLE CAUSE TO
take in the Russians. But just to cover his ass, he had called Rutledge
to get the green light. He knew full well that Rutledge would probably okay just about anything at this point.

He was right. Rutledge OK'd it immediately.

The problem was the shooter or shooters weren't going to be
hanging around, smelling like a firing range for long. They were probably in the shower right now scrubbing away all traces of the two
shots.

He waited outside the Russians' house until Ott and a pair of
backup uniforms arrived a few minutes later.

The Asian woman answered the door. Crawford badged her and
said he wanted to see the Zinovievs.

She nodded, said she'd get them, and walked away. She left the
door open. Crawford waited a second, then impatient, stepped
inside. He didn't see anyone, but heard women's voices. He and Ott
walked into the empty living room.

A moment later, Vasily stormed into the room, his short legs
churning. One of the men Crawford remembered from the day he

searched Vasily's plane—the tattooed man—was right behind him. Then, the other guy from the plane—the skinny one with acne.

Finally, Aleksandr.

"My lawyer told you not to come here anymore," Vasily said.

"Fuck your lawyer," Crawford said. "We're here 'cause you or one of your mutts just murdered two people."

Vasily looked over at his brother, who was wearing a stylish pink and blue long-sleeved shirt.

"You belief this shit?" Vasily said to his brother, then he turned slowly to Crawford. "You are getting extremely irritating."

"All four of you are under arrest," Crawford said. "We're taking you down to my station on suspicion of murder."

None of the Russians moved.

"Let's go," Ott said, flicking his Glock. "You heard the man."

They still didn't move.

"Okay," said Crawford to Ott and the uniforms, "cuff 'em."

Ott smiled as he snapped open his handcuffs.

THIRTY-FOUR

THEY DID GSRs—GUNSHOT RESIDUE TESTS—ON ALL FOUR OF them. The Zinoviev brothers were clean. But to Crawford's surprise, the tattooed man's fingers were covered with paraffin.

After the test, when Crawford started to question him, the tattooed man's grasp of the English language started to fail him. He did answer Crawford's first question, though.

His name was Evsei Nemchenov.

On the way to the station, Vasily had said something to Evsei in Russian. Crawford figured Vasily was feeding him an alibi. The translator Crawford called in when they got to the station did a double take when Evsei casually explained that the reason he had gunpowder residue on his hands was because he was target-shooting at cans on the beach behind the house.

"Are you kidding?" Crawford said, glaring at Nemchenov. "Target-shooting on a beach people walk on all day and all night?"

But Crawford knew the alibi was going to stand up. Vasily wouldn't have fed it to Evsei otherwise. And, as outrageous as it was, it was exactly something the Russians would do. Sure, they'd know shooting cans on a public beach was against the law. And, yes, they'd know it was dangerous. But they came from a place that was dangerous and lawless, a place where, to men like them, laws were like yellow traffic lights.

Nevertheless, Crawford sent Ott up to the Russians' house to check out the beach for signs of target practice. Ott left right before the Russians' lawyers showed up.

Crawford was not surprised to see Maddy Sorenson again. But this time her boss, Chris Kirk, was with her. Maddy was dressed in a gray chalk-striped pantsuit that looked like Armani. Her glasses were different from the ones she was wearing before, Crawford noticed. The lenses had a light blue tint and the frame was tortoiseshell. Chris Kirk had a paunch and his undistinguished brown suit strained a little at the gut. He was rumpled and not quite pulled together. Crawford was familiar with the look. It was an intentional one, calculated so you'd underestimate him—and also so clients wouldn't belly-ache about all the Brioni suits they were paying for.

Crawford walked up to Maddy.

"This is getting really old, Charlie," she said.

He looked around and lowered his voice.

"I gotta tell you," he said, "your clients are a bunch of stone-cold killers."

"I'm their lawyer," she said, "not a judge."

It was a good answer.

He heard steps, then felt a hand pull at his arm. It was Rutledge.

"I need to speak to you," he said.

Crawford just shook his head at Maddy and walked away with Rutledge.

Ott came back in from his run up to the Russians' house and walked up to Crawford and Rutledge.

"Find anything?" Crawford asked.

Ott nodded. "A bunch of beer cans with holes in 'em."

"I figured," Crawford said. "And no way the slugs are gonna match up to the ones they get from the couple."

Another nod from Ott.

"All right, talk to me," Rutledge said, eyeing Vasily and the tattooed man across the room. "Are these definitely our guys?"

Ott and Crawford exchanged glances. "Yeah, my guess is the guy with the tat. Maybe that other one too," Crawford said, flicking his head toward the guy with acne standing next to Vasily.

He filled Rutledge in on the GSR results, as well as the circumstances leading up to the murders—how an obviously stressed-out Calhoun-Jones had set up a meeting with Crawford only minutes before.

"Okay," Rutledge said, twitching the way he did when things got hairy, "lay it out for me again."

"Like I told you," Crawford said, "the Russians tried to buy the Poinciana. Told the Poinciana guys they wanted to turn it into a high-end development."

"And the Poinciana guys shot it down?" Rutledge asked.

"Right," Crawford said, "so a couple days after that, the golf course gets nuked. So now the Russians got the Poinciana guys' attention. All of a sudden they start taking 'em very seriously. Not quick enough for the Russians, though. So, they go and take out the president and his wife."

"And you're not buyin' the Russians want the Poinciana for condos?" Rutledge asked.

"No," Crawford said.

"Why not?" Rutledge asked.

"Because there's more to it than that," Crawford answered. "The numbers don't make sense."

Rutledge shook his head skeptically.

"Just what the fuck do you know about real estate and high finance?" he asked.

"I consulted with a local realtor," Crawford said. "I can run you through the whole thing."

Rutledge shook his head. "I'll take your word for it. But we need something to hang these guys on now. You got anything at all?"

Crawford exhaled.

"Right now... no," he said.

Rutledge flung his arms up in the air. The man could do drama.

"Why the hell not? We got three people dead and we know who did it," he said. "Take a guess how many calls I got in the short time since the hit on the Calhoun-Joneses?"

Crawford had heard it all before.

"Norm, we're doing everything—"

"—one from the fucking city manager, another from some guy on the Chamber of Commerce who informs me dead people are bad for tourism, then another from some whack-job at Neighborhood Crime Watch, saying it's time to take back the streets—"

"We're gonna put the heat on the tat guy,'" Crawford said.

"How you gonna do that?"

"Hold him," Crawford said, "for discharging a weapon on the beach."

Rutledge rolled his eyes. "Whoop-de-fuckin'-do. You gotta be kidding me."

"What do you expect me to do?" Crawford was losing patience. "Pull a rabbit out of thin air?"

"How 'bout a goddamn smoking gun?"

"We got one," Crawford sighed. "It just wasn't used for the murders."

THIRTY-FIVE

"I GOT A SERIOUS CRAVING FOR A TALL, COLD ONE," CRAWFORD said as he followed Ott into his office. It was 7:10 at night.

"This thing driving you to drink?"

"No, fuckhead is," Crawford said, grabbing his jacket from the hanger behind his door.

"You got more damn nicknames for the guy," Ott said with a smile. "Let's see, there's fuckhead, fuckface...dickhead, dipshit, shithead...I forget any?"

Crawford laughed as they got to the elevator. "Yeah, shit-for-brains."

"Oh, right."

AN HOUR LATER, OTT HAD A HALF-EMPTY YUENGLING IN FRONT of him and Crawford had one sip of his Bud left.

"I dug around a little more and found out, according to the zoning code, there's definitely no way they can knock down those Poinciana buildings," Crawford said.

"Yeah, but you really think some damn zoning law is gonna stop these guys?" Ott said. "What do you think they'd be looking to do with the Poinciana if not build condos?"

"That's the three-hundred-million-dollar question," Crawford said as Ott's cell phone rang.

"Hello," Ott said.

He listened, apologized to someone, then hung up.

"Christ, I forgot," he said. "I promised my sister I'd go to my niece's basketball game."

"You mean you actually got a life?"

"Fuck no, I'm goin' back to the station right after." He got up. "See you there."

"Later," Crawford said.

He decided to move up to the bar. Jack Scarsiola, an ex-cop and the owner of Mookie's, was bartending.

He sat down at the bar. "So where'd you used to work, Jack?" Crawford asked Scarsiola after a while.

"The fourteenth, West Palm," Scarsiola said, filling a couple of sixteen-ounce beer mugs.

"How was it?"

"It was okay. I even miss it once in a while," said Scarsiola.

"What were you in?"

"Burglary," he answered, tapping the head off two mugs of Pabst Blue Ribbon.

"People actually drink that PBR shit?" Crawford whispered.

Scarsiola flicked his head in the direction of two young cops and took the mugs over to them. Crawford guessed they hadn't been out of the academy long. Didn't know their beers yet.

Crawford drained his. Scarsiola came back over.

"Tell you what I don't miss at all," Scarsiola said. "The fact that nowadays all the mutts got automatics. Crank out fifty rounds in two seconds or whatever. Didn't used to be like that."

Crawford nodded.

"How's your case goin'?" Scarsiola asked.

"Which one?"

"Got another?"

"A double."

"Jesus, stiffs piling up over there in Palm Beach, huh?"

Crawford nodded again.

"Hey, you ever meet Don Scarpa?" asked Scarsiola, looking down the bar.

"No, why?"

"Just figured he'd be a good guy to shoot the shit with," Scarsiola said. "Man spent close to twenty years on the Palm Beach force. That's him down at the end."

Scarsiola pointed to a man in a blue windbreaker smoking a cigarette and sitting alone at the end of the bar. Crawford had heard of Scarpa. Heard he was a stand-up cop.

"Gonna go say hello," he said, getting up.

He grabbed his beer and walked over to Scarpa.

Scarpa looked up.

"Hi Don, my name's Charlie Crawford. I work your old stomping grounds," Crawford said, putting his hand out.

Scarpa shook it.

"I heard about you," said Scarpa, friendly enough. "From New York, right? Pretty new on the job?"

Crawford nodded and sat down next to him.

"Word is you butt heads with Rutledge," Scarpa said.

"Yeah," Crawford said, "ten times a day."

Scarpa smiled. "That's good," he said. "You'd have to be a shitty cop not to. He and I went at it all the time."

Scarpa lit a Winston off the one he was smoking.

Crawford had the urge for one. He still missed the cozy partnership of a cigarette and a beer.

"What was it with you and Rutledge?" Crawford asked.

"You mean, aside from the fact the guy's an asshole?"

Crawford laughed. "That's just the tip of the iceberg."

"I know. He's a suck-up too."

"How do you mean?"

"You know, you been around him enough," Scarpa said. "The mayor or anybody with a little juice, he kisses ass."

"I hear you," Crawford said.

Scarpa waved his hand and caught Scarsiola's attention. "One more time, Scar. And one for Charlie here."

Scarsiola nodded, walked over, picked up their mugs, and went up to the tap.

"You run across the Steering Committee yet?" Scarpa asked.

"No," said Crawford. "What's that?"

"How 'bout the Cadillac Fund?"

Crawford shook his head.

"You will," Scarpa said. "The Steering Committee goes way back, before I got there. This rich guy named P.D. Miller came up with it. Him and a bunch of other rich guys who donated money to the department. That made 'em like, off limits to us...untouchables, kinda. You'd see one of 'em weaving down South Ocean on a Saturday night, you'd let 'em weave. Hear about one with an underage girl, you'd leave him alone. I didn't, but everyone else did."

"You're kidding.'"

"Nah, it's still goin' on, I hear. Just a little more subtle maybe," he said, locking onto Crawford's eyes. "That's just the way it is."

Crawford took a sip of his beer. He eyed Scarpa's pack of Winstons.

"Hey, Don, mind if I bum—"

Scarpa slid the pack over to him. Crawford pulled one out and stuck it in his mouth. Scarpa lit it with his silver Zippo.

Crawford took a drag. Goddamn, it was strong.

Scarpa slid the Zippo back in his breast pocket.

"The Steering Committee got its name from when one of those guys crashed into a big ficus hedge and somebody had to 'steer' him home," Scarpa said. "Might have even been Rutledge, now that I think about it. Guy's always looking out for his rich buddies."

"Like, what? He's got some deal with 'em, you mean?"

Scarpa shrugged.

"No, just... he knows where the bread is buttered."

Crawford stubbed out the half-finished cigarette. It was a lousy idea.

"The Cadillac Fund," Scarpa went on, "it's still around, just maybe more discreet now."

"But it's different from the Steering Committee?"

Scarpa nodded. "Yeah. Know how they have all those charity balls in Palm Beach?"

Crawford knew. He had actually been to one. One too many, it turned out. "Yeah, I know about 'em."

"Well, the Cadillac Fund is this charity ball they have for us," he said. "Come to think of it, I'm pretty sure it's coming up any day now. They always have a guest of honor, raise a bunch of money for the department and donate cars to guys on the job. But usually it's just certain guys get 'em, guys they know'll bail 'em out in a jam. They're nice cars too, like three-year-old Caddies, Mercedes, you name it. Ever notice how Rutledge always drives nice wheels?"

Crawford pictured Rutledge's shiny Lexus parked next to his tired Camry with the rust spot on the side.

"Yeah, I know exactly what you mean," Crawford said. "So you're saying it's a payoff or something?"

Scarpa coughed and held up both hands.

"Hey, I'm not sayin' anything as crass as that, Charlie. Just makin' conversation. You decide what it all means. Me, I'm retired. Got nothing to do with shit over there," he said, sucking hard on his cigarette. "There was this one time, though, the granddaughter of a certain guy who owns a certain baseball team up in New York, who shall go nameless. She got into the rum pretty good one night. A party at the Poinciana, I'm pretty sure. Anyway, after it was over she decided to take a shortcut home. Rutledge found her passed out in her BMW in a goddamn sand trap on the Poinciana golf course."

"Come on," said Crawford.

"Yeah, first she took out a couple of greens, then sideswiped a palm tree," Scarpa said, hacking a laugh.

"What did Rutledge do?" Crawford asked.

"He called up Grandpa and said he'd bring her home, no problem," Scarpa said. "So then the old man got on the phone and sends out a squad of gardeners in the middle of the night. Next morning the golf course...like nothing ever happened."

Crawford shook his head.

"The Poinciana golf course doesn't look too good at the moment," he said.

"So I hear."

Scarpa downed the last of his beer and looked over at Crawford. "You ever go to the movies, Charlie?" He took another long drag.

"Yeah, sometimes. Why?"

"You ever see that old one, on cable maybe. *Pulp Fiction*?"

"Yeah, sure, one of the best."

"Well, 'member when that black guy, Samuel L. Jackson or whatever, blows away the guy in the back seat of his car?"

"Yeah, blood and guts all over." Then Crawford added, "It was John Travolta by the way."

"Whatever. So, they call in that guy, Harvey...I forget his last name."

"Keitel."

Scarpa smiled. "You know your shit, Charlie."

"Yeah, well, I just remember he played Winston Wolf. Guy who cleans up, makes it all go away."

"Exactly," Scarpa said. "So anyway, old Harvey kind of reminds me of Rutledge."

Crawford frowned and tapped his finger on the bar a few times. "With all due respect, Don, you're way off base," he said. "Winston Wolf woulda mopped the floor with fuckin' Norm Rutledge."

THIRTY-SIX

REGGIE HENDERSON WAS ACTING HEAD OF THE EXECUTIVE
committee in the absence of the late John Calhoun-Jones. Not that
Henderson had volunteered for the job, because what sane man
would? No, Henderson had made it very clear he wanted no part of
the president's job. But, the reality was, the job was about to become
extinct anyway. Because the way it looked anyway, history would
show that John Calhoun-Jones was the last president of the venerable
Poinciana Club. Not to mention the man with the shortest reign.
After the murders of John and Susan Calhoun-Jones, the executive
committee had voted—with deep regret—to sell the club by a vote of
ten to two. What choice did they have? Who knew who might be in
the Russians' sights next?

Dave Broxall, who was both a member of the executive
committee and a real-estate attorney, was already drafting a contract.
He was careful not to make it look like it was a panic sale but even
more careful to make sure it didn't have any deal-breakers in the
contract that would anger Vasily Zinoviev.

Zinoviev had been contacted a short while ago by Broxall. After introducing himself, Broxall had said, "Mr. Zinoviev, we've reconsidered and decided to accept your offer for the Poinciana."

Zinoviev had been waiting for the call.

"You mean the offer I made two days ago, Mr..."

"Broxall...yes."

"The one I made to my old friend, Mr. Calhoun-Jones?"

"Yes," said Broxall.

Vasily's pause was deliberately long.

"Oh, but Mr. Broxall, that offer has expired."

Along with Calhoun-Jones, thought Broxall.

"What do you mean? You're no longer interested in the purchase of the Poinciana?" asked Broxall, trying to hide his alarm.

"No, I'm still interested," said Vasily, smiling at his brother, who was listening on speaker, "but the price is now two-hundred-seventy million."

Broxall looked at the price in the contract in front of him. "What? Two-hundred-seventy million? You offered three-hundred million."

"Yes, but the real-estate market has gotten softer," Vasily said. "Haven't you been reading the newspapers? The bubble is bursting again, Mr. Broxall."

Broxall didn't know how to react.

"But you just made the offer the day before yesterday."

Aleksandr, who was sitting opposite his brother, gave Vasily a smile and a thumbs-up.

"Sorry, but things have changed, my friend," said Vasily, showing off his hard-nosed negotiating skills for his brother.

Broxall thought for a minute. What the hell did he care? It wasn't about the money. But Christ, his reputation was built on being a cutthroat deal-maker. He'd lose face if word got out he had rolled so easily.

"I can't go less than two-hundred-ninety," Broxall said resolutely.

"Then you better find another buyer," said Vasily without hesitating.

Broxall chewed on a pencil. "Will you close in two months?" he asked, trying to salvage something.

Vasily looked over at his brother and smiled. Aleksandr gave him the thumbs-down sign.

"Sorry, Mr. Broxall. It has to be three weeks."

Broxall knew he held no cards.

"Who is going to be your attorney on this, Mr. Zinoviev?"

"Chris Kirk of—"

Aleksandr shook his head vigorously and mouthed, "Madeline Sorenson."

"Ah, no, make that Madeline Sorenson," Vasily said, rolling his eyes.

"I know Maddy," said Broxall. "I'll fax the papers over to her right away. Contract should be ready for you to pick up later this afternoon."

"At two-hundred-seventy-million dollars?"

Broxall sighed deeply. "Yes, at two-hundred-seventy-million."

"Excellent." Vasily hung up and eyed his brother.

Then he shook his finger at Aleksandr and said in Russian, "Madeline Sorenson? Think with your head, Aleksi...not your dick."

<hr />

LATER THAT AFTERNOON, VASILY CALLED P. D. MILLER AND said that the contract signed by an attorney who had power of attorney for the Poinciana Club had just been dropped off with him.

Vasily asked him if he wanted them to deliver the contract to their usual venue, the parking lot of John Smith's Subs.

"No," Miller said, "come to my house."

Then he proceeded to give Vasily the address of the house that Rose Clarke had just put in contract for him.

Vasily drove and Aleksandr rode shotgun on the way there. Instead of the Aston Martin, Vasily was driving the Mercedes CLK.

He had heard that's what Hugh Hefner drove—on those rare occasions he got out of his pajamas and went somewhere.

As he always did, Aleksandr kept an eye peeled for the newest pretty face in town.

P.D. MILLER, WEARING A SHORT-SLEEVE YELLOW POLO SHIRT with a blue horseman logo, met the brothers at the front door. They followed him back to a massive room with a pool table and vintage slot machines lined up along one wall. The brothers looked around, impressed by the expensive leather chairs, sofas, bamboo wallpaper, and elaborate chandelier. But what really caught their fancy were the antique slot machines, which ingested quarters.

Vasily handed Miller the contract. Miller went to a corner of the room, switched on a light over a leather chair, sat down, and started reading the contract. Aleksandr, who had followed him with his eyes, winked at his brother, then whispered in Russian, "I wonder how long it's going to take."

Vasily smiled back at him, fished into his pocket and pulled out a handful of change. He plucked out five quarters, then turned to his brother.

"You have any?" he asked, leading his brother over to the slot machines.

Aleksandr reached into his pocket and gave his brother three quarters.

"You owe me a dollar," said Aleksandr, his blue eyes twinkling. "Twenty-five cents' interest."

Vasily snorted, rolled his eyes, and stuck a quarter into the slot machine. He pulled the lever and the cylinders freewheeled for a few seconds, then ca-chunked to three separate stops.

A banana, a bunch of cherries, and a jackpot sign.

"Do you hear how mechanically perfect it sounds?" said Vasily admiringly.

"Yes, beautiful," Aleksandr responded.

Vasily put in another quarter and pulled the handle.

Jackpot sign, banana, and a lemon.

Vasily fed the machine another quarter, then pulled its metal arm.

The three cylinders freewheeled silently.

Jackpot. Jackpot. Jackpot.

A pause, then quarters came pouring out of the machine.

"Our lucky day," Aleksandr said, as the machine made a cacophonous racket, disgorging twenty-four-and-a-half dollars' worth of quarters.

Aleksandr high-fived his brother and took four quarters from him, while out of the corner of his eye he saw Miller thrust up out of his chair, a huge frown on his face, and walk quickly toward them.

From ten feet away, stabbing a finger at the contract, he bellowed: "What the hell is this?"

Aleksandr stepped toward him. "Is there a problem?" he asked solicitously.

"Yeah, there's a problem, a big fucking problem," Miller said. "You were supposed to deliver this contract with the seller's signature on it—"

"Which is there," Aleksandr said, pointing at the contract.

"Yes, but the line where it says buyer is supposed to be my LLC: 357 Worth Avenue Partners," said Miller, raising his arms in utter confusion.

He looked like his blood pressure had shot through the roof. His face was matador-cape red.

Aleksandr said nothing. Miller's eyes searched Aleksandr's, then Vasily's.

Then it sank in. Miller shook his head slowly. "You bastards don't really think you're gonna get away with this." He wagged his finger at them.

Aleksandr shot him his leading-man smile. "But, my friend, we already have. We are the new owners of the Poinciana. You want it, you have to buy it from us."

"My brother," Vasily said with a look of pride, "is a very good businessman, don't you think?"

Miller wanted to strangle them both. "Nobody screws me on a deal. We had an agreement. I pay you five million dollars, you deliver me a contract in the name of my LLC."

"Yes, well, we did so much work," Aleksandr said, "that we ended up getting very attached to the Poinciana."

Miller shook his head so hard spit was flying. "You... bastards. You complete and total—"

"Now, now, Mr. Miller." Aleksandr raised a hand. "Please, no harsh words. We can always get...un-attached to the Poinciana...for, say, twenty-five million dollars."

Aleksandr took a document out of the breast pocket of his jacket. "This is a contract which assigns the Poinciana from us to your LLC. I would be very happy to sign it when you give me a check for twenty-five million dollars."

Miller's glasses looked steamed up.

He was shaking his head so hard it looked like it might go flying off his shoulders.

Finally, he seemed to pull himself together.

"I'll give you ten million dollars," he said very deliberately, white spittle in the corners of his mouth.

"My brother and I have decided that twenty-five million is a fair price," Aleksandr said.

Miller took a step closer to Aleksandr as a nasty, sardonic look swept across his face.

"Oh, have you now?" he said. "That's what you decided, huh? And I have no say in the matter?"

Aleksandr returned the smile. "Of course you do. You can decide that is too much. But the fact of the matter is we saved you *more* than twenty-five million dollars," he explained patiently. "You were prepared to pay three-hundred-twelve-million dollars and we got it for two-hundred-and-seventy million. You do the math, Mr. Miller."

Miller cupped his elbow with one hand and put his other hand on his chin. He had sausage-sized fingers and protruding knuckles. If he was packing a gun, he would have used it already.

"So, you're going back on your word? On our deal?" Miller said again. "Is that what you're doing?"

"No, what we did was make a better deal for you," Aleksandr said. "So it should be better for us too. Don't you think? I believe you would call that a 'win-win' situation."

To Miller, one thing was sacred: A deal was a deal.

But he calmly took out his checkbook and started writing.

Then he handed a check to Aleksandr.

Aleksandr examined the check and frowned. Then he tore it up. "Not fifteen million, twenty-five, Mr. Miller. And in two minutes, it will go up to thirty."

Miller, fuming, scribbled first the date, then Zinoviev's name, then twenty-five million dollars, and finally, his signature. Then he handed the check to Aleksandr.

"Thank you," said Aleksandr, examining the new check. Then he and Vasily signed the document Aleksandr had prepared and handed it to Miller. "Here you go. Our assignment of the contract to your LLC. You are now the proud new owner of the Poinicana. I hope we can do business again."

Aleksandr, followed by his brother, headed for the door. Then Vasily turned back to Miller. "Don't even think about canceling the check, Mr. Miller. You saw what happened to poor Mr. Calhoun-Jones."

Miller just glared back at him.

He had anticipated that the Zinovievs might try to pull something. He was just not sure what.

He took out his cell phone and punched seven numbers.

Nobody screwed him on a deal.

Nobody.

THIRTY-SEVEN

CRAWFORD COULDN'T SLEEP, SO HE WENT TO THE STATION AT four in the morning.

It was lunchtime now. He normally ate at his desk in his office. He'd go get a sandwich at a nearby shop and bring it back. Not today, though. His plan was to go up to Three Pete's deli, sit down in a nice leatherette booth, get a bowl of chili, toss in a packet of Saltines, and get away from work for an hour. He had been looking forward to the brief respite since earlier that morning. He went down the elevator and out the front door of the station, intent on putting the case and all the murders out of his mind for the next hour.

On his way through the little park in front of the station, he saw a familiar face sitting on a stone bench, reading a magazine, a half-eaten sandwich on a plastic tray in front of her. He spotted her before she saw him.

God, she looked good. He thought it might be better if he just snuck past her and didn't say a word. But, damn, he'd missed being around her.

"Hey, Mac," he said, "what are you doing hangin' out here?"

Dominica McCarthy looked up from her magazine, smiled, and shaded her eyes.

"Workin' on my tan," she said.

He came closer.

"So haven't seen you in a while. How you doin'?" he asked. "Been busy?"

"Yeah, pretty busy," she said. "Working on those murders you can't seem to solve."

"Yeah, yeah, rub it in," Crawford said. "I was going to get a little lunch. Want to join me?"

"Sure," she said, pointing to her half-eaten sandwich. "This tuna didn't really do it for me."

"Three Pete's okay?" he asked.

"Sounds good."

***

THE SKINNY PETE WITH THE COMB-OVER SEATED THEM.

"So what you gonna have?" Crawford asked.

"Piece of blueberry pie," she said, curling a strand of hair. "À la mode, I'm thinking."

He remembered how much she loved dessert as he spent a moment taking her in.

His cell phone rang.

"'Scuse me a sec," he said.

"Go ahead."

It was Rutledge. He wanted to meet. Crawford set a time.

"Sorry," he said after hanging up.

"That's okay. You must be flat-out," she said. "That Calhoun-Jones couple was horrible."

Crawford suddenly caught David Balfour out of the corner of his eye, headed in the direction of the nearby men's room.

Balfour glanced over and spotted them. Palm Beach was a small town and Crawford remembered Balfour knew Dominica. In fact, he remembered Balfour had taken several unsuccessful runs at trying to date her.

Balfour beelined over. "Well, look at this, you two lovebirds back together?" he said, leaning forward to give Dominica a double-cheeker.

Dominica rolled her eyes and said, "Don't be a jerk, David."

"That didn't sound like a no to me," said Balfour.

"No," Dominica and Crawford said simultaneously.

"That's too bad. You were kind of the all-American dream couple."

"Oh God, please," she said. "Weren't you on your way somewhere?"

He nodded and shrugged. "Just thought I had a scoop."

"Well, you don't," said Dominica.

"Anyway, nice to see you two. Have a good lunch," Balfour said and headed toward the men's room.

She looked up at Crawford. "He'll probably blast it all over town in five seconds," she said. "Why people would care is beyond me."

Crawford's phone rang again. He did a fast scan of the number and didn't recognize it. He punched the red button.

"I'm gonna ignore that one," he said.

She knew that was a major concession. Back when they were dating, she'd referred to the constant ring of his phone at all hours as Chinese water torture.

He used to shift it to vibrate when he was around Dominica. He had done that one time, right before a passionate couch session with her when the two were pressed tightly together, kissing feverishly. What happened was his phone, which was on vibrate, had started hopping around in the pocket of his shirt and Dominica, who was pushed up against it, had no idea what it was at first.

"Je-sus—" she had said, pulling back.

"Sorry," he said, fishing the offending device from his pocket.

She smiled her little beguiling smile and said, "I gotta admit, I kinda liked it."

Another time he had put it on a coffee table at her house while they were watching a movie. It started flopping around like a fish on a dock until she grabbed it and said, "Either it goes or I do."

At the time, he was pretty sure she was kidding, but three weeks later, she was gone.

The phone was only a symbol, she'd told him. He took her for granted, she observed. 'Maybe a little too into your job, Charlie,' she suggested. 'Ever heard of the word compromise?' she asked.

But maybe... just maybe, he was getting a second chance today. And maybe... just maybe, it wasn't too late to change a few things. Learn from his mistakes. After all, she was the smartest, funniest, most down-to-earth woman within a thousand-mile radius of Palm Beach. And yes, there were those incredible eyes.

His phone rang again. He looked down at the caller.

"Oh, Christ, I am so sorry," he said. "I gotta take this one. It's Ott."

"Don't worry about it," she said, probably not meaning it.

He clicked on the green button. "Charlie, you're not going to believe this," Ott said.

"What?"

"I'm at the Russians' house," he answered.

Crawford listened intently for a few seconds. He tried to keep his expression steady and not react.

"I'll be right there," he said finally.

He clicked the phone.

"What's wrong?" Dominica asked.

He wasn't as poker-faced as he hoped.

"I'm really sorry, but I gotta go," he said. "Got another bad one."

He got up and pulled two twenties out of his pocket, then put them on the table. "I was really looking forward to that chili," he said. "And catching up a little."

He wondered if he should have reversed the order. He leaned down to give her a kiss on the cheek. But she turned toward him at the last second and they kissed on the lips.

"Bye," she said. "Call me after you've rounded up all the bad guys."

THIRTY-EIGHT

EVSEI'S FIRST LOYALTY WAS TO THE ALMIGHTY AMERICAN BUCK.

But, for a guy who had grown up in the industrial grayness of Grozny and had the equivalent of an eighth-grade education, the tattooed hit man had also developed a prolific creative side. It helped that his boss Vasily had given him some latitude. It wasn't as though Vasily had said, "Hey, why don't you go dump some poisonous snakes over the wall at Churchill Ames's house?" Hardly. Vasily didn't have that much of an imagination. What he had said was something like, 'I need you to intimidate someone. And if it means that person gets injured, crippled, or even killed, well, I can live with that.'

For the latest job, Evsei's initial plan was to either employ the big-bang approach, i.e., a homemade, but highly effective bomb, which had proved effective for him in the past, or else do something entirely new. The new thing was inspired by something that happened down in Pompano Beach a few years back.

As far as explosives went, he was an expert at rigging a car bomb that would detonate when the ignition key was turned. He was supremely confident he could—based on the amount of Semtex used —either scare the hell out of a target, maim them extensively, or else launch their mangled torso into a nearby palm tree. The new alternative—which had been used to kill a man at the National Enquirer headquarters in Pompano Beach—was anthrax. His thought was to sneak it into the target's house and let it do its thing. The only problem with anthrax, he had read, was that it could be kind of random. And it could take a while.

In the end, though, he decided on something similar to anthrax but way more deadly. And *way, way* quicker.

The day after the snake attack, Evsei was at a newsstand in Palm Beach getting a Russian magazine for Vasily, and it was the only thing people were talking about. He was rapturous as he observed the horrified expressions on people's faces as they talked about what had happened at Churchill Ames's house. He almost wanted to announce to them, "It was me! I was the mastermind behind that."

This time he felt challenged to top that. While guns, knives and bombs all had their places, he prided himself on being a strictly disciplined professional, but even more, a pioneering one. A man who set the killing bar at the highest level of innovation and imagination. He aspired to be someone future assassins spoke of in hushed, reverential tones. And speaking of assassins—from the moment he first heard that English word, he loved its sound. How it sang with menace and malevolence. Assassin. The word's sibilance, it had the hiss of a snake.

Evsei wanted to be remembered for the genius and inventiveness of his work, not just as a man who could shoot straight. But when he first came up with his most recent idea, he thought it might be over-the-top. Like something out of a comic book rather than real life. And the biggest challenge was getting the murder weapon. Yes, murder weapon, because this time there was no intention of merely intimidating or injuring his victims.

No, this time the targets were going to be killed. Horrifically, but creatively.

And the more he looked into it, the more he hammered out the details, the more he knew he could pull it off.

But if he couldn't—if there was a glitch or the whole thing went up in smoke—he always had a plan B. The 9mm. Glock 17. It had proved itself very reliable.

Immediately after the woman hired him to do the job, he jumped into action. He snuck into the utility room off of the laundry room on North Lake Way and crawled into the air-conditioning ducts of the house. The purpose was to make sure that the passageway was unobstructed and he could get to where he needed to. Then, with a screwdriver, he loosened two vents directly above where he intended the executions to take place.

To his amazement, there had been room to spare in the rectangular aluminum channels. The ducts were extra-large because the air-conditioning system of Vasily and Aleksandr's house was commercial-grade, the kind you generally found in office buildings.

He had spent the last twelve hours preparing everything. Working out every detail.

He couldn't wait to hear people talk about it. With those horrified looks on their faces.

THIRTY-NINE

WHILE AN AMERICAN MAN'S SATURDAY AFTERNOON MIGHT typically consist of a game of golf, mowing the lawn, or relaxing while watching a baseball game on TV, Vasily and Aleksandr Zinoviev had their own particular Saturday-afternoon ritual. You could set your watch by it—always the exact same routine at the exact same time. It began with a swim in the ocean at 1:00 on the dot. Having grown up in the Caucasus Mountains with the Black Sea to the west and the Caspian to the southeast, the brothers shared a small number of good childhood memories. One was their family's summer weekend trips to the Caspian, where they'd swim all day long despite water temperatures in the low sixties.

What they really got to like in Florida was bodysurfing, something they could never do in Russia. Aleksandr had also become a quite competent surfer in Palm Beach and, though older than most of the others, blended in with the young guys who surfed the north end. But Vasily didn't surf, so the brothers' Saturday afternoon custom was two vigorous hours of bodysurfing.

They had been in the ocean for an hour and a half already. The waves were big and they were both getting good rides. The last one

Vasily caught had whirled him around underwater like he was in a giant clothes washer. He secretly liked the sensation: the momentary loss of control. The thing he had to be careful about, though, was not to get slammed to the ocean floor headfirst. That's how people broke their necks.

The brothers had slightly different techniques. Aleksandr would position himself ahead of a breaking wave and then paddle gently into it, while Vasily would start a little later, then thrash furiously until he caught up with the wave. Aleksandr would ride as far as a wave took him. Vasily, impatient for the next one, would pull out early, then race back to get another one. They rarely talked when they were out in the ocean. They just went about their business. Aleksandr's face had an expression of enjoyment, while to Vasily it was just another task he needed to excel at.

After two hours of bodysurfing, right at 3:00, Vasily started walking toward the shore. That was the way it always ended. Aleksandr would take the cue from his older brother, follow him, then catch up with him.

They separated once they got inside the house and Aleksandr walked down to the wing of the house where the girls stayed. This was his domain; he was the liaison with the girls.

There were usually anywhere from seven to ten women living there at any given time. Nadia had been there the longest, over four years. She was Aleksandr's favorite.

The layout of the house and guesthouse was an inch-for-inch exact replica of the Playboy Mansion in Holmby Hills, California. The brothers had gotten the plans and had re-created it. They had spared no expense, and the Spanish movie director, Pedro Schiff, who had been to both places, told them their Palm Beach version was far superior because of the breathtaking ocean vista.

In the guest wing was a long, central corridor with bedrooms and baths on either side. Upstairs, it was a similar layout. The girls had their own pool too, the infinity-edged kind, which had a square fifteen-by-fifteen section that was only one foot deep. The girls put their chaise longues in the water there and thus were partially submerged as they sunbathed. It was a very effective body-cooling system.

The other half of the brothers' Saturday afternoon ritual was getting together with several of the girls at their indoor pool. Aleksandr knocked on one of the solid mahogany doors. He knew where each of the girls' rooms were, of course.

Nadia came out wearing only a pair of low-slung black panties.

"Aleksandr," she said with an inviting smile.

"Nadia, my dear, my brother and I would be flattered if you would join us in the grotto," Aleksandr said in Russian, in his courtly manner.

Aleksandr had watched every James Bond movie a hundred times and affected 007's manner. He once ordered a martini "shaken, not stirred," but his brother's mocking frown made it the last time he did. Though he had once been told he bore a resemblance to the actor Roger Moore, who had played James Bond several times, to Aleksandr there was only one Bond: the Scottish version.

"I would love to join you," Nadia said. "Just give me a second."

She started to go back inside.

"You can come just as you are," he said.

"But I want to look beautiful for you," she purred.

"You do now," he said. She had a way of getting Aleksandr immediately in the mood.

Then he went to Yulena's room. She was taking a nap and said she would be there in ten minutes.

They always seemed so flattered, Aleksandr thought. It was human nature, he supposed. They had been chosen. They were desired.

EVSEI CRAWLED THROUGH THE WIDE DUCTS OF THE commercial air conditioner. In front of him, he pushed the same Igloo cooler he had used several weeks before at Churchill Ames' house to contain the water moccasins. This time his cargo was even more deadly. It had taken a little doing to get the liquid sarin, but Evsei was a resourceful man. He had spent two years in a prison cell next to the man who had sent anthrax through the mail and killed a photo editor at the National Enquirer headquarters. Evsei had stayed in touch with the man, thinking one day he might need him. And he did.

The liquid sarin was in six plastic bags. Each one had sixteen ounces in them. Evsei was using as his blueprint the 1995 attack on the Toyko subway by five members of a cult group called Aum Shin-rikyo. Originally, the five were going to spread the sarin in aerosol form, but ultimately considered it too risky. What they ended up doing was dropping the bags on the floor of the subway, puncturing them with the tips of umbrellas, then running out of there as fast as they could.

Twelve people were killed and nobody could quite figure out what the cult's motive was.

Evsei assumed that the bags would burst upon impact being dropped from a height of about fifteen feet. But just to be sure, he dropped several bags filled with water onto a sidewalk from his second story bedroom as a test, and they all broke.

Now he was ready for the real thing.

FORTY

.

ALEKSANDR SUSPECTED HIS BROTHER WORE THE BLACK SPEEDO because he was less endowed than him. The women and Aleksandr—who was opening a second bottle of Cristal—were all naked as they lounged around the pool. They had gone through the first bottle fast. Vasily was a gulper, not a sipper. Nadia was sitting on the side of the pool. She seemed to be enjoying herself. What Aleksandr loved about Nadia was how natural she was, never the least bit self-conscious.

They were talking about swimming in the Sea of Azov. It was cold and rocky there, the opposite of what it was like in Florida. They all agreed that they were lucky to be in America. Aleksandr walked down the steps into the pool. Yulena was on top of Vasily, massaging his back and neck. Vasily was lying on his stomach on the pool's edge and she was straddling him.

He suddenly grunted in Russian, "Get up," as if he was uncomfortable.

Yulena got up and then Vasily followed. He picked up his champagne glass and went down the steps to the pool. She followed him.

Then suddenly they heard a sharp, unfamiliar sound from somewhere above.

"What was that?" Aleksandr asked his brother.

Vasily shrugged.

Aleksandr looked concerned.

"I'm going to go check," he said, heading toward the steps.

Then Vasily held up his hand. "I remember. Evsei told me he was having someone fix something with the air-conditioning."

"I didn't notice anything wrong with it," said Aleksandr.

Vasily shrugged again.

Then there was a scratching sound that seemed close.

"What the hell is that?" Aleksandr asked again, looking up at the air-conditioning vent above them.

Yulena moved a little closer to Vasily who was looking up.

Suddenly, a grated vent fell from above and landed with a clank on the coping around the pool.

Then came the six plastic bags, one after the other, all landing on the hard surfaces around the pool. Each one of them burst and their deadly contents poured out.

FORTY-ONE

Crawford and Ott had gotten there ten minutes after the first uniform. The uniform had sized up the scene and advised everyone coming there to wear gas masks or surgical masks. When Crawford and Ott arrived, there were two Russian women and a man near the pool. They lived in the house, they explained, and had heard screams. One of the women was just staring blankly into space. The other women had gotten sick after seeing the bodies. Crawford could empathize. Not only was this crime scene one of the grisliest he had ever seen, but there also was a pervasive stench of death and vomit in the air. That, combined with the grotto's chlorinated water, created a rancid stink.

There was yellow liquid in close proximity to the three victims and Crawford wondered if it was the deadly agent that had killed them. Then he noticed some of it in the corner of the mouth of the woman and realized it was vomit. He noticed foam in the mouth of one of the men.

Besides Crawford and Ott, six other people were working the crime scene. Two evidence techs, dressed in scrubs with masks over their noses and mouths, looked like they didn't know where to start at first. The place was a grisly battlefield. But now the techs were methodically going around, first retrieving the bodies, then filling their evidence bags. Crawford was just glad that Dominica hadn't caught the job, particularly because of her relationship with Aleksandr.

The ME, Bob Hawes, who Crawford had seen entirely too much of in the last couple of weeks, was taking pictures with his digital camera. After Hawes finished doing that, Crawford knew that he would videotape the scene. At Churchill Ames's house, Crawford had noticed that Hawes's technique was to start at the center, meaning where the victim was located, then work his way out. But in this case, since there were three scattered victims, Crawford wasn't quite sure what his MO would be.

He walked up to Hawes. Hawes looked up at him. "Sarin?" was all Crawford said.

"Yup," Hawes said. "Dropped it in bags. Like water bombs."

"I saw," Crawford said. "That AC vent."

"Yeah, stuff goes from liquid to gas, then dissipates pretty quick," Hawes said, shaking his head. "Poor bastards musta really suffered. Puking, twitching, paralyzed, dead. Just wonder how they got that shit."

Crawford shrugged, then slowly walked away from Hawes.

Right after Crawford got there, Ott told him that one of the Russian women had said in broken English that there had been an eyewitness. Her name was Nadia. She had escaped and was the first one to call 911.

Crawford and Ott left the grotto and went back to the part of the house where they'd been told Nadia was hiding. She wouldn't unlock her door at first. When she finally did, her chest was heaving and she had a glazed look on her face. She was shivering, arms crossed over her breasts.

Crawford knew right away she was in shock. He had seen the distracted, zombie-like state many times before.

"I'm Detective Crawford, this is Detective Ott," he said as clearly and deliberately as he could. "We're very sorry about what happened. What is your name, please?"

The woman looked blankly at him for a second, then said, "I am Nadia."

"Are you okay?" asked Ott. "Is there anything we can do for you?"

"I'm okay," she said. "Thank you."

"You were there when it happened, right?" Crawford confirmed.

"Yes, I was," she said robotically.

"I'm sorry, but we need to ask you what you saw," Crawford said. "Can we sit down somewhere?"

Nadia nodded and started walking stiffly down the hallway. They followed her as she led them down a foyer and through French doors that went outside to another pool. She sat down at a round, glass-topped table with an umbrella and four chairs, as Crawford and Ott sat down on either side of her.

Nadia looked away, unfocused, at the ocean.

"So if you would tell us exactly happened, please, Nadia?" Ott asked gently.

That's when Nadia lost control. She started to cry, then it ratcheted up to almost a wail, her hands pressed hard over her eyes.

After a few moments, she recovered and took her hands away from her red-rimmed eyes.

"Yulena was my best friend." Nadia said. "And Aleksandr..." Her voice trailed off.

Ott said, "I'm sorry. Please, any details you could give us would be greatly appreciated."

"We were all in the grotto, swimming and drinking champagne—"

"Vasily, Alkesandr, you, and the other woman?" asked Crawford, looking down at his notebook.

"Yes," she said. "Yulena is her name. And then I hear a noise. We all did. I did not know what it was. It sounded in the ceiling or the roof. And then—oh, my God—these plastic bags came out of that place..."

"Keep going, please," said Ott.

Crawford saw Nadia's expression change. She was now locked in an expression of focused concentration, as if she was willing herself to get through the story.

"They broke on the floor near us and I saw Yulena, water pouring from out of her eyes, then she had this very bad shaking. That was when I...threw up near the edge of the pool. Then I just started to run. I knew I should not stay there. Something terrible was in those bags. I didn't even look back, I was so afraid for my life. I got to my room and I was sick again. I didn't dare come out."

"So you didn't see what happened to Vasily, Aleksandr and Yulena?" Crawford asked.

"No, I just stay in my room," Nadia said. "I wanted to help, but I—I—"

Crawford put his hand on Nadia's arm.

"Had you noticed anything unusual happening around the house before?" Crawford asked. "Anybody doing something that didn't look right?"

Nadia thought for a second, then shook her head. "Sorry, I was in my room before."

Then Crawford saw the French doors open and Norm Rutledge barged through. He looked like he was on the warpath.

"Norm," Crawford said, getting up. "This is Nadia, she was there when—when it happened."

"Let me talk to you a second," said Rutledge, giving Crawford a head flick.

Crawford followed him away from the others.

"The fuck is going on?" said Rutledge. "We got six stiffs in just over a week in our tropical little paradise. Just what the fuck is going on here?"

Ott and Nadia heard the agitation in Rutledge's voice and swung around to where the two were huddled.

"Norm, you gotta calm down," Crawford said.

"I gotta calm down...is that your answer?" Rutledge said. "No, you gotta find out who did this. You gotta catch 'em. That's what's gotta happen."

Rutledge had been Chief of Detectives for an eight-year stretch when one of the worst crimes in Palm Beach had been a three-man burglary team that hit houses when their owners were at charity benefits. Yes, he was in charge when Crawford and Ott solved the Daryl Bill murder, but his involvement had been minimal. Now, in only nine days, he'd had a woman killed by snakes, a prominent couple shot between the eyes, three Russians die horribly from sarin gas, and an entire golf course poisoned and ruined.

Rutledge's hysteria, though maybe understandable, was a far cry from professional.

Crawford was recapping what had happened to Rutledge. "So the question is who did Vasily and Aleksandr Zinoviev burn—"

"Know what it looks like to me, Crawford? Looks like you're better at asking questions than answering them," Rutledge said, shaking his head slowly.

Crawford ignored the taunt.

Ott and Nadia walked past them. Ott was taking Nadia back to her room. She had no more to offer them.

"So who you think could have done it?" Rutledge asked.

"Either someone who worked for the Russians who could be bought, or used to work for the Russians, but got a better offer, is my guess."

"That doesn't narrow it down much," Rutledge said.

Crawford sighed, wishing he had left with Ott. "Here's the thing, Norm: You show up at a crime scene and either expect us to know exactly who did it or have 'em cuffed already. Sorry, it doesn't work that way."

"Okay, we don't need a debate," said Rutledge. "But I want to see you and all seven deltas right after you're done here."

A delta was the department's designation for a detective.

"Okay, it's gonna be awhile, though," Crawford said. "I'll notify the others."

Whatever the meeting was going to be about, Crawford could safely assume it would be the mother of all clusterfucks.

Rutledge turned and left without another word.

Crawford walked back into the house and spotted Ott coming out of Nadia's room. "She all right?"

"Better," Ott said. "Told her we'd probably need to talk to her again."

Crawford nodded. "The tattooed guy, Evsei," he said. "I haven't seen him around. Or that other mutt, the one with the acne. We gotta talk to them. See if you can you find out from Nadia where they live."

FORTY-TWO

Ott came back out to the pool where Crawford was snapping pictures of the AC duct with his cell phone.

"She told me Evsei's got a bedroom on the third floor," he said to Crawford. "Other guy lives up there too."

Crawford slid his cell into his breast pocket and he and Ott walked into the main house.

Evsei's bedroom had a king-sized bed and a beveled-edge mirror over it. There was a little sitting room off of it, with various kinds of electronic equipment and wires. Evsei was not there. Three drawers were open and empty.

Evsei was in the wind.

Ott went over to one of the closets.

The room was like a bedroom in a frat house, a long way from what you'd expect in a sixteen-million-dollar Palm Beach house. It looked like it had been left off the cleaning ladies' route for at least a year. One of the pillows on the unmade bed had no pillowcase and was stained a yellowish brown. On the floor, dust balls were mixed in with paper clips, shirt buttons, candy wrappers, and discarded match-books. Clothes hangers also littered the floor, along with receipts, a lottery ticket, pennies, and a dirty, white strappy T-shirt off in the corner.

Crawford walked over to the bedroom's walk-in closet, pulling on white vinyl gloves. Strewn around the floor were various articles of dirty, wadded-up clothing. Crawford looked up and spotted a small box tucked back on a high shelf, slightly above eye level. He stood on his toes and reached up for it.

It was a box of Black Talon shell cartridges.

"Hey, Mort, take a look at this," he said, walking out of the closet and holding the box in his gloved hand. "I think we got one mystery solved."

Ott eyed the box. "Well, look at that. Just the caliber we been lookin' for."

"Yup, I'll give 'em to Hawes," Crawford said. "No question they're gonna match up with the slugs that killed the Calhoun-Joneses. You got anything?"

"Naw," he said, shaking his head. "Place is a fuckin' dump."

Crawford nodded.

A few minutes later, as they were about to leave, the door opened.

It was the man they had first seen on the Zinovievs' plane and who they took in after the Calhoun-Jones murders. The one with the acne.

The man spun around and started to run.

"Hold it," said Crawford, going after him.

The man bolted down a long corridor, but Crawford gained on him fast. Crawford dived, catching him around the shoulders, and they went down onto the carpeted floor just short of the end of the corridor. It looked like they might crash into a wall, but Crawford yanked him back like a cowboy wrestling a steer to the ground.

He reached for his handcuffs and cuffed him.

"Nice goin'," said Ott, coming up behind them. "Still got your speed, I see."

"Yeah, well, Nikita here's no Hussain Bolt," Crawford said.

He got to his feet and yanked the Russian up by an arm, then turned him around. The Russian's nose was bleeding.

"What's your name?" Crawford demanded.

The man felt his nose gingerly.

"Nikita," he said, his eyes darting around.

Ott laughed.

"No shit, really?" Crawford said.

The man nodded. "I have done nothing wrong."

"How come you ran, then?" Crawford asked.

The man had no answer.

"Where's your buddy, Evsei?" asked Ott.

"He was here," Nikita said. "I do not know where he went."

Ott held up the box of Black Talons. "You ever seen these before?"

"No."

"Bullshit," said Crawford. "There are two missing. You and your buddy Vasily used 'em a couple nights ago."

"I never saw those in my life, I swear," Nikita insisted.

Crawford nodded skeptically.

"Where's your crib?" Ott asked.

Nikita looked blank.

"Your bedroom."

"Just down the hall."

"Let's go have a look."

Nikita led the way.

Unlike Evsei, Nikita had a neat room. Until Ott and Crawford tossed it. They didn't find anything incriminating. After they were done, Crawford went over to Nikita, who he had handcuffed to a metal bedpost, and got in his face. "How well you speak English?"

"Not too good," Nikita said.

"Then I'll talk real slow," said Crawford. "How would you like us hanging the murder of that nice couple on you?"

"But I did not do it," Nikita protested loudly.

"Know what? I don't really give a shit whether you did or didn't," Crawford said. "I'm going to hang it on you anyway."

Nikita didn't say anything. He just looked scared.

"Thing is, I think you did it, and I'll tell you why," Crawford said. "Know what a 'retina slide' is, harelip?"

Judging by his reaction, Nikita didn't know what a retina slide or a harelip was.

"No," he said.

"It's simple," said Crawford. "A retina slide is what crime-scene technicians use after someone gets killed. You with me so far?"

Nikita nodded tentatively.

"They take a picture, arthroscopically, of the victim's retina…got it?"

Nikita didn't get it. "Retina?"

"Eyeball, dumbo," Crawford said impatiently.

Nikita nodded tentatively again.

"You know what it shows?"

Nikita shook his head.

Crawford pointed to his right eye. "It shows the last impression in the victim's eyes," he said. "Which means the last thing those two saw before you killed 'em."

Nikita looked like he was having difficulty processing the concept. "But I did not kill them."

"Know what else?" Crawford said. "It takes exactly two days for the ME to develop the slide. And an hour ago he called me and said it was ready. It's going to be a whole lot better for you if you confess now, before I see it."

"But I said, I did not do it," he answered again.

"Come on, Nikita," Crawford said. "Cut the bullshit."

Then Ott approached Nikita. "How come a couple of smart guys like you and Evsei didn't shoot 'em in the eyeballs?" he asked. "That way the retina slide wouldn't be any good."

"It was Evsei who did it, by himself," Nikita blurted. "You will see. It will be him on the retina slide, not me."

"What did Evsei do with the gun?" Ott asked.

"I do not know anything, just that Vasily ordered Evsei to kill those two."

"And what about what happened at the pool? To Vasily and Aleksandr?"

"I know nothing about that."

"Somebody comes here with poisonous gas and kills Vasily and Aleksandr and you know nothing about it?" Ott said. "Ain't buyin' it."

Nikita shook his head again.

Crawford stepped back. "Innocent little Nikita, huh?"

Ott laughed.

"I did noth—"

"Put a fuckin' lid on it," said Crawford. "Give this guy the Miranda, Mort. Something I doubt they got back in the gulag."

"Yeah, then we're taking a ride to the station," Ott said to Nikita. "You'll be wantin' to pack your toothbrush, 'cause you're gonna be there a while."

FORTY-THREE

After depositing Nikita in a cell, they went in to Crawford's office.

"I tell ya, Charlie, you oughta be in Hollywood," said Ott. "That retina-slide thing. Oscar material, man."

"Kind of had myself believin' it," Crawford said. "Hey, give me a few minutes. I gotta make a call."

Ott nodded and walked out.

Crawford sat down at his desk and reluctantly picked up the phone. Then he put it down and thought for a few moments. The call he was about to make was going to be a tough one.

Finally, he dialed.

Dominica picked up after two rings.

"Dominica, it's Charlie."

"Hi," she said. "Thanks for lunch, even though you ditched out on me."

"Sorry 'bout that," he said. "That call I got at Three Pete's was about something that happened at Aleksandr and Vasily Zinoviev's house. I'm really, sorry to have to tell you this, but they were both killed."

Dead silence.

"Oh, my God, what happened?" she said at last.

"It was a terrible thing," Crawford said. "It happened in their pool."

"Tell me what happened," she said, her voice quaking.

"It might be better if I come over, face-to-face, if that's okay with you," he said, looking at his watch. "I just have a few things to wrap up first. Can I stop by in, say, about forty-five minutes?"

"Sure, I'll see you then," she said, sounding badly shaken.

"Can I bring you something? Is there anything I can get for you?"

"Thanks, Charlie, I appreciate it. I'm okay."

"Okay," he said. "See you in a little while."

WEARING A PINK POLO SHIRT, THIS TIME WITH A LITTLE BLUE horseman on the chest, Miller was tapping his fingers on his Bentley's steering wheel. The wheel probably cost more than the stubby little Geo sedan that he was staring at disdainfully. Evsei was supposed to have been there fifteen minutes ago, and Miller was in a hurry to go see his architect. And, the reality was, Tim Kurchon really was *his* architect, based on the sheer monumentality of the project, the whole incredible scope of it, not to mention how much he was paying Kurchon. He had told Kurchon that he didn't want him accepting any new work until his job was done. He suggested—no, insisted—that Kurchon's partner, or one of the junior guys, take care of the firm's other jobs.

Kurchon, who had a fully developed ego of his own, had looked at him contemptuously, as if he might just pitch a full-blown fit, one of his well-known trademarks. Then he seemed to temper his reaction.

"You know, I have to hand it to you," Kurchon said in his difficult-to-place accent. "You have absolutely no problem asking anyone to do anything, do you?"

Demanding would have been a more accurate word than asking.

It was a rhetorical question anyway, and Miller knew it didn't require a response.

"This is the biggest job you've ever had, right?" Miller asked.

"Square-footage-wise, you mean?" asked Kurchon.

"You know damn well what I mean: square-footage-wise, prestige-wise, win-all-the-goddamn-architectural-awards-wise."

Kurchon gave him his imperious look. "It's up there, I suppose."

Up there, my ass, Miller thought. No way Kurchon had ever had anything close to the magnitude of this job.

Kurchon was always throwing around his regal tone. It was basically his way of saying, you may be worth billions of dollars through some curious combination of luck, ruthlessness, and chicanery, but I...I am an incorruptible artiste and aesthete.

Miller snickered and went on. "Then, seeing how it's the biggest commission you've ever had, by a factor of a hundred probably," he said, "why wouldn't you want to focus on it solely? To make it as singularly distinctive as you possibly can."

He could see that the singularly distinctive line had registered with Kurchon. Got him thinking Pritzker Prize or something.

"Singularly distinctively is how I do all my jobs," Kurchon said with a cocksure smile, clearly pleased with his retort.

Miller had not yet been able to locate Kurchon's Achilles' heel, but he wouldn't stop until he found it.

He saw the Aston Martin pull into the lot of John Smith's Subs and come over to where he was parked. Miller had been here so often lately he wondered when John Smith would hit him up with a rent bill.

Evsei pulled up alongside the Bentley and lowered his window.

"So is it a done deal?" Miller asked, poking his head out of the Bentley's window.

"Yes," Evsei said, "trust me, I would not be driving this car if Vasily was still alive."

"Both brothers are dead?"

"Of course. And there was what you call collateral damage."

"I don't need to know about that."

"One million dollars, please," said Evsei.

Miller looked around, saw no one nearby, and held up a leather suitcase.

"This is one million five-hundred-thousand dollars," he said.

Evsei smiled and took the suitcase. He felt as though he fully deserved the bonus, based on the job's cold-blooded creativity.

"The other half million is for you to get out of the country right away. And never come back."

Evsei thought about it. "And you will pay for a first-class ticket?"

"My friend, even better. My jet is waiting at Talon Air to take you to Moscow. The flight plan has been approved, and there is caviar and champagne on board. I'm assuming, of course, that you're a gourmet," said Miller, not attempting to hide his sarcasm.

It was lost on Evsei, who was thinking he'd grab a bag of John Smith meat bombs for the trip.

"That's very thoughtful of you," Evsei said.

CRAWFORD WAS ON HIS WAY TO DOMINICA MCCARTHY'S. IT was a little past nine. The meeting with Rutledge and the deltas was over, and the only good news was that Rutledge was going to be the point man at the station house and exercise what he considered to be his masterful organizational skills. That was good for Crawford, who planned to avoid the office and do his thing alone or with Ott.

He hit Dominica's number on speed dial. He had never removed it.

She answered.

"Hi, Mac, it's me," he said. "Sorry, I'm running a few minutes late. But I'm on my way now."

"That's okay," she said, "see you in a little while."

"Yeah, be there shortly."

A few minutes later he pulled into her driveway on Queens Lane. He had spent many a cozy night there.

He knocked. She came to the door. She was wearing a blouse he had the fond memory of removing once or twice.

"You look nice," he said.

"Thanks," she said. "Come on in."

Crawford looked around—stalling the big conversation—and pointed to a sisal rug off the kitchen. "That's new."

"Very observant," said Dominica, going over to the refrigerator. She pulled out a Sierra Nevada for him, then reached for a half-opened bottle of pinot grigio.

"Thanks," he said. "I've been craving my first beer of the day."

She handed him the bottle and poured a glass of pinot grigio for herself. He didn't like using a glass, having once explained to her how the transfer process—from bottle to glass—meant a three-degree loss in temperature along with a not-insignificant flavor reduction. He didn't know whether it was true or not, but it sounded good.

He followed her into the combination living and dining room.

She sat down in a sofa and tucked one leg under her.

"I just want to say again, I'm very sorry about what happened to Aleksandr Zinoviev."

She bowed her head a little. "Thanks. Me too. Rose called after you did and told me all about it."

"How'd she know?" Crawford asked. "It just happened."

"You know Rose," Dominica said with a shrug. "He was a nice guy, Aleksandr. But Rose said he and his brother were into some bad stuff. When I was around him, he was always the perfect gentleman. What is going on, Charlie? I mean, all these murders? They're connected somehow, right?"

"Yeah, they are," Crawford said, observing her closely. "Sure you're okay?"

She sighed. "Yeah. I mean, how okay can you be when someone who was a friend and nice to you gets killed? Especially like that."

"I know." He walked over and sat down beside her on the couch.

He thought about putting his arm around her, comfortingly, but wasn't sure it was the right thing. "We can talk tomorrow if you prefer."

"No, that's okay, I know you have things you need to ask me," she said. "I mean, we are in the same line of work and all."

Crawford smiled. "You sure?"

"Yeah, I'm sure. I just don't know how helpful I'm going to be. But go ahead."

He leaned forward.

"Okay, well, thanks. Did you ever—when you and Aleksandr went out—ever notice or hear anything suspicious? You know, unusual, out of the ordinary? A phone conversation? Or maybe something he said to his brother when he didn't think you were listening? Anything at all that might be useful?"

"No, nothing," she said. "I just met his brother once. We went out on his boat and water-skied, mainly. I didn't really even talk to Vasily. He was kind of a moody guy, didn't really have much to say."

"But did Aleksandr ever talk about...I don't know, business rivals or maybe political enemies? Anybody at all who might have been behind what happened today?"

"You know I'd like to help you, Charlie, I really would, but there wasn't much to it. We water-skied, had lunch, water-skied some more, had a drink, then he took me home."

"So the only times you were with him were on his boat?"

"Times? Charlie, it was just three times. The third one was last Sunday." She must have spotted a tell on his face. "Why? What did you think?"

He was usually pretty good about keeping business and personal separate.

"I didn't think anything. Your private life is your private life."

"Oh, come on, Charlie, I know you too well." She smiled and brushed her hair back over behind her ear.

"What do you mean by that?"

"What do I mean?" she said. "I'll tell you exactly what I mean. I think...I think you've missed me terribly."

"Well, will you listen to this," he said with a smile. "And exactly where did you get that from?"

She paused. "Rose. She thinks you're still pining for me."

"Oh, I see, the gospel according to the gossip queen," he said. "You know, I have a theory of my own."

"You have theories on every conceivable subject."

It was true. She had heard more than a few from him.

"Maybe I do," he said, "but yesterday, when you were outside the station, reading your magazine—"

"Yes?"

"You were actually waiting for me to happen along," he said. "You know my routine. You were lying in wait."

"Is that a fact?" she said, sitting up straighter and shaking her head. "You know, that is just so incredibly vain."

She cracked a tiny smile.

"You were, weren't you?" he said, returning the smile.

"Um, maybe."

"I think the fact is, you've missed me terribly," he said, "Even though you've made a huge effort to put me out of your mind. I have evidence too."

"Oh, do you now?"

He nodded. "Those Sierra Nevadas in your refrigerator, prima facie evidence," he said. "I suppose you just...happened to have them there."

She laughed.

"They were, ah, on sale—"

"Come on," he said.

He had a sudden, overwhelming urge to kiss her. She was just two feet away. But it was weird, him coming there to console her about the death of a guy she had gone out with.

His cell phone rang. Thank God, he thought.

She rolled her eyes. "Here we go again."

He reached into his pocket and slid the phone out.

"Hello."

"Detective Crawford?"

"Yes."

"Detective, it's Mary Ann Walling at Talon Air—"

"Yes, Mary Ann, I remember. What's up?"

"Sorry to call so late, but you said if I ever saw anything suspicious—"

"Yes?"

"You know the man with the tattoo who was on the Zinoviev plane?"

He bolted upright.

"Yes," he said, pushing the phone tight to his ear.

"Well, I just saw him get on a plane headed for Moscow."

Crawford got to his feet. "Whatever you gotta do, stop that plane."

"It's too late, it just took off."

"I'll be right there," he said, then hung up.

Dominica grabbed a pillow from the sofa and whacked him with it.

"The old Crawford MO," she said, her eyes flashing. "We're having a nice conversation and ring-a-ling."

"I'm sorry," he said, "it's just someone I really gotta see—"

"I know, I know," she said. "Someone by the name of Mary Ann."

"Yeah, Mary Ann Walling," he said, "around sixty-five, sixty-six. I'm guessing probably eight grandchildren."

Dominica started nodding. "Uh-huh, that's your story and you're stickin' to it," she said. "Well, guess I can't accuse you of robbing the cradle anyway."

FORTY-FOUR

CRAWFORD GOT TO TALON AIR IN LESS THAN FIFTEEN MINUTES. In her office, Mary Ann Walling described having seen the man run on board a large private airplane.

"Whose plane was it?" asked Crawford, hunched forward.

"A man named P.D. Miller," Walling said.

Him again, thought Crawford. "Any idea why this guy would get on Miller's plane?"

Walling shrugged and said, "No."

"Did you ever see them talking? Or together?"

"No, sorry, I didn't."

"Was Miller on the plane?"

"No, definitely not."

"The tattoo, right here on his neck, right?" asked Crawford, pointing to where he had seen it close up.

"Well, actually, I didn't see the tattoo," she said, "but I'm sure it was him."

"Why?"

"Well, 'cause his walk is real stiff, like he had a back injury. Kind of jerky, like a robot."

Crawford remembered seeing that.

"But he didn't come through the terminal here?" asked Crawford, figuring if he had, someone might be able to positively ID him.

"No, he must have parked and gone around, straight out onto the tarmac."

"Parked where, do you have any idea?" he asked.

"I don't know for sure. Probably in the front lot somewhere."

"What was he wearing?"

"Black pants, a black shirt."

"A hat?"

"A baseball cap. White."

Crawford's mind was racing. Where to go next? It was obvious. It was time to talk to the guy whose name kept popping up. P.D. Miller.

"Did this man have a suitcase?" Crawford asked.

"He had one of those silver aluminum ones," Walling said. "Not too big. And a computer; I saw a strap over his shoulder."

"And how soon after he got on the plane did it leave?"

"Right away," Walling said. "It started taxiing and took off almost immediately."

Crawford stood up abruptly.

"Thank you, Mary Ann." He shook her hand. "I really appreciate it. You wouldn't have a phone number for Miller, would you?"

She looked apprehensive. "I do, but you can't say you got it from me."

He said he wouldn't.

She got a hardbound blue book with gold lettering out of a drawer, turned the pages, then gave him the number.

Crawford wrote it down in his murder book, thanked her, and walked quickly to his car.

He dialed the number as he pulled out of the Talon parking lot. After a few rings, a recording said, *You know the drill,* then there was a beep. Crawford decided not to leave a message.

Then he dialed Rose Clarke's number. "Hey, Rose, it's Charlie.

Sorry to call so late, but I have a quick question: Where does your client, P.D. Miller, live?"

"Thought you were going over to Dominica's?" Rose said.

"Do you have a GPS on me or something?"

"Why in God's name do you want—"

"It's a long story."

"Okay," she said, "right next to Rod Stewart. One house to the north."

"Like I'd know where Rod Stewart lives," Crawford said.

"Jesus, Charlie, you gotta take the celebrity tour," Rose said. "Okay, a few houses south of the Racquet and Beach Club. 1208 South Ocean."

"Thanks."

"One more IOU, Charlie."

Crawford thanked her again.

As he drove across the south bridge, he tried the number for Miller again, but got the same recording.

He started looking for street numbers.

He saw 1204 South Ocean. Then he saw 1208 and made the turn in. A lot of the big houses on the ocean had massive wrought-iron gates and fences, often with a man in a gatehouse. But, surprisingly, not the eighty-eight-million, five-hundred-thousand-dollar digs of P.D. Miller. It had a long, twisting driveway, then opened up to the big façade of the house.

The house was Mediterranean-style, Crawford's least favorite kind. The parking court looked big enough for fifty cars.

He looked at his watch. It was a few minutes after eleven. He didn't see any lights on inside.

He walked up the steps to the front door. He pressed the doorbell and guessed who would answer. A sleepy-looking butler? Mrs. P.D. Miller, irate at being disturbed at such an hour? Then he remembered what Rose had told him: There was no Mrs. P.D. Miller. Currently, anyway. The man was between wives. Crawford speculated there were probably at least twenty single women in Palm

Beach scratching each other's eyeballs out, trying to get to old P.D. and his checkbook.

Crawford tried rapping on the door with his knuckles. A minute later, the door opened. A man with Coke-bottle glasses looked down at him, not the welcoming sort.

"Who the hell are you?"

"Mr. Miller?"

Louder. "I said, who the hell are you?"

"Sorry it's so late. I'm Detective Crawford, Palm Beach—"

"What do you want?"

The man had the advantage of being one step higher up than Crawford. He was standing in a giant foyer of the house. Crawford first impression was that Miller didn't look at all Palm Beach. In fact, he looked like a chunkier, taller version of the rich guy from Texas who took a run at the presidency ten or fifteen years back. He had a crew cut, Alfred E. Neuman ears, and was about six feet tall. He could have been a Marine drill instructor, right down to the intimidating style and booming voice. He was wearing a button-down dress shirt tucked into twelve-dollar burgundy sweatpants. He had a Bluetooth hooked on to his right ear. For a big-time captain of industry, he looked kind of ridiculous.

"I need to ask you a few questions, Mr. Miller. Can I come inside?"

"This is fine right here," said Miller. "Last time: What the hell do you want?"

"Just want to confirm that your private plane left a little while ago for Moscow."

"So?"

The wrinkles on Miller's forehead were illuminated by the chunky brass lanterns on either side of the front door.

"Why was it going there?" Crawford asked.

"It's none of your goddamn business," Miller said.

Crawford knew rich guys didn't like answering questions. They didn't feel they had to explain anything to anyone. Figured their money did that.

"Actually, it is. It's police business. I need to know why your jet was going to Moscow."

"'Cause I got business there. It probably flies there ten, fifteen times a year," Miller said, his voice thick with condescension. "To Kazakhstan, Tajikistan, places you probably never even heard of."

Crawford ignored the insult. "Was there a man named Evsei on board?"

Miller slowly moved his head to one side, then back.

"Maybe you're not aware of who I am," Miller said. "You should ask around about me. Rutledge or somebody. I'm a big supporter of you guys. I take real good care of you."

"I asked if there was a man named Evsei on board?"

Miller's lips twitched menacingly.

"No. There was nobody named Evsei on board."

"Do you know who the Zinoviev brothers are, Mr. Miller?"

"Of course I do. Bunch of goddamn thugs."

"Were," said Crawford.

"What do you mean?" asked Miller, stepping closer.

"They're dead," said Crawford, studying Miller's reaction.

"You're kidding. What happened?"

"It would take a while to explain," Crawford said. "Who was on your jet, Mr. Miller?"

"Bunch of guys who work for me."

"Do you have an employee who walks kind of hunched over, like he's got a bad back maybe?"

Miller hesitated.

"Matter of fact, I do," he said. "Why?"

"'Cause someone fitting that description was seen boarding right before takeoff."

"It's a guy named Kelter," Miller said. "Broke his back heli-skiing or some goddamn thing."

"What's he do for you?"

"He's a trader. Arbitrage. You do know what arbitrage is, don't you, Detective?"

Crawford remembered a Forbes article in his dentist's office entitled "Arrogance as an Asset in Today's Super-Rich."

"This man Kelter, can you describe the way he walks?" Crawford asked.

Miller shook his head.

"You got to be fucking kidding me," he said. "It's almost midnight and you're on my doorstep asking me to describe how an employee of mine walks."

"I apologize about the time, Mr. Miller," Crawford said. "But I'm looking for a man responsible for five homicides, and an eyewitness told me he saw him get onto your jet."

He thought it was a good idea to change Mary Ann Walling's gender.

"Your eyewitness has shitty eyesight," Miller said. "Why the hell would I have someone who works for those lowlife Zinovievs on my jet?"

"That's what I'm trying to figure out."

"Who told you this bullshit story anyway?"

"You don't need to know."

Miller moved closer.

"Who told you?" His voice doubled in decibels.

"It's confidential," Crawford said.

"Let me tell you about the Zinovievs," Miller said. "They are—or were—nothing but lowlife, gutter thugs. You ever heard of the Vory v Zakone, Detective?"

Crawford shook his head.

"No, course you haven't," Miller said. "They fancy themselves an elite class of professional criminal. Wear these eight-point-star tattoos on their chests. They're into everything: murder, counterfeiting, arms trafficking, kidnapping, you name it. They're Chechens, bad actors. Getting the picture here, Detective?"

Crawford made a mental note to check the brothers' bodies for eight-point tattoos.

"Why are you telling me this? The Zinovievs are dead."

"I just want to help you with your investigation," Miller said with a sneer. "You need it. A lot of people seem to be getting killed and you clowns don't have a clue."

"I appreciate your help, Mr. Miller." Crawford had grown tired of Miller's sarcastic act and figured it was time to throw it back. "You ever get sick of the hedge-fund business and arbitrage, we could use you. I'm sure you'd make a hell of a crime fighter."

"You're a funny man, Detective. Now get the fuck off my property."

FORTY-FIVE

P.D Miller was slouched over the slanted wooden architect's table, surveying his plans. He was almost salivating he was so excited. Kurchon was standing above him, erect and imperious, with a self-satisfied look that said, *Ah yes, I've done it again.*

Miller looked up and asked the same question he'd asked before, a little differently this time. "This is the biggest project you've ever done. By far, right?"

The two were still jockeying.

"Like I told you before, it's up there," Kurchon said. "The question is: Are we ever going to get it approved?"

"Oh, trust me, it's definitely gonna happen."

"How can you be so sure?" Kurchon said. "Palm Beach has never had a personal residence anywhere close to this size before. You know what the zoning board's like, and the architectural review board. And that pain-in-the-ass building department guy, Paul Nicastro."

"Yeah, I know. But don't worry about him. He's on the team."

Kurchon nodded. "You seem pretty sure about it."

"Damn straight I am."

Kurchon smiled knowingly. "I didn't know you could do that anymore."

"Do what?"

Kurchon seemed reluctant to use the word that came to mind.

"Well, you know, pay someone to get something you want."

"Jesus, don't be so crude. Who said anything about bribing someone? I just was able to exert certain leverage."

Kurchon nodded, not sure what he meant. "So when does the closing take place?"

"Two weeks."

"So we can get the contractor started right away?"

"Yeah, and I've already lined up people to fix the golf course."

Kurchon looked up from the plans. "What the hell happened there anyway?"

"I don't know exactly," Miller said. "It'll be as good as new, though, in six months."

Kurchon ran his hand through his salt-and-pepper beard. "I mean, between that and the president getting killed, the place is kind of blemished, wouldn't you say?"

Miller shook his head and gave him a look like he was dealing with a child. "Listen, Kurchon, any place that's of any consequence probably has some kind of a history behind it. So, don't you worry your pretty little head about some 'blemish.' Guys get killed every day, grass dies every day. You know what they say: Shit happens."

FORTY-SIX

CRAWFORD CAME INTO OTT'S OFFICE AT FOUR IN THE afternoon. Ott had been checking out a few things. The first was whether one of the Zinovievs' cars driven by Evsei Nemchenov was parked somewhere in the vicinity of Talon Air. So far, no car had been found. He was also looking into Miller's employee, Geoff Kelter, to determine whether he was on the plane to Moscow and had a walk similar to Evsei's.

Crawford had gone down to forensics, which confirmed that both the caliber of the bullets that killed the Calhoun-Joneses and the rifling marks matched the caliber and brand of the rounds found in Evsei's closet, as well as the barrel of the gun.

Crawford had told Ott about his rancorous visit to P.D. Miller's house.

"You think he was lying about Evsei?" Ott asked Crawford.

"I don't know, it was hard to tell," Crawford said as Norm Rutledge walked in.

"Hey, Norm," said Ott.

"I need to see you alone, Charlie," Rutledge said to Crawford.

That was a bad sign. Calling him Charlie.

"What is it now, Norm?" Crawford asked, though he knew exactly what it was.

Rutledge stared hard at Ott, who had not moved.

"Go solve a murder, huh, Ott," Rutledge said.

"Okay, okay, I'm going," Ott said, putting his hands up.

Rutledge closed the door behind Ott.

Crawford's cell phone rang. He looked down and saw it was Rose Clarke.

He held up one hand to Rutledge and punched the green button.

"Hi, Rose, gonna have to call you right back."

"As soon as you can," she said. "It's important."

"Will do," he said and hung up.

He decided to head Rutledge off at the pass.

"So I take it you heard from my new buddy, P.D. Miller?"

Rutledge dropped down heavily in the chair opposite Crawford.

"Yeah, he called," Rutledge said with a heavy sigh. "Said you were over at his house harassing him in the middle of the night. Accusing him of flying a fugitive out of the country or some bullshit like that. I gotta tell you, that's not the way we do things down here."

"Hey, Norm, it's called investigating a lead, not harassment," Crawford said. "The lead suspect in the Zinoviev and Calhoun-Jones murders is Evsei Nemchenov, who I believe was last seen getting on Miller's plane."

"Miller said it was a guy who works for him," Rutledge said.

"My witness was pretty sure it was Evsei."

"'Pretty sure,' huh?" Rutledge said. "And that was good enough for you to go wake up one of the most prominent citizens in Palm Beach in the middle of the night and accuse him of flying a fugitive out of the country? 'Cause you're pretty sure? You don't seriously think Miller's involved in this, do you?"

"If this guy Evsei was on his plane, I sure as hell do," Crawford said. "Just so you know, Miller wasn't a big fan of the Zinovievs. Guy does a lot of business in Russia, apparently. I'm guessing they might have butted heads."

"Come on, for Chrissakes," said Rutledge, "Miller's a goddamn businessman who runs a bunch of stock funds."

"Norm, you ever hear of a businessman committing a crime before?" Crawford said. "Maybe you've heard of Bernie Madoff; used to have a house down here. You know, now hangin' his hat in a cell up in North Carolina."

"Yeah, but you're talking about being involved in a homicide."

"Yes, I am," said Crawford. "Six, in fact."

Rutledge, twisting his face into a smirk, said, "Come on, Charlie, really?"

"Yeah, really," Crawford said. "And I like it better when you call me Crawford. Look, you want to take me off it, take me off."

Rutledge was silent.

"What is it with Miller anyway?" Crawford said. "Ask him a couple questions and he runs off and cries to Mommy."

Rutledge got up, started walking out of Crawford's office, then turned back.

"You know what it is," he said. "It's like you watched one too many Dirty Harry movies. Always fighting city hall, telling the boss to go fuck himself, but the difference is, Harry gets his guy. You, on the other hand, don't got shit."

"Yeah, well, the movie ain't over yet," Crawford said. "Like I said, you want me on this or not?"

Rutledge looked away and grimaced. "For now, you're on it."

"Don't go doin' me any favors, Norm."

"I said you're on it," Rutledge said, shaking his head. "What is it anyway? You got a hard-on about rich people or something?"

Crawford shook his head and chuckled.

"Well, if I do, then I'm sure as hell in the wrong goddamn town."

FORTY-SEVEN

Crawford gave Rose Clarke a call right after Rutledge left.

"I got something important," she said, "but I'm right in the middle of a showing. Can I call you in an hour?"

"Sure. What are you selling?"

"A fixer-upper on Jungle."

"Good luck."

"Thanks."

Just as he clicked off, Ott walked into his office.

"Guess who's still around?" Ott asked.

"Who?"

"Evsei."

"No shit. So it wasn't him on Miller's plane the other night?" Crawford asked.

"I guess not."

"How'd you find out?" he asked.

"Guess maybe I forgot to tell you," Ott said, sheepishly. "I planted a bug in the Russkies' house."

Crawford could barely hide his glee.

"Good goin', man. But, in my official capacity, I gotta tell you, that's not legal or admissible."

"Yeah, I know," Ott said, "but turns out it's pretty goddamn helpful. I got the translator to listen in and he heard one of the girls tell another one that Evsei came to the house today and took one of the girls with him."

"Got lonely, huh?" Crawford said.

"I guess."

"You get a description of her?"

"Yeah, I went there and Nadia described her. Blonde, tall, late twenties or so."

"Maybe he'll be easier to find with a woman in tow," Crawford said. "We gotta find him fast."

Ott nodded.

"I need you to do something for me," Crawford said.

"What's that?"

"Get everybody into the soft room ASAP. Round 'em up wherever they are."

"Okay." Ott headed for the door, then turned. "Why, what's your plan?"

"You'll see," Crawford said, going toward Rutledge's office.

He knocked hard on Rutledge's door.

"Yeah?" Rutledge said.

Crawford opened the door and walked in.

"Hey, Norm, you'll be happy to know, I fucked up," Crawford said. "Turns out that guy Evsei's still around." He raised his arms, surrender-style. "I'll call Miller and apologize, if you want."

Rutledge thought for a second. "Let's just forget it and move on," he said.

Crawford was surprised.

"Thanks," Crawford said. "It's time to take this guy down. Ott's rounding up everybody in the soft room. I got a plan. I just need you to back me on it."

Rutledge looked Crawford in the eyes, then stood up. "Okay, what the fuck, nothing else is working. Let's hear what you got."

A few minutes later they took the elevator to the third floor and went into the soft room, a room where suspects were interrogated.

Side by side, Crawford and Rutledge walked to the front of the room, then turned to face the six detectives already present. Rutledge folded his arms and nodded to Crawford.

"Okay, listen up," Crawford said. "I don't know how much you guys know, but here's the long and the short: A Russian named Evsei Nemchenov is our target. The guy's scary dangerous and we gotta put him away. Like right now. Today. Chances are he's with a woman—blonde, tall, late twenties, probably Slavic. I want all of you fitted out with throat mikes and earpieces. Drago, get three uniforms and go to the airport. Put out a BOLO with all the airlines, especially international ones. We don't know exactly what the guy's up to, but he's not going to hang around forever. Get copies of this picture of him out to everyone who could have run across him already or who might in the future."

Crawford pulled out a stack of nine-by-twelve glossies Gus Wilmer had taken of Evsei the day they were at the airport searching the Zinovievs' plane.

"Guy knows we're after him, and he's maybe wearing something covering a big tattoo on his neck," Crawford said, pointing at the picture. "Bernstein, you go to the private airport with a uniform and check Talon Air. Take a bunch of these with you and see if anyone's seen him."

Drago and Bernstein nodded, took a few glossies from him, and walked out.

Crawford looked around at the others and saw Shimkus slip into the room.

"Shim, you and Sullivan, get out the yellow pages and start calling every hotel, motel, and fleabag within a twenty-mile radius. Fax 'em a picture of this guy and ask if anyone fitting Evsei's description is staying there."

"There gotta be a hundred places on Dixie alone," said Sullivan.

"Yeah, so?" Crawford said. "Make a hundred calls."

Shimkus and Sullivan walked up to him, took a handful of pictures, and walked out of the room.

Kerns, Williams, Bayliss, and Gonzales were the ones left.

"Kerns and Williams, here's what I need you to do," Crawford said. "Stake out the Russians' house, see who comes and goes. Keep an eye out for someone sneaking up to the house, from the beach, maybe. The judge just authorized it, so go get the papers from him. It's Judge Canet."

Kerns nodded and he and Williams walked out.

Crawford turned to Rutledge.

"About how many houses are vacant this time of year, Norm?" he asked.

Rutledge thought for a second. "Probably about fifty percent."

"You guys got a big job," Crawford said, turning to Bayliss and Gonzales. "That's why I saved you for last. Go around first and check houses that are closed up; you know, shuttered or whatever. Start at the Zinoviev residence and fan out from there. Keep an eye out for a light on, a car parked around back, anything suspicious. If you see something funny, try to figure out how to get inside. Call around to real-estate offices: They have keys to lots of houses. Once you're in, be real careful. One possibility is this guy and the girl might have already broken into a place."

As Bayliss and Gonzales started to walk out, Crawford called to them.

"You guys be careful," he said. "Guy's a stone-cold killer."

Gonzales nodded.

Now it was just Ott, Rutledge, and him.

"Mort, I'm thinking you and I just cruise, keep track of everybody," Crawford said. "Norm, how 'bout you? Stay here and monitor everything?"

"Yeah, but I want you guys to check back with me from time to time," Rutledge said. "No goin' rogue on me now."

"Us?" Crawford said. "We're strictly by-the-book guys."

OTT WAS DRIVING. CRAWFORD WAS COORDINATING THE SEARCH, fielding calls from the different teams. Shimkus called to report that a man matching Evsei's description was staying at the Blue Wave Motel up in Riviera Beach. Crawford ordered him to go there with two other men. But when they got there, it turned out to be a biker with tattoos from head to toe.

Then Gonzales checked in to say that a woman who lived on South Ocean had called to report seeing lights on at her neighbor's house, which had been closed up for the season, and weren't on the day before. Gonzales called her back and found out that the owner had shuttered it last month and had gone home to Chicago. Gonzales drove over and noticed a car that was pulled around to the back of the house. He was running a search on it now. His partner, Rod Bayliss, had circled around to the beach side of the house and Gonzales was covering the front.

Crawford told him they'd be right there. He gave Ott the address. Ott accelerated hard, snapping Crawford's head back.

"Whoa. We out at Moroso, Mort?"

That was the racetrack out west where Ott had gone to learn how to become the world's oldest stock-car driver in case murder ever dried up in Palm Beach. Ott turned to Crawford, smiled, and patted the steering wheel of his Crown Vic. "Just wanted to see what this old girl's got."

A few minutes later, Ott pulled in to a house on the beach and they saw Gonzales's car behind a hedge in a corner of the driveway. Crawford noticed the front end of a green MINI, sticking out in the back of the house. Gonzales, in the driver's seat of his car, shot them a wave. Ott backed up so that the Crown Vic was blocking the MINI's escape.

Crawford nodded at Ott and pulled his Sig Sauer out of its holster.

"Ready to rock?"

"Ready," Ott said.

Crawford got out of the car, went around, and got into the passenger side of Gonzales's car. Ott slipped into the back seat.

"Did one of you call the people who own the house?" Crawford asked.

"Yeah, I did," Gonzales said. "Owner told me nobody's supposed to be there."

"Okay, what's Bayliss's number?"

Gonzales gave him the cell number and Crawford dialed it.

"Bayliss, it's Crawford. See anything?"

"No, man, nothing."

"All right. Ott and I are going in," Crawford said. "You stay where you are. 'Case they come out the back."

"Copy that."

Crawford punched off.

"You don't want any more backup?" Gonzales asked.

"Nah, we're good. It's just one guy."

Crawford grabbed the door handle, opened it, and got out. Ott did the same.

They walked to the front door, guns drawn.

Crawford reached for the front doorknob, expecting it to be locked, but it wasn't.

He nodded to Ott, then turned the doorknob and pushed the door open. It was pitch-black inside. Ott turned on his flashlight and pointed it straight ahead. They were in a foyer with a powder room off it. Straight ahead was a cavernous living room with a ceiling that had to be sixteen feet high. There was a musty smell, possibly from the dark furniture that looked old and tired.

They took a few steps into the living room, then Crawford held up his hand. They listened. Nothing. Crawford started walking again and Ott stayed with him. They went from the living room to the library, then to the kitchen. Then started up the stairs.

When they got to the landing, they stopped and listened again. They heard voices. Two men were arguing. They walked toward the room it was coming from. One voice sounded familiar. Then he recognized it. Russell Crowe, in a movie he couldn't remember the name of. At the door, Crawford held up his hand. One finger. Then two. Then three.

Crawford burst through the door and saw a blonde woman in bed. He thought she might be one of the women he saw in Vasily Zinoviev's bedroom on the Citation X jet. Ott aimed his gun at the woman and put one finger up to his lips. The woman looked terrified but didn't scream.

Crawford heard a shower running and saw the closed bathroom door. He went to the door, put his left hand on the knob, then threw it open.

A tall, dark-haired man was in the shower, his back to Crawford. Crawford checked his neck. No tattoo.

Then the man turned around. He was a kid—maybe twenty or so. He saw Crawford and his drawn gun and freaked. He bent over, covering himself, then held up his hands and yelled, "Don't shoot! Jesus Christ!"

"Police," Crawford yelled. "Come on out."

The kid came out, grabbing a towel as he did.

"Who the hell are you?" Crawford shouted as the kid dripped water onto the floor.

"Walt Meyer," the kid said, shaking. "Th—this is my grandparents' house."

Crawford glanced into the bedroom.

"Who are you?" Ott asked the girl, turning off the TV set at the head of the bed.

"Miranda," said the girl. "I'm—I'm—"

"She's my girlfriend," explained the kid.

"Your grandparents know you're here?" asked Crawford.

"No, they—"

Crawford was dialing Gonzales.

Gonzales picked up.

"False alarm, man. Tell Bayliss," he said, then turned back to the kid. "What are you doing here?"

"We just came down," the kid said, "to get away from school for a few days."

"What school?"

"Rollins."

Crawford shook his head. "Here's what you're gonna do. Call your grandparents, tell 'em about your bright idea."

He turned to the girl and realized she was probably ten years younger than the Russian girl on the jet.

The kid nodded. "Yes, sir, I will."

"I find out you didn't, I'm comin' up to your school and handcuffing you in front of all your frat bros."

He and Ott left the room and ran down the staircase. When he got to the front door, Crawford kicked it open so hard it made a small dent in the solid mahogany.

Outside the house, Crawford glanced over at the kid's green MINI, then to Gonzales, who was walking toward him. Then he swung back to the green MINI. It reminded him of the car he had seen Dominica McCarthy and Aleksandr Zinoviev in a few days before.

He pulled out his cell and dialed fast.

Norm Rutledge answered.

"Norm, I bet I know what our guy's driving," he said. "It's a green Aston Martin. Aleksandr Zinoviev's car. It wasn't in the garage when we were up there yesterday. Can you get the chopper in the air, have the guy go down every street until he spots it?"

Silence. Then: "What if it's in a garage?"

That would be Rutledge's response.

FORTY-EIGHT

"I am just curious, what is your net worth?" Evsei asked P.D. Miller in the parking lot of John Smith Subs.

Miller just laughed. It was amusing—bizarre, actually—the Neanderthal thug asking him a *Wall Street Journal* reporter kind of question.

John Smith Subs had the usual collection of Toyotas and Chevy beaters parked there. His Bentley and Evsei's green Aston Martin—formerly Vasily Zinoviev's green Aston Martin—stood out like thirty-karat diamonds in a coal bin.

Miller ignored Evsei's question.

"Why'd you come back, anyway?" he asked, even though he knew the answer.

"I thought about things right after I took off on your plane," he said. "How cold it is in Russia. How there's no ocean. No good strip clubs. I went up to your pilot, offered him a lot of money to stop in Atlanta."

"They let you land?" Miller asked.

"Your pilot was very persuasive," Evsei said. "Told the people it was a medical emergency."

"I repeat my question: Why did you come back?" Miller asked.

Evsei smiled, revealing bulbous gums and nicotine-stained teeth. "I decided if I was going to live in a place that had no ocean and shitty strip clubs, I needed a lot more money."

Miller just waited.

"Twenty million dollars," Evsei said. "That's like a tip to you."

Miller shook his head.

"So let me get this straight," he said. "You want twenty million dollars for what?"

"For a nice, quiet life in Sochi," Evsei said. "Or somewhere warm like that."

Miller was so sick of all these Russians holding him up all the time.

He had his Ruger on him. He felt like just popping him right here and being done with the whole damn thing.

"I've seen this movie before," Miller said.

Evsei looked puzzled.

"You'll just come back again in a few years and want more."

"Mr. Miller, it is much harder to spend twenty million dollars in Russia than here," said Evsei. "I promise you, you will never hear from me again."

He had heard their promises before. He had totally had it with them making deals, then breaking them. Bastards had absolutely no integrity at all.

"So I suppose you expect me to just write you a check right here and now?" Miller said, leaning forward and starting his engine.

"No," Evsei said, "you can have until the end of the day."

Miller shook his head and smiled contemptuously.

"So do we have a deal, Mr. Miller?" asked Evsei.

"No, Evsei, we do not have a deal. I'll wire five million to an account in Russia, but first, you have to go there. And stay there."

"Fifteen million," Evsei demanded.

"No way."

Evsei just stared Miller down, hoping he could intimidate him with all his tattoos, scowls, and nasty looks.

But Miller just smiled and put the Bentley in drive. "Five million. I'll wire it to you over there. Then you can open your own strip club."

FORTY-NINE

CRAWFORD'S CELL PHONE RANG WHEN HE AND OTT WERE headed north on South Ocean Road.

"Crawford," he answered.

"Hi, this is Brisbane in the chopper," the man said. "I got a green Aston Martin coming over the South Bridge from West Palm."

"Can you see the driver?"

"No."

"Okay, thanks," Crawford said. "Stay on him."

"You got it."

Crawford fist-pumped Ott. "Our guy may be coming over the South Bridge."

Ott didn't hesitate. He pulled a hard U-turn, going a few feet onto a lawn, then stomped on the accelerator. Tires squealing, the Crown Vic Interceptor's modular V-8 roared as it headed into the sharp turn right after Mar-a-Lago.

Suddenly a green car, coming around the bend, came into sight.

Crawford recognized it as an Aston Martin. "That's the car," he said.

Ott pulled over to the side of the road and waited.

A few seconds later, the car passed them. The driver looked over. It was Evsei.

He recognized them.

"Okay, Mort, let's see what this thing can do."

Ott didn't have to be told. He goosed the accelerator and yanked the wheel hard left. The Vic got back onto the pavement and left a thirty-foot long patch behind it.

Evsei had a big jump and the Aston Martin was up to seventy already.

Crawford dialed the dispatcher:

"This is Crawford," he said. "We're right behind our perp, Evsei Nemchenov. Girl's not with him. We're at Clarendon and South Ocean going north. I need all units in play."

"Ten-four," the dispatcher said.

"Stay with me on the phone," Crawford said, then he looked over at Ott. "Just pretend you're out at Moroso."

Ott smiled. He was not backing down, but the Aston Martin had a big head start. Not to mention a lot more agility than the Vic.

Suddenly Evsei took a left off of Ocean onto South County Road.

"Okay, off Ocean onto County now," Crawford said, "just before the turn to Everglades Island."

"Got it," said dispatch.

It flashed through Crawford's mind that it was going to get hairy if they got into the commercial part of Palm Beach, both going like a bat out of hell. A lot of people would be walking around there, crossing the streets. His mind was going as fast as the Vic, which wasn't going fast enough.

There was no time to get a roadblock set up.

"Block the middle and north bridges," Crawford said into his phone.

"Copy," the dispatcher said.

All of a sudden, Evsei changed direction, almost like he was in Crawford's head. He hit his brake and Crawford heard the whining of a downshift as Evsei skidded onto El Vedato. Then the Aston

Martin's tires squealed loudly as it accelerated straight toward the Intracoastal. Ott was doing well, not losing ground. Crawford glanced over. His partner was all gritted teeth, unblinking eyes, and race-car-driver intensity.

"Suspect's on El Brillo," Crawford said. "You got someone in the area, send 'em down Jungle to cut him off."

"Nobody's that close yet," said dispatch. "Bernstein's comin' up Ocean."

All of a sudden the Aston Martin skidded off the road. Crawford realized it was intentional. Evsei took a ninety-degree left turn between two Brazilian palms and through the backyard of a brick British Colonial. They caught up in time to see the Aston Martin crash through a low ficus hedge.

———

To Leon Barnes, it was a pretty straightforward job the woman had hired him for: Find a Russian guy driving a green sports car with a big tattoo on his neck and smoke him. But, as it turned out, the cops were making it even easier. Leon had picked up the cops chasing the guy on his police scanner. As his car idled in a restaurant parking lot, Leon chambered a cartridge into the M14, put the butt of the rifle down on the floor on the passenger side with the barrel resting on the seat, and floored it. He didn't want to get in between the cops and his target. He wanted to get ahead of them, take out the Russian, then score a nice, big payday. He had some debts to pay off and had his eye on a Sony 85-inch 4K UHDTV. Sucker went for pretty close to fifteen grand.

There were three possible outcomes to the cops' chase: One, they'd catch the guy and he'd surrender. Two, the guy would get away. Or three, the cops would kill him.

Two out of three of those scenarios didn't work for Leon or the woman who had hired him. He knew he didn't have much time.

OTT MADE A SPLIT-SECOND DECISION TO TAKE THE NARROW north-south road that connected El Bravo to Jungle. Problem was, it was slower and less direct than Evsei's route. He jammed the accelerator to the floor, but the road was bumpy. When they got to Via Bellaria, Crawford looked left and saw the Aston Martin pull onto South County, going south this time.

Ott punched it and it took a second for the squealing tires to get traction.

Crawford spoke into his throat mike: "Any unit around South County and Mar-a-Lago, block the road. We're headed south now."

"Roger that," said someone whose voice he didn't recognize.

Then Crawford, not turning his head, said, "Make up the distance, Mort."

A car suddenly came out of Banyan. Ott had almost no time to react. He jerked the wheel hard and Crawford heard metal screech as the Crown Vic nicked the other car and kept going.

"Thatta boy," Crawford said.

Ott was too focused to even hear him.

They were coming up to the intersection of Ocean and County now. Ott craned his neck to the left as they approached the stop sign. He saw no one coming and gunned it. Just as he did, Crawford saw the Aston Martin go right onto Clarendon Street, two hundred yards ahead. Then he saw why. Two marked cars were perpendicular on South Ocean, blocking the way. Crawford couldn't see the uniforms, but figured they were down behind the cars.

Then he saw Bernstein pull up behind the uniforms. He knew it was him because he had the only unmarked Taurus.

A second later, Ott took the turn onto Clarendon, fishtailing again, his tires smoking. Then he slammed on the brakes and skidded up to within ten feet of the Aston Martin. Its door was open and it was stopped in the middle of the road.

Crawford, with his gun out, was trying to make out Evsei through the screen of blue and gray smoke from both cars tires.

Then he spotted him, running toward the Intracoastal. Crawford thought about yelling for him to surrender, but knew that was a waste of time.

He glanced over at Ott, who looked like he had just done fifteen rounds with Muhammad Ali.

"Let's go," Crawford said, as another car screeched to a skidding stop right behind them.

It was Shimkus and Drago.

Crawford yelled to them, pointing. "Up there."

They nodded. Shimkus pumped a shell into his shotgun and started running. Drago unholstered his automatic and took off down the street. Evsei was just about at the Intracoastal. He had two choices: Jump in and swim for it or go left along the Intracoastal. He couldn't go right because of an eight-foot stucco wall that ran up to the water.

Evsei'd be a sitting duck in the water, Crawford knew, so his only play was to go left and try to lose them on foot or maybe take a hostage somewhere along the way.

Shimkus and Drago were fifty feet behind Crawford, who was running as fast as he had since lacrosse in college. Crawford suddenly veered to his left and took a shortcut through a stand of sabal palms in an attempt to cut off Evsei. Ott, twenty feet back, took the same course.

"Bernstein, you still on Ocean?" Crawford said into his throat mike.

"Yeah," said Bernstein. "I'm here."

"Get over to the Southern Bridge. Work your way up towards Mar-a-Lago. He's comin' that way on foot."

"Roger that," said Bernstein.

"Take him alive," Crawford said, "if you can."

Leon Barnes heard Crawford's order to Bernstein and figured odds were pretty good that he'd have a clean shot. He was coming down Flagler just north of the Southern Bridge. The chase was going on directly across from him, on the other side of the Intracoastal. He figured his shot would be either from the bridge or just on the other side of it. He knew he had to get in position quick.

He started taking long, deep breaths the way he always did. His relaxation technique.

Crawford was just past Woodbridge Street now, cutting through the backyard of a house. Ott was a little behind him. Crawford couldn't see Evsei up ahead.

"Shim, where are you?" he asked.

"Going along the water; subjects's thirty yards ahead of me," said Shimkus, panting. "Should I take him?"

"No, I want him alive if we can," Crawford said. "Bernstein, where are you?"

"Just south of Mar-a-Lago. That little beach there," Bernstein said.

"Good," said Crawford, "we got all sides covered."

Leon could see the guy he'd just heard on the scanner. The one named Bernstein. He was on one knee on a little beach, his pump gun aimed, just waiting. A Crown Vic, its lights flashing, was blocking the bridge up ahead of Leon now. He guessed it was the one named Bernstein's car. That he had positioned it there so no civilians could drive over and get in the line of fire. There were a lot of cars on the bridge, headed east toward the ocean, blocked by Bernstein's Crown Vic. Several of them started backing up, having realized they couldn't get through. Leon waved at the driver of a car between him and the cops' Vic to back around him.

The guy gave him a dirty look as he backed past.

Leon was still doing his breathing exercises. He felt like his pulse was slower now. He reached over for the M14, his favorite piece. He adjusted the scope. Then he looked behind him. Everyone had turned around and gone back off the bridge. He pushed the button to lower the window. Then he rested the barrel of the rifle on the window frame and sighted in Bernstein.

Boom, he said to himself, imagining Bernstein was the Russian.

Taking the Russian out was going to be a piece of cake, assuming the guy got into his line of sight before the cops got him.

He shifted his aim farther north, the direction Evsei would be coming from. It was like a cattle drive, the cops chasing the target right into his crosshairs.

Then he saw him.

Exactly how he had been described. Through his scope he saw the sweat-shiny tattoo on his neck. Two cops about fifty yards behind him, chasing him. Then, off to the right, another one, even closer.

Evsei suddenly raised his hands in surrender. He had spotted Bernstein in front of him down on one knee, aiming at his chest. Evsei had stopped and was facing him.

Leon slowly exhaled.

Calmly, he squeezed the trigger.

Boom. The explosion reverberated in the car.

Evsei fell backwards. Leon saw a flash of blood on his chest, exactly where he had aimed.

Bull's-eye.

The cop nearest the Russian looked up and yelled something into his throat mike.

Leon tossed the rifle through the open window over the side of the bridge. He turned on the ignition and jammed the car into reverse. Then he swung the wheel hard, did a backwards U, and gunned it. In a few seconds, he was at the crest of the bridge.

That's when he saw the two Chargers, lights flashing but no siren, screech to a stop on the far side of the bridge. One cop, inside his car, was aiming something at him outside his window. He couldn't tell whether it was a rifle or a pistol. Another one jumped out, a shotgun in his hands, and took a position on the other side of his car. He rested the shotgun on the roof of the car and aimed. The man inside his car now had a bullhorn in his left hand, and Leon could see an automatic in his right.

"Hold it right there," the voice said through the bullhorn. "Stop your car and get out—hands on your head then down on the pavement."

Crawford could see the whole thing play out from where he was. After a few moments, the man opened his car door, got out, and put his hands up.

It was complete luck, Crawford knew: Gonzales and Bayliss being where they were when he put out the call.

Every once in a while, you caught a break.

FIFTY

EVSEI WASN'T GOING TO MAKE IT, THAT MUCH WAS CLEAR TO Crawford. The Russian was looking up at him with vacant, flickering shark eyes as Crawford called for an ambulance anyway.

Evsei was on his side, his head wrenched around like a doll that had been tossed across a room.

Then his breathing stopped and his eyes froze into a dead man's stare.

GONZALES AND BAYLISS HAD TAKEN IN THE HITTER, WHO THEY'D ID'd as Leon Barnes, and put him in the basement jail of the station house on South County. He was just down the hall from Nikita.

It was time for Crawford to talk to him. He had gone to his computer and found a sheet on the guy. It was a long one, dating back to when Barnes was sixteen years old.

Crawford walked down to the basement and approached the cell. Leon was a light-skinned black man who weighed in at over two hundred pounds and had long, braided hair.

Crawford pulled up a metal folding chair in front of Leon's cell door and peered in through the bars.

"My name's Detective Crawford," he said. "How 'bout we have a little chat?"

Leon shrugged.

"Just so you know, Leon, we got you cold on that residue test," Crawford said.

When they first brought him in, they had found trace particles of the explosive primer from a gun all over his right hand and shirt.

"You got the wrong guy," Leon said.

"Whatever you say," Crawford said.

Leon scowled.

"Next thing we're gonna do is match you up to the murder weapon," Crawford went on.

Crawford had seen Leon throw a rifle into the water. The scuba guys were in the water now looking for it.

"It wasn't me," said Leon.

Crawford nodded. "Let me ask you: Have you thought this through, Leon? Your options aren't all that promising."

Leon gave him a blank look.

"Way I see it," Crawford said, "you're either gonna get the gas or someone inside's gonna take you out."

"You talkin' about, man?" said Leon.

"That guy who hired you," Crawford said. "P.D. Miller. You're gonna be his next victim."

"Never hearda him," Leon said.

"Well, then, let me tell you about him. He did those Russians, the brothers who got killed. I'm sure you heard about that," Crawford said. "Actually, he hired Evsei—the guy you just capped—to do it. Then you come along and take out Evsei. Seeing any kind of pattern?"

Leon just stared back.

"Pattern is, you're next, bro," Crawford said.

"Told you," Leon said, "don't know what you're talkin' about."

"I'll break it down," Crawford said. "You're in a position to finger Miller. Meaning he's gotta take you out, so you can't finger him."

Leon was trying to look bored with the whole thing. But he wasn't pulling it off too well. A few sweat beads had broken out on his forehead and upper lip.

"Way I figure it," Crawford said, "he'll have a lawyer tell you he's gonna get you off. Promise you a bunch of money to keep quiet. Then a few days later, he's gonna have a guy—a guy just like you—make sure you keep quiet on a permanent basis."

Leon seemed to be listening more attentively now.

"I said I didn't do it."

Crawford pushed back the chair. "Okay, okay. I don't want to hear your broken record any more."

Crawford walked out and went back upstairs to his office.

He wanted to get back to Rose Clarke. She had said it was important. He looked at his watch; her showing would be over now.

He dialed her number from his office.

"Rose, it's Charlie," he said when she answered.

"Hey, Charlie," she said. "You all right?"

The woman never failed to amaze him. How her radar picked things up five minutes after they happened. "You heard about—"

"A guy was killed?"

"Yeah."

"Can you come over?" she asked.

"I'm kinda right in the middle of something," he said.

"It's important," she responded.

"Okay, but it's gotta be quick."

"Typical," she said, "slam-bam, thank-you-ma'am."

But just as he was about to get in his car, she called back.

"I'm sorry, I didn't realize it was so late," she said. "Can I meet you at my open house instead?"

"Sure, where is it?"

"On Eden Way. Two-twenty-three."

CRAWFORD GOT THERE JUST IN TIME TO SEE HER SILVER JAG roll up in front of the house. He watched her get out and pull an OPEN HOUSE sign from her car trunk and plunk it down in the front yard facing the street.

He turned off the ignition and took in the house. He figured it was on the low end of Rose's typical listing. A mere four or five million, he guessed.

He walked in as she was putting brochures and some kind of a sign-in book on a table.

"So," he said, admiring the sweeping circular staircase up to the second floor, "how much do you want for this little beauty?"

"For you, five-point-five. Everyone else, six," she said, and came over to him. They exchanged a single-cheeker.

Rose was dressed to sell. A charcoal-gray suit that showed a lot of leg, a beige silk shirt, fairly light on the bling.

"So, I'm all ears," he said.

Rose looked at him like a stern hostess eyeballing a gauche houseguest. "You know what I think, Charlie?"

"No, what?" he asked, not sure what he had done wrong this time.

"You need to brush up on your foreplay a little," she said. "It's always straight to business."

"I'm sorry," he said. "Just got a lot goin' on."

Rose nodded. "Anyway, so last night I had dinner with P.D. Miller at Amici."

She had Crawford's full, undivided attention. Must have been right before he went to Miller's house. "Yeah, and?"

"We had a few drinks and then a bottle of wine at dinner and he's telling me all about his Harvard Business School reunion—" She noticed Crawford was about to cut in. "I know, I know, 'cut to the chase, Rose.' So, he tells me about this new house he's building. Renovating, actually. On two hundred and ten acres right smack in the middle of Palm Beach."

It hit Crawford like the proverbial ton of bricks.

"Only place that big is the Poinciana."

"Bingo."

"He bought it?" Crawford asked, the adrenaline starting to pound.

Rose nodded.

"Who'd he buy it from?" he asked.

"I don't know exactly," she said. "Guys on the Poinciana Executive Committee, I guess."

"And what's he going to do with it?"

Rose started to walk in tight little circles.

"That's the amazing part," she said. "He's going to live there."

"What do you mean, live there? It's a club," said Crawford.

"I'm aware of that, Charlie. I've lived in this town a little longer than you," she said. "He told me he's going to do a major renovation to the main club-house building and live in it."

So, the Russians had been Miller's front.

The whole luxury-condo development scenario...one big diversionary tactic.

Crawford tried to picture one man padding around inside the cavernous Poinciana.

Cozy didn't come to mind.

"He's already got plans drawn up, he told me," Rose said. "Plus, he quietly negotiated to buy another house close to it—on the Intracoastal—just so he could have a dock for his Feadship."

Crawford had no idea what a Feadship was, but figured it was big and expensive.

"I was the broker on that deal," Rose added with a dry smile.

"Of course you were," Crawford said. "So he's gonna turn the Poinciana into his personal residence. What's he gonna do with the golf course?"

"Fix it up, make it his own private golf course."

"You're kidding," Crawford said, shaking his head. "I don't get it."

"What don't you get?"

"I mean, why's he doing all this? I understand wanting to have a big house and a big boat, but—"

"Charlie, that's just it: You'll never understand a guy like P. D. Miller. I'm not sure I do either, but as usual, I have a theory," Rose said. "He's a man who started with nothing. A nothing little guy from nowhere. There are a lot of men like him who—even with the biggest house and the biggest boat around—still think, deep down, they're nothing."

"Wow, that's pretty heavy, Rose," Crawford said. "You a shrink too?"

Rose laughed. "In my business, you have to be."

Crawford's cell rang.

He clicked it.

"Yeah, Mort," he said.

"I got something big, Charlie," Ott said.

"Guarantee you, whatever you got, I got something bigger," Crawford said.

"Well, just listen a minute," Ott said. "When you sent Shimkus down to the airport he showed around that picture of Evsei. Some guy saw it and said, 'Oh yeah, I saw that guy get into a green sports car in the main parking lot yesterday.'"

"So?"

"So, it *was* Evsei on Miller's plane. Turns out he got off in Atlanta. An unscheduled stop. Then he got a car at Avis and drove back here."

Crawford let it sink in.

"So he must have thought it over," Crawford said. "Figured he could squeeze Miller for a big, early retirement score."

"Exactly," Ott said.

"Good work, Mort," Crawford said. "But I still got you topped. Meet me at the station in a half hour, I'll tell you what I got."

Crawford hung up, then looked up at Rose.

"Rose, I owe you big. Like Café Boulud big, with three bottles of expensive French wine."

She smiled.

"I accept. No more IOUs. Plus," she said with a wink, "I'd love it if you paid another visit to my pool, once you've rounded up all the bad guys."

He smiled and stood to go.

"Where are your open-house people, anyway?" he asked.

"It's slow this time of year."

He went over and gave her a kiss on the cheek.

"Thanks for everything," he said.

They both heard a shuffling sound and turned.

A wizened man in long green shorts and a gray cardigan, black elastic socks up over his puny calves, walked in and spotted them.

Crawford had a hunch who he was.

"Oh, hi," said Rose, giving the man a big smile. She went over and gave him a peck on his liver-spotted cheek. "This is my friend, Charlie Crawford. Charlie, this is Dirk Burke."

Yup.

The old man looked Crawford over disapprovingly. Crawford reached out and shook his limp hand.

"So, are you a realtor, too, Lawford?" Burke asked.

Rose laughed and said, "No, Mr. Burke, he's a detective. Palm Beach's finest. And it's Crawford."

"A detective?" Burke said. "Well, hell, shouldn't you be out solving those murders instead of tomcatting around in here?"

Crawford flicked him a salute.

"I'll get right on it, Mr. Burke," he said, starting to walk away. Then he stopped. "Oh, by the way, the sound system in this house is amazing. Old Blue Eyes never sounded better."

Rose struggled to suppress a laugh.

FIFTY-ONE

CRAWFORD HAD ONE THING TO DO BEFORE HE WENT AFTER P.D. Miller. He wanted to get David Balfour's take on the man. Balfour had money invested with Miller, so chances were good he could shed some light on him.

He called Balfour on his cell phone, got his machine, and left a quick message. Then he called him at home.

"Hello?" Balfour answered.

"David, it's Charlie Crawford," he said. "Mind if I stop by for a few minutes?"

"Yeah, sure, Charlie, come on over."

FIFTEEN MINUTES LATER, CRAWFORD PUSHED THE BUZZER AT David Balfour's house. Balfour opened the door. His hair was wet and he had a big, fluffy white towel around his waist.

"Hey, Charlie, come on in," Balfour said, shaking Crawford's hand. "Just doing a few laps."

Crawford followed Balfour through the house and out back to a loggia overlooking the pool. Balfour sat down in a wrought-iron pool chair covered in a blue pad.

"I heard the Poinciana got sold," Crawford said.

A deep frown cut into Balfour's face.

"Yeah, you believe it? I'm just hoping we can get it back somehow, now that the Russians are dead."

"Don't count on it," Crawford said. "They sold it right before they died."

"What?" said Balfour, leaning forward.

"To your friend, P.D. Miller."

"You gotta be kidding," said Balfour, enunciating each word like he was speaking to a small child.

"He's going to make it into his very own personal kingdom," Crawford said. "Complete with his own private golf course."

Balfour took a long sip from a bottle of water. He had a faraway look, like he was connecting dots.

"Now that I think about it," he said, "that actually doesn't surprise me much."

"Really? So, tell me about the guy, will you?" said Crawford. "You've got money invested with him; you know him."

Balfour slowly shook his head. "Problem is, there are so many bullshit stories out there about him."

"Like what?" asked Crawford.

"Well, I read this article somewhere—actually in some credible magazine like Forbes or something—about Miller growing up in Texas, one of those hardscrabble, one-room schoolhouse childhoods. Then supposedly, five years after that he's summa cum laude at Harvard Business School. I mean, it's all total bullshit. I know for a fact he grew up right here in West Palm. He was this little hustler, I heard. Used to caddie at the Poinciana."

Crawford nodded, sensing that might have taken on major significance in Miller's life.

"When he was eighteen, he went to Vietnam, volunteered to be one of those tunnel rats—"

"Wait, where'd you get this from?" Crawford asked, scribbling fast in his murder book.

"Right off his résumé," Balfour said. "He tried to get into the Poinciana three years ago."

"And?" Crawford said.

"Got hit with an avalanche of blackballs," said Balfour.

"Why?"

"All the money in the world couldn't buy his way in," Balfour said. "The long knives came out."

"What do you mean? Why?"

"Miller made a bunch of enemies in the business world. I mean, the guy's ego was one thing, but a few Poinciana members were at the wrong end of his deals. I guess he had a few bad ones when he first started out. Investors lost money, but not Miller. One guy even swore Miller was psychotic," Balfour said, pausing to dry his wet hair with the towel.

Crawford looked up from his notes. "What else was on his résumé?"

"Well, after he got back from Vietnam—this is actually something I heard from another guy—he got a scholarship to Stetson and hooked up with this rich kid from up north. The kid had all kinds of connections. Miller figured he could use him, I heard. After college, they raised some money from the guy's parents, blew it all, raised some more, bought a little company, then sold it and made a small fortune. At that point, Miller cut the guy loose and went solo. Didn't need him anymore."

"He's got a bunch of investments in Russia, right?" Crawford asked.

"Yeah, huge oil and gas holdings, largest shareholder in the second-biggest bank over there too. He went in right after communism flamed out," Balfour said. "Supposedly hired himself these Red Army guys—they were his muscle. Strong-armed his way in. We're not talking a J.P. Morgan, Goldman Sachs kind of guy here."

"I get that," Crawford said. "When did he start his fund?"

"Right around then. About twenty years ago or so," Balfour said. "He's got something like ten billion under management now. Supposedly he personally made two-hundred-thirty million last year."

"So buying the Poinciana—"

"Chump change," said Balfour, nodding.

Crawford did some quick math.

"And killing seven people?"

"I don't know," Balfour said grimly, "the cost of doing business maybe?"

"So you're telling me people invest billions of dollars with a guy like him?"

Balfour nodded. "In a heartbeat," he said, "if they get a thirty-percent return."

Crawford nodded. "One thing I don't get at all," he said.

"What's that?"

"The Poinciana is now completely tainted. With murder and every other crime under the sun. It's like it's been poisoned..." He smiled as it clicked. "Come to think of it, it *has* been poisoned, plus it's got blood all over it."

Balfour thought for a second, then shrugged. "Miller doesn't give a shit," he said. "Not like it's his blood."

FIFTY-TWO

CRAWFORD WENT AND LOOKED AT WHAT THE SCUBA GUYS HAD brought up from the bottom of the Intracoastal. It looked like a tag sale of rusty and gunk-coated items. There was a standing lamp that still had a hundred-watt bulb in it, a valuable-looking table missing a leg, a full set of golf clubs in a heavy leather bag that looked like it hadn't been in the water that long. Like somebody had a bad eighteen and tossed them over the side of the bridge on their way back home.

Crawford pulled a five-hundred-dollar Big Bertha driver out of the golf bag, thinking it might help him drive the ball further than his old Nike Sasquatch.

Then he had a better idea.

He put the oversized head of the driver up to his shoulder and aimed it. It was time to pay Leon Barnes another visit.

"LEON," CRAWFORD SAID, PULLING UP A CHAIR NEXT TO THE man's cell door, "guess what the scuba guys just brought up from under the bridge?"

Leon tried to maintain his world-weary look.

"Hint: it's long and skinny," Crawford said, putting up his arms as if he was aiming a rifle. "And, I'm sure, it has your fingerprints all over it. My guys just dusted it. You thought about what I said?"

"About what?"

"About being next on Miller's hit list."

"Don't know any dude named Mill—"

"Cut the shit, man," Crawford said. "I told you we found it. Want me to bring it down and show it to you?"

He was ninety percent sure Leon wouldn't call his bluff.

Leon was silent.

"You ever take any history back in high school?" Crawford asked.

Leon just evil-eyed him and swatted at a fly.

"'Cause they got this saying, something like, 'Guys who don't learn from history are doomed to repeat it.'"

Leon scratched his chin. "The hell's that s'posed to mean?"

It came out as one long word.

"I'll spell it out," Crawford said. "See, Miller's history is killing people. And you... you're in the on-deck circle."

Crawford looked into Leon's eyes. He guessed Leon knew baseball.

"Like I said before," Crawford said. "First, Miller gets Evsei to take out the Russians with the sarin, then you take out Evsei with the gun we found, then...well, you get the idea."

Crawford paused. He could see he had the hook into him.

"I mean, there are two ways to go," Crawford went on. "You cop a plea, the prosecutor spares you a date with Old Sparky. Or, you do what Miller wants you to do: Keep your mouth shut, then one night when you're off in dreamland..."

"What's your offer?" Leon demanded.

Crawford shrugged. "I don't have the authority to offer you anything, my man."

"How 'bout like ten years?" Leon said, animated for the first time.

Crawford smiled and leaned back in the plastic chair. "That's a tad optimistic, I'd say, Leon."

"What then?"

"First, you gotta sign a confession. Say you did it. Miller hired you. Then I put in a good word. The prosecutor, he likes guys who cooperate."

"First you gotta tell me what I get," Leon demanded.

Crawford stood up.

"Leon, I don't gotta tell you shit," he said and started to walk away.

Then he turned back.

"You ever watch CNN?" Crawford asked.

"Never heard of it."

"That's kinda your mantra, Leon."

"Huh?"

"Nothing,'" Crawford said. "So this reporter did a story on Miller once, which, I guess, wasn't too complimentary. Then the reporter mysteriously disappeared. Never heard from him ever again. Some people think he's right next to Jimmy Hoffa. End zone of Giants Stadium."

Leon's eyes narrowed and his toes started tapping fast.

Crawford walked away, sorry Ott wasn't around to hear the last one. It wasn't as good as the retina slide, but it was up there.

FIFTY-THREE

WHEN CRAWFORD GOT BACK TO HIS OFFICE, HE HAD A MESSAGE to see Rutledge. He went down the hallway and walked in. Rutledge looked up.

"Barnes is bonding out," Rutledge said.

"You gotta be kidding."

"I just found out," he said.

"On what grounds?"

"We got no murder weapon," Rutledge answered. "No hard evidence."

The Big Bertha driver wasn't going to cut it.

"But I saw him toss the gun. And what about the GSR?"

"Not enough, we gotta have the gun," said Rutledge. "That was the judge's call."

"I just came from the guy's cell," Crawford said. "As of two minutes ago, he didn't know anything about bonding out."

Rutledge shrugged. "What can I tell you?"

Crawford turned and walked out.

On his way back to his office, Crawford realized that maybe this was the best thing that could have happened. He went back down to

Leon's cell, dragged the folding metal chair out in front of his cell again, and straddled it.

Leon was lying on his back, studying the ceiling.

"You look like a goddamn corpse, Leon," Crawford said.

Leon snapped up into a sitting position. "What'd he say?" he asked, his eyes bugged out.

"What'd *who* say?" asked Crawford.

"The prosecutor."

"You thought I was going to speak to the prosecutor?" Crawford asked.

Leon's shoulders slumped forward and a frown creased his face.

"What about? I had nothing to say to him," said Crawford with a shrug.

"You know, if I cooperated?" Leon said.

"Yeah, but, you haven't," Crawford said, getting up from the chair. "Doesn't matter now, anyway."

"What are you talking about?" Leon said, swinging his feet around so he was sitting on the edge of the bed.

"'Cause, my brother, you're hittin' the streets."

Leon's face didn't reflect the jubilation of someone about to be sprung from jail. "What you talkin' about, man?"

"Your lawyer posted and you're bonding out."

"What lawyer?" Leon's right leg on top of his left started jiggling fast.

"The one Miller provided you with, I assume."

"Hey man, why didn't you go to the prosecutor?"

"I already told you."

Leon started furiously itching his three-day old growth.

"Maybe it'll all work out in the end, Leon."

Leon didn't look as though he had much faith in that. "Can you talk to him now?"

"Your lawyer's going to be here any second."

Leon put his hands tightly around the bars.

"I'm stayin'," he said.

"Sorry," Crawford said, turning to go.

"Please, man, come on," Leon pleaded.

Crawford turned back. "If I keep you in here, you're gonna do exactly what I tell you, right?"

Leon didn't respond.

Crawford turned again to go.

"All right, all right," Leon said.

LEON'S ATTORNEY GOT THERE FORTY-FIVE MINUTES LATER. HE was a guy Crawford had run across once before. He had been instructed to go to Crawford's office.

"Detective," he said, "nice to see you again."

"Yeah," said Crawford, standing up and folding his arms.

The attorney smiled and rocked back and forth on his heels. "He ready?"

"Who?"

"Leon Barnes."

"Leon? He's history."

"What do you mean?" The lawyer's eyes got big. "You're supposed to release him to my custody."

"Well, theoretically," Crawford said, "but Leon got sick of waiting. And, I figured, why not let him go? We can't hold him."

The attorney's face went slack.

"Seriously. Where'd he go?" the lawyer asked, impatiently.

"I don't know," Crawford said.

"Well, shit," the lawyer said, his hand scratching the back of his head. "That's just not protocol."

Crawford just shrugged as the lawyer turned and stormed out.

Crawford walked back to Ott's cubicle, where Leon Barnes was slouched down in a chair facing Ott's desk, a handcuff on his wrist attached to another one around his ankle.

Crawford walked around his desk and sat down. "Okay, Leon," he said, "Miller's guy came and went."

"Can you take these things off me?"

"Not yet," Crawford said. "You don't have that high a trust quotient."

Leon shook his head. "When I told you before I didn't know no guy named Miller, I wasn't lyin'."

Crawford eyed him closely.

"Then who hired you?"

"Some woman," Leon said.

"What's her name?"

"Never said," Leon answered. "Just told me to call this other woman, who'd tell me where to meet up. So, I called the other woman, told me to meet her at this place."

"So you met her and she told you what the job was?" Crawford asked.

Leon nodded.

"And paid you for it?"

Leon nodded again. "Half of it. We went out to her car, gave me a bag of cash."

Crawford snapped his fingers.

"Perfect. You got a number for her?"

Leon nodded. "Right here."

Leon turned over his wrist. Written on it, in faded blue ink, it said 724- 3401.

"Her number would also come up on your phone," Crawford said.

"Yeah," said Leon, "but it said unknown number."

Ott walked in as Crawford was writing the number down.

"Hey, Charlie." Ott nodded, then he looked over at Leon. "So I'm guessing you must be the dude who took out Evsei?"

"That's him," Crawford said. "But old Leon here just flipped over to the good guys' side."

"Well, welcome aboard," Ott said.

Leon grunted something unintelligible.

"So I'll get you up to speed, Mort," Crawford said to Ott. "Leon here's gonna call the woman who hired him to do Evsei."

"Woman?" Ott said.

"Yeah, we don't have a name yet," Crawford said, typing something on his computer. "Leon's gonna set up a meet so she can give him the other half of the hit money."

"And we'll be hidin' in the bushes?" Ott said.

"Something like that," Crawford said, looking down at his computer. "I've been checkin' the reverse directory to see if I can come up with her name."

"Anything?" Ott asked.

Crawford closed his computer. "Nah, nothing comes up."

He reached into a manila envelope that was sitting on a corner of his desk and pulled out a cell phone.

"Okay, Leon," he said, putting the phone on his desk. "Here's your phone. Give the mystery woman a call."

Crawford walked around his desk and undid the handcuffs.

Leon took the phone. "You mind givin' me back my wallet too?"

Crawford reached back into the manila envelope.

"Sure," Crawford said, "but that money you had in it, we had to confiscate that."

Leon didn't look happy.

"It's evidence, my friend," Crawford said. "So go on, dial her up. And, hey, be chill, huh?"

FIFTY-FOUR

"IT'S LEON," HE SAID INTO THE CELL PHONE. "I WANT THE REST of my money."

Crawford nodded approvingly.

His head was close to Leon's phone, listening in. The woman barely hesitated, said to meet her in the Home Depot parking lot on Okeechobee. Park in an area where there were no other cars around, she told him.

"Same red Lexus?" Leon asked.

She said yes, told him 4:00 that afternoon, and hung up.

Leon clicked off.

"You're a man of few words, Leon," Crawford said. "I like that about you." Then he turned to Ott. "The woman's voice...it was familiar."

"Really?"

"Yeah, I can't remember from where, though," Crawfod said. "It'll come to me."

Leon was driving north on Flagler in West Palm. Crawford was lagging back, a half-block behind him. What Leon didn't know was that if he ever decided to try to lose Crawford, Ott had hidden a GPS device in the trunk of Leon's car. Not only that, Crawford had made Leon wear a Kevlar chest protector, onto which he had attached a tiny microscopic tracking device Leon couldn't see. No way Leon was going to be losing him. Plus, Crawford had done a very convincing job of selling Leon on the fact that he was better off in their protection than out on his own.

Speaking of sell jobs, Crawford and Ott had gone to Rutledge and told him they thought they were getting close to busting the case. It was possible they had exaggerated a little. In any case, Rutledge had authorized the somewhat sketchy, hastily conceived plan they had outlined in his office.

Crawford bought Leon a couple of hamburgers at the Checkerburger on Dixie Highway. A half-hour later, at 3:30, he met Ott at the Home Depot parking lot. Ott brought along Gonzales and Bayliss, just in case they needed backup. They positioned Leon in his jacked-up Nissan Altima equidistant between the Crown Vic Crawford and Ott were in and the Charger that Gonzales and Bayliss drove. All four Palm Beach detectives had slid down in their seats, just able to see out their front windows.

"Haven't figured it out yet," Ott asked, "that woman on the phone?"

"No, not yet. She had an accent, is all I know," Crawford said, looking at the time on the dashboard clock.

It was 3:55.

"What are the odds the woman shows up with the money?" Ott asked.

"You mean, instead of three guys with Uzis?" Crawford said. "I'd say about one in five."

"I'd say one in ten," Ott said.

"I got three squads of under covers ready to seal off the exits," Crawford said.

"I figured you had it covered," Ott said, nodding. "So ten of us altogether?"

Crawford nodded.

"That oughta do it," Ott said.

Crawford looked at his watch again: 4:01. He took his Sig Sauer semi out of its shoulder holster and clicked the safety off. Ott did the same with his Glock.

"Get ready, boys," Crawford said into his throat mike. "Could be just a quiet little meeting, or Fourth of July fireworks."

"My money's on the latter," Ott said.

Crawford hit a button and the driver's side window rolled down.

He looked at his watch again: 4:05.

"What did you expect," Ott said with a shrug. "Women...always late."

Crawford smiled, then a noise off in the distance caught his attention.

"The hell's that?"

"What?" Ott turned to him.

"That sound," Crawford said, scanning the parking lot.

Then Ott heard it.

"That buzzing?" Ott said.

"Yeah."

Both of their heads were zigzagging around the parking lot, trying to see what it was.

"Getting louder," Ott said.

Then Crawford saw it.

"Leon," he shouted into his throat mike, "get the hell out of the car!" Then to the others: "There's a fuckin' drone up there."

Leon's door opened and he bolted from the car, just as a line of bullets cut across the front windshield of his Altima.

Crawford ran out of his car, grabbed Leon, and pulled him toward the Crown Vic.

Ott reached behind him and opened a back door as Crawford

shoved Leon toward it. Leon dived into the back seat like a baseball player going for home plate in the last game of the World Series.

Crawford ran around and got back in the driver's side. The drone was hovering over the Leon's Altima, strafing it with bullets.

Crawford leaned outside his window and aimed his Sig Sauer. "Okay, Mort, let's take it down." Then into the throat mike: "Okay, boys, blow it out of the fucking sky."

Ten sets of automatic weapons opened up on the drone.

FIFTY-FIVE

THE DRONE WAS A SMOKING METAL CARCASS, LYING UPSIDE down five feet from Leon's Altima.

Crawford turned around and looked in the back seat. Leon was trying to look cool, like getting attacked by a drone shooting twenty bullets a second wasn't really such a big deal. But he was sweating like he had just finished a marathon.

"You okay?" Crawford asked.

"Yeah, I'm okay," he said. "You get that thing?"

"We got it," Crawford said. "That other women you mentioned, she have a name or a phone number?"

"A number," Leon said, pulling up the shirtsleeve of his left arm.

The number was written in ink on the inside of his forearm: 813-2525.

"Guess you don't needs tats with all those numbers," Crawford said.

Leon smiled. "Can you read it?"

"Yeah," Crawford said.

"Want me to call?" Leon asked.

"I'll do it this time," Crawford said.

He dialed the number.

A woman answered on the third ring.

"Hello."

Crawford recognized the voice, but couldn't place it right away.

"Who is this?" he asked.

"Who do you think it is, Charlie?" she said. "You called me. It's Maddy Sorenson."

FIFTY-SIX

CRAWFORD WENT STRAIGHT TO MADDY SORENSON'S OFFICE. IT was 5:30, but the receptionist was still there.

He walked past her. She tried to stop him, but he went right into Sorenson's office.

She was on her computer. She looked up at him and raised her arms.

"Well, Charlie, why don't you just break the door down?" she said. "What the hell's this about, anyway?"

"That's my question to you."

"Sit down, for God's sake." Sorenson motioned to the chair. "You look like you ran all the way here."

"Why did you call Leon Barnes?"

She took off her glasses and put them down.

"Because one of my clients asked me to," she said. "That's what I do: What my clients pay me to do."

"Who's your client?"

"Why don't you tell me what this is about?"

"A murder," Crawford said. "A murder Leon Barnes committed. That your client hired him to do."

She drew back. "That's a very serious charge."

"Yeah, it's a very serious crime," Crawford said. "Who was the woman you put Leon in touch with?"

"Sorry, attorney-client privilege prevents me from—"

Crawford placed his hands firmly on her desk and leaned down close to her.

"Fuck attorney-client privilege," he said. "Do you want me to arrest you for conspiracy, for your involvement in knowingly commissioning a murder?"

"I didn't do anything like that. You could never—"

"I know you represent scumbags," he cut in, "but you've been handing out free passes to murderers. First, the one who killed John Calhoun-Jones and his wife. Now this woman. Is this really who you want to be, a woman who puts cold-blooded killers back on the street?"

Sorenson was silent. She put her glasses back on. He had never seen her at a loss for words before. Finally, she leaned across her desk and whispered.

"You know that woman at the door of the Zinovievs' house?"

"Yeah?" he said, flashing to the quiet, petite Asian women. Then he realized that was the voice he couldn't place.

Sorenson stood. "I have my five-forty-five arriving any minute, Charlie."

"So you represented her and the Russian brothers?"

She nodded. "She contacted me right after they were killed," Maddy said. "Offered me a very substantial retainer."

Crawford started walking toward the door. "Thanks, Maddy. You did the right thing," he said. "Finally."

FIFTY-SEVEN

CRAWFORD CALLED OTT AND TOLD HIM TO MEET HIM AT THE Russians' house.

"Sure," Ott said, "but there aren't too many people still alive up there."

"Except that sweet Asian chick at the door," Crawford said.

"Yeah, Miss Personality," Ott said. "What's she got to do with—"

"Everything," Crawford said.

CRAWFORD GOT THERE FIRST AND WAITED A FEW MINUTES FOR Ott. There was still yellow crime-scene tape around the house. The detectives, Kerns and Williams, were still there on stakeout. Kerns said that two of the crime-scene techs had just left.

Crawford and Ott got out of their cars and walked toward each other.

"I still got a few questions," Ott said.

"So do I," Crawford said. "For one thing, I assumed P.D. Miller was behind the hit on Evsei. Now it doesn't look like it."

Ott unholstered his Glock. "Just in case our little Asian friend has another trick up her sleeve."

"Yeah," Crawford said. "Another drone, maybe?"

Crawford leaned on the doorbell.

A full thirty seconds went by. Crawford hit it again. The door suddenly opened and it was Nadia, the woman who had been in the pool when the brothers were killed.

"Hi, Nadia," Crawford said. "How are you doing?"

"I'm okay," Nadia said. "I was packing my suitcase along with the other girls."

"Where are you going?" Ott asked.

"Back to Russia," Nadia said. "Some of the girls are staying here."

"Well, good luck," Crawford said. "We need to talk to the woman who usually answers the door."

"Ming-Hua," Nadia said. "Sorry, but she is not here now."

"Do you know where she is?" Crawford asked.

"She went somewhere a little while ago. She was all dressed up," Nadia said.

Crawford looked at Ott.

"Why don't we check her room?" Ott said.

Crawford turned back to Nadia.

"Can you take us to her room?"

She nodded.

She led them to the guest wing of the house. Ming-Hua had a large bedroom, painted powder blue, off of which was a sitting room with an expensive-looking desk and chair.

Crawford reached into his pocket and pulled out a pair of white latex gloves.

"I'll check out her desk," he said to Ott, walking over to it.

He scanned the top of the desk. Nothing caught his attention.

He opened a drawer and saw a stack of photos, then riffled through them.

One close to the bottom was of Ming-Hua, with a man who had

his arm around her shoulder. They were both smiling and it looked very cozy.

The man was P.D. Miller.

"I got something here, Charlie," Ott said from across the room, picking up a card off the top of Ming-Hua's bureau.

"Me too," Crawford said, walking over to Ott.

Crawford flashed the photo to Ott.

"Cute couple," Ott said, then handed something to Crawford. "Check this out."

It was an engraved vellum invitation that said, in raised letter-head: You are cordially invited to honor Mr. P.D. Miller as he is presented with the Humanitarian of the Year Award by the founding members of the Cadillac Fund. It went on to give details about the time and the place.

"You check out the date?" Ott said, pointing.

Crawford nodded. "In an hour, at the Breakers," he said. "I don't know about you, Mort, but I wouldn't miss it for the world."

"I had plans," Ott said, "but to honor the great man, I'll just have to cancel 'em."

Crawford nodded, walked to a closet, and opened it. It was a walk-in the size of his bedroom. There were a lot of expensive-looking dresses and a shoe collection on two walls worthy of Imelda Marcos.

Then Crawford looked down and saw something. "Check this out," he said.

Ott walked over. Crawford pointed at something on the floor.

They both crouched down to look at it. It was an elaborate remote-control device.

"She not only opens doors," Crawford said, "but pilots drones as well."

FIFTY-EIGHT

The large room at the Breakers glittered with opulence. The charity-ball crowd in attendance was a mix of disparate professions, such as Midwestern tire kings, wildly successful Botox doctors, retired bank presidents, and other captains of industry, all squiring their socially ambitious, dressed-to-the-nines wives or significant others. Giving money with ballyhooed fanfare and Glossy publicity was the quickest way to burst onto the Palm Beach social scene. It was either that or take up polo. Such transparent social-climbing displays were frowned upon by many old-line WASPs and members of exclusive clubs, but to that fact this charity-ball crowd seemed indifferent. They didn't have time to change their stripes and reinvent themselves. It was too late in life for eastern prep schools and the exalted game of squash.

Twenty-four tables boasted ten people per table. The centerpieces were glorious floral displays of peonies, lilacs, and roses surrounded by scores of flickering tea lights. They were screwed to the tables because past partygoers had felt it their right—at a thousand bucks a pop—to spirit them away at the end of the night. The two hundred and forty assembled ranged in age from mid-forties to late-seventies, the crème du lait of Palm Beach society. Not A-listers, but all solid B's and B-minuses, with maybe a few C-pluses thrown in. One thing was certain: Nobody scrimped on evening clothes, precious stones, or fancy watches. Prada was everywhere, of course, along with Versace and Badgley Mischka. As were Harry Winston and Bulgari jewels and Franck Muller and diamond Rolex watches by the score. Cocktail hour had been going for over an hour, mostly top-shelf bubbly. Gaiety and giving was in the air as the attendees sat down for dinner and the special presentation later in the evening.

P.D. Miller was tanned and confident-looking in his perfectly-cut dinner jacket. He was judiciously sipping his Johnnie Walker Blue, trying to remain clearheaded and sharp for his humble acceptance speech. At his side was Ming-Hua, glowing, radiant, and large-breasted.

"We can't just walk up and handcuff him, can we?" Ott asked as he and Crawford got out of their Crown Vic and approached the front door of the Breakers.

"Why not?" Crawford said.

"Well, Christ, in front of all these people. At the Breakers?"

"Hey, as good a place as any," Crawford said.

Crawford had once arrested a guy at halftime at a Knicks game in Madison Square Garden, after having spotted him on TV during the first quarter sitting next to Spike Lee.

Two uniforms—Hearn and Munoz—had come along with them, just in case Miller tried to make a run for it. As they were about to walk into the large room where the charity ball was being held, Crawford stopped and turned to the other three.

"We're going to the back of the room, so he can't see us. I'll give you the word."

Ott and the uniforms nodded.

THE FABULOUS TWO HUNDRED AND FORTY WERE HAVING dessert now. A man with a bulbous nose and a showbiz presence strode up to the elevated podium. He tapped the microphone.

"This thing working?" he asked. "Can you hear me out there?"

A few shouted yeses from the middle and back of the room.

"Hello and welcome, I'm your roast—excuse me—host, Larry Peal. We are here tonight to celebrate the extraordinary life and incredible accomplishments of one P. D. Miller," Peal said, then took a sip of water. "Over the years, I've heard people speculate what P.D. actually stands for. For those of you who don't know, it's actually Philip Daryl—"

Miller, at a front table near the dais, smiled at Ming-Hua and patted her hand.

"—but just the other day, someone told me that he thought P.D. stood for *plethora of divorces*."

Waves of cackling swept through the room as Miller thumped the table and laughed heartily. Then he dabbed at his eyes with a handkerchief.

"Another one I've heard is *plenty of dough*," Peal said. "You know, from all those *profitable deals* of his. Sure wish I was in on a few of 'em, instead of my money going down the tubes with Lehman Brothers."

The crowd roared, happy they hadn't sunk with that particular ill-fated Wall Street ship.

Crawford, Ott, Hearn, and Munoz were in the back of the room now, blocked from Miller's view by two enormous fluted columns.

Larry Peal raised his arms, like Billy Graham addressing his adoring congregants. "By the way, before we go any further, I just want to recognize the lovely Ming-Hua, P.D.'s sweet, enchanting, and thoroughly delightful fiancée. In her gentle, unassuming, Oriental way, Ming-Hua has made Palm Beach a far better place for all of us who have had the pleasure of knowing her."

Ott leaned over to Crawford. "So the enchanting Ming-hua was Miller's spy in the Russians' house?"

Crawford nodded. "Exactly," he said, "not to mention kamikaze pilot."

Larry Peal was building to a crescendo: "So, if you would—Ming-Hua, please take a bow."

Ming-Hua stood, put her hands together, bowed slowly, then blew a kiss to Larry Peal.

As she sat back down, she kissed Miller.

"The lovely Ming-Hua, ladies and gentleman," Peal said, gesturing toward her. "First, the beauty, now the beast"—gesturing toward Miller.

"Just kidding." Peal took another sip of water. "Seriously, folks, we're here tonight to honor a businessman, a decorated Vietnam vet, a sportsman, a philanthropist, and, yes, a humanitarian. A man whose success is well-documented and whose generosity is boundless. I'd like to just catalogue a few of P.D.'s contributions. His charitable work in New York is well-known, particularly his having been a founding father of the Robin Hood Foundation. But here on the local scene, he's a major benefactor of the Red Cross, the Hurricane Disaster Relief Fund, the Boys and Girls Club, and probably biggest of all, a contributor to local law enforcement. Whether it's the Policemen's Benevolent Fund, the Palm Beach Police Department, or the auspicious Cadillac Fund, which sponsors this event tonight, there's no bigger supporter of our men and women in blue."

"Hear! Hear!" A man stood up at his table, looking slightly wobbly from alcohol, age, or both. He raised his near-empty glass. "Here's to P.D."

Everyone rose to their feet.

"To P.D.," they said in chorus.

Larry Peal glanced down at the man who had made the toast.

"Hey, Herm," he said. "You trying to butter him up? Need a loan or something?"

The charity-ballers howled.

"But seriously," said Peal, eager to get the spotlight back, "P.D. is a man who will do anything for the cops. He's supported them so generously and for so many years with his heart and his checkbook. And for that reason, we are all pleased and proud to name P.D. Miller the Cadillac Fund's Humanitarian of the Year. Ladies and gentlemen, I give you P.D. Miller."

"Okay, guys," Crawford said, "let's do it."

Crawford, Ott, and the two uniforms started down the center aisle just as Miller ascended the dais.

Larry Peal pumped Miller's hand and the assembled guests once again rose to their feet. Peal handed Miller the microphone. It was time for the multitudes to settle back and listen to a few well-chosen words from the great man himself.

Miller looked up. "Ladies and gentlemen—" At that exact moment he saw Crawford, Ott, and the uniforms walking down the aisle some thirty feet away.

Crawford had his handcuffs out.

"What the hell?" said Miller, shocked.

The guests craned their necks to see. Crawford climbed the dais and did a fast Miranda on Miller, as Ott did the same with Ming-Hua.

The hall became deathly silent.

Then someone in the audience started to laugh.

"How good is this?" he said.

"Larry set the whole thing up," whispered another.

Then more laughter.

Larry Peal wondered whose idea the gag was. He laughed heartily and grabbed the microphone. "Ladies and gentlemen, I give you Palm Beach's finest, doing what they do best," said Peal, his arm raised high in tribute.

The fab two hundred and forty were on their feet again.

Crawford roughly cuffed Miller's hands together behind his back, then grabbed one arm and started pulling him back down the aisle toward the rear exit. Ott was right behind him with Ming-Hua.

Laughter and raucous applause reached a crescendo.

"Old P.D," someone said. "Dontcha just love how he played along with it."

"Yeah, the man ought to be up for an Academy Award," said another.

"It didn't look like he was too happy," said a third.

"That was all part of the act," said someone else.

"You think they were real cops?"

"No, that guy in charge was definitely an actor."

Miller paused halfway down the aisle and set his heels, like a mule digging in.

Crawford shoved him roughly on the shoulder. "Come on, Mr. Humanitarian...we got a cell to get you to."

FIFTY-NINE

"So he never got to deliver his acceptance speech?" Dominica asked.

"Maybe to Leon Barnes," Crawford said.

Miller was in jail and Crawford was stretched out on a sofa at Dominica's house on Queens Lane. He was on his second Sierra Nevada.

"Incredible," she said. "That Larry Peal. I've seen him in action before; he's like some old vaudeville guy."

"Yeah, probably still waiting for his buddy to return to the dais and give his acceptance speech," Crawford said.

"So I have a million questions," said Dominica.

"I'll give you...three." He took a sip of his beer.

"Well, for one thing, what's going to happen to the Poinciana?" she asked.

"That's a good question. My guess is that the Poinciana guys will make a good case that they were coerced into selling it," Crawford said. "But stay tuned."

Dominica, bare feet up on a bamboo table, was twirling a strand of hair. "What about Miller?" she said, frowning. "He really had all those people killed just for those Poinciana buildings and its golf course?"

Crawford shook his head. "You need an army of shrinks to figure that guy out," he said, "but I think the Poinciana was a lot more than some old buildings and a golf course to him. You know anything about him?"

"Just by reputation," she said, getting up. "He gives that big party for the department every year."

"Gave," Crawford said.

"So the Chinese woman," Dominica said. "She was like a mole? To keep an eye on the Russians?"

"Yeah, among other things," Crawford said.

Dominica shook her head. "Incredible."

"I know," Crawford said. "So is that it for your questions?"

"For now," she said. "I'm going to get another glass of wine. You okay?"

He nodded.

A minute later she was back with her pinot grigio.

He slapped the cushion on the sofa next to him.

"Come on over here," he said. "We need to pick up where we left off a few nights ago."

"You mean, when we were so rudely interrupted by your friend, Mary Jo."

"Mary Ann."

She cozied up into his arm, looked up at him, and they kissed.

She looked down at the handcuffs on his belt, then leaned back.

"Do I need to cuff you to me this time?" she asked. "So you don't go running off again?"

"There's nobody left to arrest," he said with a little shrug.

She put her arm around his waist and they kissed again.

His cell phone rang.

But this time, Dominica was ready and in perfect position. She reached into his breast pocket, pulled out the offending cell phone and, with a spirited flick of the wrist, flung it across the room, then resumed the kiss.

The kiss was barely broken. The phone...well, Crawford could always get another one.

THE END

PALM BEACH DEADLY (BOOK 3): Talk show host Knight Mulcahy makes $65 million a year insulting people. Until the night he's found, skivvies around his ankles, a bullet in his heart.

Tap here to get Palm Beach Deadly (Book 3) on Amazon

AFTERWORD

I hope you liked *Palm Beach Poison*. If you did, please **leave a quick review on Amazon**. Thank you!

Charlie Crawford and Mort Ott return for another murder investigation in *Palm Beach Deadly*—**now available on Amazon**.

And to receive an email when the next Charlie Crawford Palm Beach Mystery comes out, be sure to sign up for my free author newsletter at **tomturnerbooks.com/news**.

Best,
Tom

PALM BEACH DEADLY
(EXCERPT)

ONE

Roughly two hundred people were assembled at the thirty-five-million-dollar oceanfront mansion of Knight Mulcahy—yes, *the* Knight Mulcahy—to celebrate his being clean and sober for three long months. The vast majority of attendees, however, were celebrating with hi-powered cocktails—shaken, stirred, and otherwise mixed—by bartenders who didn't hold back on the pour. The fact was, only about twenty percent of those present were actual teetotalers and many of them were being sorely tested by the sight of unrepressed inebriants whooping it up and clearly having a hell of a lot more fun than they were.

Mulcahy stood at the alcohol-free bar, a tall goblet of freshly squeezed grapefruit juice in hand, doing what he did best: Bloviate. In fact, *the Bloviator* was one of several nicknames the press had dubbed him. Another was the *Billion-Dollar Gasbag*, which was an overstatement of his net worth, but not by much.

Manning the alcohol-free bar was a white-jacketed man with spiky platinum hair. Behind him were four shelves, all featuring bottles of water. Very, very expensive bottles of water...there to slake the thirst of Mulcahy and his fellow twenty percenters. On the top shelf was the exotic Kona Nigari at $419 a bottle, next to the more reasonably-priced Fillico (a mere $219), both products of Japan. On the shelf below was one called Bling, which had a champagne-style cork and stood tall and proud next to Veen, a product of Finland. Below them were two from Canada—One Thousand B.C. and AcquaDeco—which bookended a long, svelte bottle of Tasmanian Rain, from the small island down under the Down Under continent. Below them came the more mundane Perrier, Pellegrino, and other familiar brands.

For those teetotalers who wanted more than exorbitantly priced water, the bartender was whipping up non-alcoholic concoctions with flamboyant names like Fuzzless Navel (peach nectar and OJ) and Innocent Passion (passion fruit syrup, cranberry and lemon juice) and its apparent nemesis, the Evil Princess (grenadine, apple juice and a dash of vanilla syrup.)

Knight Mulcahy peered out over a cluster of his guests and saw his son, Paul, walking across the room with his arm around the shoulder of a woman Knight had never seen before. She was wearing a black silk dress designed to display maximum cleavage. She had beautiful azure blue eyes, high cheekbones and a confident walk.

Paul had done his job better than usual.

As Knight watched his son chat up the top-heavy beauty, Ned Durrell wandered into his periphery. Ned took a four-dollar sip from his Kona Nigari and sidled up to Knight.

Knight acknowledged him with a curt nod. "Hey, Ned, what's happening, bro?"

Knight—at sixty-one—was way too old for 'bro' and the soul knob that sprouted out below his lower lip.

Durrell gave him a withering frown. "Been meaning to take you out behind the woodshed, Knight, bitch-slap you around a little."

"The hell you talking about?" Knight asked, clearly not alarmed by the threat.

"That comment on your show about *Night Wolf*," said Durrell.

Durrell was a thriller writer who'd had a modest bestseller eleven years before but not much since. *Night Wolf* was his latest, a *USA Today* bestseller, which lacked the clout of being a *New York Times* bestseller, but was still nothing to be sneezed at. A thumbs-up from Knight on his number-one rated radio talk show could have meant the sale of thousands of copies, but Knight had panned it. Called it a "sleeper...as in snore," among other snarky put-downs.

"What can I tell you?" Knight said. "I knew who did it on page nine. And that sex scene"—he shook his head and frowned— "I mean did you really use the phrase, 'quivering pudenda?' I guess your editor must've fallen asleep by then, huh?"

No sugar-coater was Knight Mulcahy.

"For the record, it was not 'quivering,'" said Durrell, "it was 'trembling.'"

Mulcahy, in mid-sip of his Fuzzless Navel, burst out laughing and sprayed peach nectar all over Durrell's chin. "What-the-fuck-ever," Mulcahy said. "It was 'pudenda' that was so lame. I mean, shit, man, how 'bout just calling it 'pussy' or 'snatch' or 'cooter,' something the common man can relate to."

Durrell dabbed his chin with a cocktail napkin. "Cooter, huh? Is that what they call it up in East Jesus, West Virginia, or whatever the hell you come from?"

"Kentucky, my friend," Mulcahy said. "And I'd say we've beaten this subject to death, but one last thing." Knight always got the last word. "Any sentence with the word pudenda in it should be outlawed. Period. End of story. Sounds so goddamn biological. If you're gonna write about sex, use words that give guys hard-ons, get women stirring in their loins. Know what I mean, bro? Christ, if you can't write a good sex scene..."

Knight shook his head and walked away, leaving Durrell to finish the sentence.

Knight Mulcahy's sixty-five-million-dollar-a-year salary gave him the right, he figured, to say any damn thing he pleased. And, the reality was, that's exactly what had made him famous. His irreverent candor. As host of a three-hour daily show focusing on politics and current events, he had thirty-five million listeners a week, who—if Knight told them to dive off a cliff—would do so in a heartbeat. But Knight was content just to tell them how to think, who to vote for, and what products to buy.

Another thing about Knight, as is often the case with men who have vast power, money, and ego: he was an inveterate skirt-chaser and assumed every woman on the planet found him devastatingly sexy, utterly irresistible. Even though the man was bald, eighty pounds overweight, and had the eyes of a newborn warthog.

After shoving off from Ned Durrell, Knight headed in the direction of who he hoped would be his next conquest. Olivia Griswold was the rare female who'd never had a drop of alcohol in her life, but was well schooled in other vices. Among them: cocaine and ménage à trois (viewed by many a Palm Beacher as not a vice at all, just good, clean fun with one extra participant.) Olivia was tall, red-haired and flat-out gorgeous. She worked at Preview Properties and sold high-end houses.

Knight snuck up behind her and put his beefy mitt on her shoulder.

"How ya doin', honey?" he said and, as she turned, kissed her on the lips.

"Just fine, Knight, lovely party," Olivia said, taking a step back.

Knight looked across the capacious living room and saw his wife, Jacqui, deep into it with a woman who never talked about anything except her unabiding commitment to the born-again movement.

"How 'bout taking a walk outside with me," Knight said. "It's kinda stuffy in here."

Stuffy was the last thing it was, but Olivia might have been hoping he'd tell her about a rich friend of his who was moving to Palm Beach and needed a good realtor. Or in her case, a fair to middling one.

They walked out the French doors to the back lawn, which was the size of three football fields laid side by side. It tapered down to the beach, the black ocean off in the distance. In between was an oversized infinity-edge swimming pool that had cost Knight more than half a million dollars.

No more than twenty steps outside the French doors, Knight turned to Olivia and asked, "Wanna fuck?"

Olivia was probably no stranger to being propositioned but, chances were, never this fast and with absolutely no foreplay. She laughed, shook her head and shot him a look that said, you naughty boy, you.

"What a romantic," she said instead. "I'm terribly flattered, but no. Just out of curiosity, where did you intend this little love-making session to take place? Roll around on the lawn or something?"

He pointed at the pool house.

"Still, no," she said.

"Okay," Knight said. "Let's go back inside."

"To that stuffy room, you mean?"

Her irony was lost on him because Knight had already moved on, wondering who to go after next. He was—quite clearly—a direct man, and of the school that if you asked enough times, someone would eventually say yes. It had worked for a number of other rich, powerful men. Ted Kennedy for one, Nelson Rockefeller for another. Kennedy had drunkenly taken Knight aside once and explained that the *wanna fuck?* gambit beat the hell out of flowers, candy, and an extended courtship.

Knight and Olivia walked inside and Knight noticed that the queen of the born-agains was still bending Jacqui's ear.

"Well, nice chatting with you, Knight," Olivia said.

Again, the irony fell on deaf ears. "Yeah," Knight said distractedly, casting his eye around the room.

And there she was on the far side of the room, ready for the taking.

Continue Reading Palm Beach Deadly

ALSO BY TOM TURNER

CHARLIE CRAWFORD PALM BEACH MYSTERIES

Palm Beach Nasty

Palm Beach Poison

Palm Beach Deadly

Palm Beach Bones

Palm Beach Pretenders

Palm Beach Predator

Palm Beach Broke

Palm Beach Bedlam

Palm Beach Blues

The Charlie Crawford Palm Beach Mystery Series: Books 1, 2 & 3

The Charlie Crawford Palm Beach Mystery Series: Books 4, 5 & 6: Box Set #2

THE SAVANNAH SERIES

The Savannah Madam

NICK JANZEK CHARLESTON MYSTERIES

Killing Time in Charleston

Charleston Buzz Kill

STANDALONES

Broken House

Dead in the Water

For a current list of all available titles, please visit
tomturnerbooks.com/books.

ACKNOWLEDGMENTS

Thanks to the usual suspects—Susan, Serena, Georgie, John and Cece. And also to the boys in LV, whose distinguished names I sprinkled throughout the pages of *Poison*. Also to loyal readers: Jennifer LePage, Natalie Saitta, Larry Libater and Peter Schiff. Finally, to Ed Stackler, best editor in the business.

ABOUT THE AUTHOR

A native New Englander, Tom dropped out of college and ran a bar in Vermont...into the ground. Limping back to get his sheepskin, he then landed in New York where he spent time as an award-winning copywriter at several Manhattan advertising agencies. After years of post-Mad Men life, he made a radical change and got a job in commercial real estate. A few years later he ended up in Palm Beach, buying, renovating and selling houses while getting material for his novels. On the side, he wrote *Palm Beach Nasty*, its sequel, *Palm Beach Poison*, and a screenplay, *Underwater*.

While at a wedding, he fell for the charm of Charleston, South Carolina. He spent six years there and completed a yet-to-be-published series set in Charleston. A year ago, Tom headed down the road to Savannah, where he just finished a novel about lust and murder among his neighbors.

Learn more about Tom's books at:
www.tomturnerbooks.com

 facebook.com/tomturner.books

Made in the USA
Middletown, DE
24 July 2021

44736449R00168